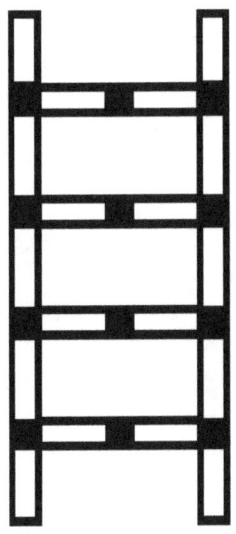

"Hail to thee, O Ladder of God, hail to thee,
O Ladder of Set. Stand up, O Ladder of God,
stand up O Ladder of Set, stand up, O Ladder of
Horus, wherein Osiris went forth into heaven...."

—Pyramid of Pepi I (South Saqqara) 2200 BCE

The Patriarch Rising

A novel by

Aaron A. Malavolti

PREFACE

London, England, 1787

John Adams was a young diplomat living in London when he wrote his three-volume *A Defence of the Constitutions of Government of the United States of America.* In a collection of writings that demonstrated the comprehensive research and depth of thought that went into the work of the Founding Fathers of the United States of America, he covered a wide range of history as he narrated various governmental structures, philosophers, and ideas, gauging the success and shortcomings of several countries, ranging from ancient times to his present day.

Halfway through the second volume, he was ready to address the Republic of Siena in Italy. He paced near his desk, with its pile of historic sources on Siena and thought: *Where to begin? There is much to learn from this region beyond the great republic of the Roman Empire.* Spanning back to the ancient Etruscans, whose wealthy country was a confederacy not unlike a young America, Siena sat at a crossroads, between Rome and the rest of Europe, between ancient nobility and modern democratic republics. He sat down and opened one of his source books, *Dell'Historia di Siena*, written by Orlando Malavolti in 1574.

John Adams began, "The antiquity of the city of Siena is proved by the notice of Pliny, Tacitus, and Ptolemy, if not by another circumstance mentioned by its historian, namely—the splendor of certain families among its citizens, nobility being only an ancient virtue, accompanied with the splendor of riches."[1]

March 16, 1961

Remarks on the occasion of the celebration of the Centennial of Italian Unificatio by President John F. Kennedy

"Many of us who are here today are not Italian by blood or by birth, but I think that we all have a more than passing interest in this anniversary. All of us, in a large sense, are beneficiaries of the Italian experience.

"It is an extraordinary fact in history that so much of what we are and so much of what we believe had its origin in this rather small spear of land stretching into the Mediterranean. All in a great sense that we fight to preserve today had its origins in Italy, and earlier than that in Greece. So that it is an honor as President of the United States to participate in this most important occasion in the life of a friendly country, The Republic of Italy.

"In addition, it is one of the strange facts of history, that this country of ours, which is important to Western civilization, was opened up first by a daring feat of navigation of an Italian, Christopher Columbus. And yet this country was nearly a century old when modern Italy began.

"So we have the old and the new bound together and inextricably linked—Italy and the United States, past, present, and we believe future.

"The Risorgimento which gave birth to modern Italy, like the American Revolution which led to the birth of our country, was the re-awakening of the most deeply-held ideals of Western civilization: the desire for freedom, for protection of the rights of the individual.

"As the Doctor said, the state exists for the protection of those rights, and those rights do not come to us because of the generosity of the state. This concept which originated in Greece and in Italy I think has been a most important factor in the development of our country here in the United States.

"And it is a source of satisfaction to us that those who built modern Italy received part of their inspiration from our experience here in the United States—as we had earlier received part of our inspiration from an older Italy. For although modern Italy is only a century old, the culture and the history of the Italian peninsula stretches back over two millenia. From the banks of the Tiber there rose Western civilization as we know it, a civilization whose traditions and spiritual values give great significance to Western life as we find it in Western Europe and in the Atlantic community."

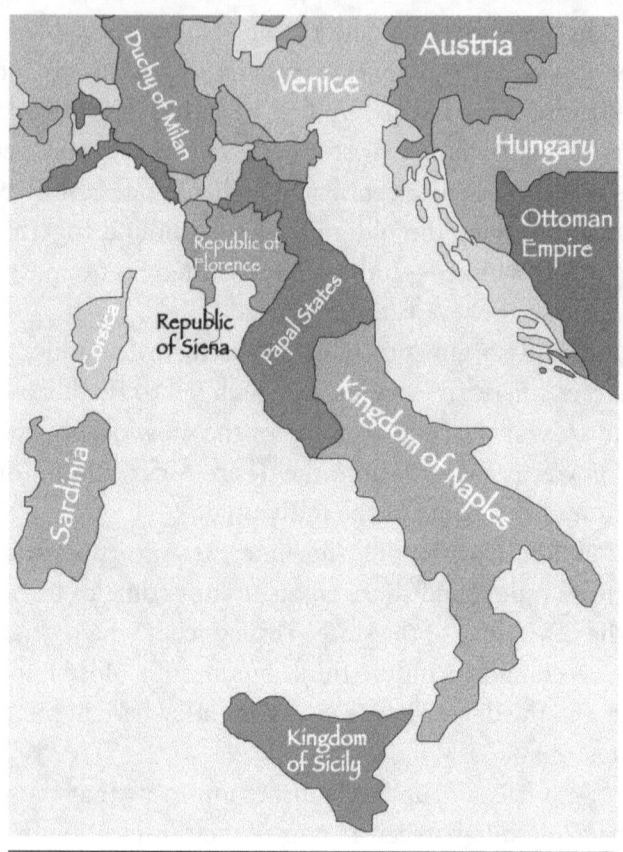

*Republic of Siena, Republic of Florence, Papal States
late 1400s*

The Patriarch Rising *is a work of fiction. I have connected a number of historical dots in a speculative manner. However, the dots—the legends, places, and historical people—do and did exist as described, as does the science used to do some of the connecting.*

CHAPTER ONE

Present-Day Rome, Italy

Professor Federico Sisti was working late in his lab, more energized than he had felt in a very long time. Many would consider his life's work tedious; tracing the migrations of prehistoric man through molecular genetics was difficult work. Sisti was a giant in the field of anthropological genetic research, an area of study that had advanced by leaps and bounds over the past twenty years, thanks partly to his own work. Despite being renowned within the field, however, few knew his name outside of academic circles. This new discovery would surely change that.

His tenure at Sapienza University allowed him to teach at a leisurely pace and follow his true passion: research. *Archeologists dig and historians debate, but when it comes to history, geneticists are helping to fill the gaps with facts*, he thought happily. The use of genetics to illuminate history's murky, distant depths was a practice that was gaining momentum in academia, even for the layperson. Anyone with 100 euros could send their saliva to a lab and find out a great deal about where their ancestors came from. The implications of where the technology was going frightened some; one might soon be able to find out every disease he was predisposed to, where his relatives had lived in the recent past, and even where some of them came from thousands of years ago. Sisti couldn't understand all the hand-wringing by some of his colleagues at the possibilities available. *The truth should always be welcomed, even when it carries unpleasant details or contradicts previously held beliefs.*

The sudden explosion of people getting their DNA sequenced provided him with an abundance of data to advance his research. He had always found himself drawn to this kind of old-fashioned detective work, piecing together history one bit of DNA at a time. Sisti had published numerous studies resulting from his completed or partly completed genetic puzzles, focused mainly on the migrations of peoples around the Mediterranean Sea, the cradle of Western civilization. His own country, Italy, afforded him an opportunity to live in one of the world's best laboratories for studying human-movement patterns from the earliest civilizations around the Mediterranean. The country of Italy itself was less than 200 years old. Previous to being one unified country, the peninsula had been a variety of smaller republics; before that, it was part of the vast Roman Empire, which was preceded by Etruscan settlements.

Italy was comprised of an amalgamation of people who had migrated there in the distant past from the Middle East, North Africa, and, of course, down from Central Europe. It was in one of the best positions on Earth to track genetic dispersion around the Mediterranean due to the various cultures and people who had melded together to form the modern country. Even though he had always felt truly passionate and drawn to genetics, never in his wildest imagination would he have thought his work would lead him to something quite like his current discovery.

I caused waves when I proved that many of the ancient Greeks descended from men who had migrated from North Africa, possibly even crossing over by boat before others thought it was possible. Nothing like this, though; what I found will be met with a furor to say the least. He hadn't told anyone yet; indeed, he didn't dare voice out loud what he was working on. Not until he had confirmed more data...

Just then, he heard glass breaking from somewhere within the lab, where he'd thought he was alone behind locked doors.

"Hello? Who's there?" Professor Sisti moved down a row of dimly lit workstations toward the source of noise. As he turned the corner, he could see a broken beaker on the floor, having fallen from the counter. Probably it had fallen on its own from the vibrations caused by one of the heavy centrifuges he had spinning. It happened sometimes. Breathing a sigh of relief, he walked toward the glass to clean it up, reaching for the broom in a nearby corner.

His last memory was of someone forcefully grabbing his neck from behind and pressing something into his face. Then everything went dark.

CHAPTER TWO

"To be ignorant of what occurred before you were born is to remain always a child. For what is the worth of human life, unless it is woven into the life of our ancestors by the records of history?"

—Marcus Tullius Cicero

Chicago, Illinois

Michael Malavolti walked aimlessly through the exhibits in the Oriental Institute of the University of Chicago, letting his mind wander while listening to rock music on his headphones. His athletic frame bounced to the beat as he meandered through the museum. It was his favorite place on campus to think. At the moment, he was pondering the complete 180-degree turn he had taken on his career path in the past year, his senior year of college. Michael had been a physics major here, one of the most prestigious universities for the discipline, and had been holding his own.

Certainly, his career path would have had several possible avenues to explore once he'd advanced through a postgraduate degree. One of his friends who had graduated last year was working for the Department of Defense, doing something he couldn't talk about. There was also the growing private space exploration sector with its deep pockets and exciting new job postings. His tutor, Reggie, who had finished a PhD last year, was working with lasers.

Weaponized lasers, for Pete's sake! What the hell am I thinking, switching majors my senior year and applying to a newly formed department offering a PhD in Renaissance Studies, of all things?

His father's response when he'd told him kept running through his head: "That's great, you're gonna borrow $200,000 to be a *teacher*?" His mother had all too predictably asked if he had prayed about it. Once he convinced her that he had, that he felt he was following his conscience, she was completely supportive, and his father then followed suit. *Was this really his conscience, though? And if so, was it the right thing to do?*

Michael had grown up in blue-collar Rockford, Illinois, one of the upper Midwest's once-great manufacturing centers—now struggling to reinvent itself and known derisively as part of the Rust Belt. His father had worked hard to make ends meet; he built houses in the summer and helped run a Christmas tree farm in the winter. His mother was a grade-school teacher. Nothing about his immediate family or any of his known relatives hinted at a grand or wealthy history. His great-grandfather on his father's side had emigrated to America in the early 1900s for the same reason so many other Italians had at that time: in the hope of finding work. They found it in the form of hard labor, in his great-grandpa's case in the coal mines of central Illinois. When Michael first discovered the Malavoltis had been a wealthy noble family during the Middle Ages, it didn't take much for him to become completely consumed with discovering their history.

As he stepped out of the university's archeology museum and into a sunny day on Chicago's South Side, he thought about his opportunity. Everyone liked a tale that involved castles and knights, fortunes gained and lost. *I never expected to find such an interesting story involving my own ancestors. Exploring their history feels like a calling, something I just can't explain.*

Michael didn't notice the burly man with the crew cut in a full-length trench coat sitting at the bus stop across from the Oriental Institute. He was doing what anyone else would be: waiting for a bus and punching the keys on his cell phone, like so many did when they were bored.

But what the man was texting was neither banal nor innocuous: *He's in that Oriental Museum again. He's been in there for at least 30 minutes. Please advise: should I take him today?* the man called Ely texted.

The response came quickly: *Negative. Your orders remain the same: observe and report back. He is scheduled to fly to Rome tomorrow. You are booked on the same flight. Don't blow your cover.*

CHAPTER THREE

Rome, Italy

Vivianna Giuseppe rushed to finish putting herself together. As she applied a dark shade of red lipstick, she paused to admire the scene from her bathroom. From her window, she had a view that looked down the Tiber River and framed the Vatican's St. Peter's Basilica in the distance. The sun was just coming up, and its early morning rays reflected off the dome. She thought about how silly it was that she rarely left her flat unless her appearance met a certain standard. *Why do I wear designer suits and heels to work when I don't give a damn what people think of me?*

Her mind snapped back to the present as she felt some satisfaction for how her career was progressing. She was one of Rome's youngest homicide detectives. Making the rank of detective in her early thirties as a female was something to be proud of; she felt it vindicated her lifestyle. As a single woman, she found herself putting in more time than her married colleagues. When she was ten, her mother had died after a short but intense battle with cancer. After a few years, her father started seeing another woman right around the time when boys really began to pursue Vivianna, but she wanted nothing to do with them. *What good was love if it was so fleeting? And how could her father love another woman?* It was several more years before she understood her father's desire to be happy again. By then, she was fiercely independent and content pursuing her own happiness from things she could control. Her career and few hobbies were enough. The hours and hard work had paid off; she had been promoted several times, and now found herself working on the types of cases she got into police work to solve: murders, rapes, and violent crime. She felt she was fighting evil now. Roman politics being what they were, it probably didn't hurt that her uncle was a well-known cardinal and personal friends with both the pope and the mayor.

Vivianna was still trying to process the message she had received after her 5:00 a.m. run. The office had called and told her to report to Sapienza University for a break-in and possible missing professor. Being at the bottom of the detective food chain, it wasn't a shock to be assigned such a case. She was, however, confused when the voice on the phone had told her that detectives Monti and Ruggero would also be on the case. *Three detectives assigned to this? And why Monti?* He was a special inspector, a rank reserved for those who had seen a lot—the kind of detective who had earned the right to pick and choose his cases. She thought of him as more of a media personality than a detective at this point in his career. He was often attached to high-profile cases where the press might be involved, so she had seen him more on TV than in person around the station. Vivianna wasn't especially happy to have two detectives who out-ranked her on the same case, but was excited to be considered for it, nonetheless. *This must be some important academic.*

As Vivianna pulled her vintage, red Fiat onto the campus, the commotion was immediately visible. Parking at a distance to avoid another lecture on the need for a more reliable automobile seemed prudent. She considered her classic Fiat another irrational fashion accessory. Approaching the science department on foot, it became evident to her that reporters and, unfortunately, both Monti and Ruggero were already on the scene. Detective Ruggero was barking orders into a walkie-talkie in-between taking drags from a cigarette. Detective Monti was pacing and talking on his phone in the general vicinity of Ruggero. *Oh, great, I'm the last one to the party.*

"About time you got here!" Ruggero snapped as he flicked his cigarette toward the ground as if it had burned him, ignoring the garbage can and ashtray a few meters away.

"It's 6:00 a.m., and I was called to report here less than an hour ago," Vivianna shot back. Detective Monti, no longer pacing, was walking directly toward her.

"Good, I'm glad you're finally here. Detective Ruggero will brief you on the case. We'll hold a small press conference in one hour; I will address the press. You will stand behind me and say nothing," barked Monti. *Now I'm beginning to see why I was assigned to this case*, she thought somewhat bitterly. *I'm the young female cop, required to lend a sense of diversity to the Roman P.D. for what is, apparently, a case that will play out on TV.*

"What's the meaning of all this?" asked Vivianna. "I was told there was a robbery, some missing computers, and possibly a missing professor?"

Monti just pointed to Ruggero and walked away to take a call.

"Here's the bio of the teacher whose laboratory was vandalized. We have reason to believe he was here working last night when this occurred." Vivianna was handed a sheet of paper by Detective Ruggero, containing Professor Federico Sisti's credentials. She quickly learned that he was not only one of the university's most decorated faculty members, but one of the world's preeminent geneticists. His expertise was anthropological genetics, the study of the human genome to determine the origins and migrations of ancient human populations.

Detective Ruggero talked as they walked into the building. "A cleaning crew was coming through early this morning and found evidence of a break-in, so they called us."

"Why is the press here? And why is Detective Monti here?" asked Vivianna. Ruggero just motioned for her to follow him as they headed deeper into the school.

They walked down a long hallway where students were beginning to congregate, buzzing about the police presence. As they turned a corner, she could see crime tape blocking entrance to an entire wing of the building. "The lab is back here," said Ruggero. "You have to see what the cleaning crew found to understand the commotion."

As they walked through rooms filled with sophisticated-looking equipment, Vivianna noticed that some computers had, in fact, been smashed, cords forlornly hanging out of them as if hard drives had been removed. Through another door into the last lab at the end of the hall, she immediately saw the reason Monti was here: The lab was filled with more equipment and workstations, all of which that appeared to be vandalized. On the far wall was a whiteboard. Someone had painted large Egyptian hieroglyphics across the board; each was at least three feet tall and painted in what looked to be blood. The blood had started to drip down the whiteboard, but the glyphs were still clearly legible:

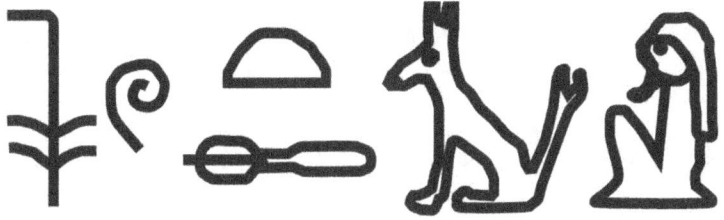

CHAPTER FOUR

Chicago, Illinois

Michael stood in the middle of a packed train, balancing his stack of luggage. *This would be so much easier if I had just taken a cab. Nah...every dollar counts, and the Red Line to the Blue Line to O'Hare will save me a $50 cab ride.* He thought about the difficulty he would face in making his student loans last while traveling around Italy using euros. Thankfully, he had lined up some free places to stay with relatives and assumed some authentic home-cooked meals might be in his future as well. At least, he hoped so.

It can't be that bad of an idea if one of the world's top geneticists has agreed to participate in my project...right? Michael was trying to convince himself. He thought about the day he'd heard back from Professor Sisti. After sending him a lengthy email and assuming it was a long shot that he'd get anything back, he was surprised not only to hear back from the professor, but that his lab wanted to participate in Michael's doctoral thesis project. The idea he had pitched was rather straightforward: The use of last names was rare during the Middle Ages. Surnames were generally only used by nobles who held land. The concept of a family surname didn't become commonplace until the mid-1400s. Michael's idea had been to explore the nature of the family structure during this dark time in history. He was going to collect saliva from any and all living male Malavoltis willing to participate in the study. On top of that, he had already started the process of documenting his own genealogy to connect himself to the Malavoltis who had helped rule the Republic of Siena for several hundred years. With documented proof and the right connections, thanks to Professor Sisti, he hoped for government permission to open and retrieve DNA samples from various Malavolti tombs scattered throughout Tuscany. Some were documented as far back as the eleventh century, with others that could be as old as the eighth or ninth century, according to the Dominican priest he had talked to about the tombs under the San Domenico Cathedral in Siena.

With DNA samples from various Malavoltis throughout a millennium, he could gain a clearer idea of what had constituted his family structure over a long stretch of time. Was there a single patriarch, or was the surname something that had been given to a group of early Siena inhabitants? How far back in time did the family have a presence in Siena? These were just a few of the questions Michael hoped to answer with the genetic component of his thesis paper. The Malavoltis presented the perfect case, having a documented history in the vicinity of Siena as far back as the time of Charlemagne. *Why would a noble family that governed their own lands use a surname that meant "the evildoers"?* he wondered.

Once the genetic relation between the Malavoltis of Middle Ages fame and the present-day Malavoltis was established, he would be able to write the "social amnesia" aspect of his thesis. Social amnesia is a well-documented phenomenon that demonstrates humanity, as a whole, isn't very good at remembering or learning from the past. He hoped to show how prevalent it is, even within one family structure throughout a millennium. The bulk of his thesis would be about the country of Siena itself, particularly how its economic prosperity in the thirteenth and fourteenth centuries had helped to kick-start the Renaissance. By doing an in-depth genealogy of one of Siena's most notable families and conducting interviews from modern-day family members, he hoped to demonstrate how common the concept of collective ignorance of our past still is.

As far as he knew, his modern relatives had little inkling of the family's past. Now a part of modern Italy, Siena had existed as an autonomous, wealthy, and important country for roughly 500 years, and the Malavoltis, through all its ups and downs, had been one of a handful of prominent families that had helped establish and run the country. Another 500 years later, and their contributions were all but forgotten.

Michael's thoughts wandered to the academic accolades that could come of this thesis; then he snorted at his own hubris. Who was he kidding? There might be a handful of modern historians who cared about the early days of Siena. *At least I'm doing a favor to all future generations of Malavoltis,* he told himself. How many families have a family historian who has access to one of the top anthropological geneticists in the world? It's possible, through the use of

Y-chromosome analysis, that the professor may even have a good guess as to where the original patriarch of the family came from before settling in Siena over a millennium ago. Maybe the family stems from a noble Etruscan family, or perhaps they were wealthy early traders on the Mediterranean Sea—maybe even Phoenicians; who knows?

All he *did* know was that he really wanted to piece together this historical mystery that maybe only a handful of historians even cared about. Oh well, Professor Sisti cared, so that was something. Then again, maybe he had agreed to do this just so some of his students would have a project. *What if Sisti thinks this is really beneath him, but here comes some American student with a grant, and he's willing to go collect samples? He could just assign some grad student to answer my emails, run the samples I turn in, and then if anything interesting comes of the study, he can always attach his name to the project and publish it at the end*, Michael worried.

Well…at the very least, he had agreed to meet with Michael the next day to go over the whole thing; that was something. And even if nothing academically interesting came out of the project, how many people ever got a chance to try to document their paternal lineage for more than 1,000 years? Michael's nerves eased as the train lurched to a stop downtown. Time for a transfer. *Ugh, why did I bring so much luggage?*

CHAPTER FIVE

Rome, Italy

Detective Monti led the meeting like a drill sergeant barking out orders. Meanwhile Vivianna looked around the room, wondering who all these people were, as there were at least a dozen people being briefed on the case. The crowd began to thin as Monti gave directives. Eventually, it thinned down to just the three lead detectives, Monti, Ruggero, and Vivianna. Monti had a report from the forensics lab on the blood from the whiteboard.

"I've got good news," he announced. "It was not the professor's blood. Not his blood type, and, in fact, not even fresh blood. A preservative was found in the blood. Whoever did this carried it in with them."

Vivianna voiced the obvious question. "This was obviously a message left for someone. But who and why?"

Monti explained that the hieroglyphs formed the name of the Egyptian god Set. As far as why that name had been left at the crime scene, they were still gathering more information on its meaning. He did have some preliminary information he had requested from the university's history department. Detective Monti read aloud the short synopsis he had been given:

"Set was one of many deities worshiped in ancient Egypt. He was viewed differently at different points in history, but he's best known now for the Osiris legend, a story that is over 4,000 years old. Osiris was a good king who was murdered by his brother Set in an attempt to steal the throne. Osiris's wife, Isis, resurrected her husband just long enough to conceive a boy by him, whom she named Horus. Horus was born, put in a reed basket, and sent down the Nile River by his mother, Isis, in order to hide his royal birth. Horus grew up and eventually went on to avenge his father's murder and retake the throne of Egypt. It is widely believed that Set went on to become a symbol of evil and disorder and, eventually, influenced the name for the Abrahamic devil, Satan.

"So…this could be a message for someone unknown to us regarding the doctor's work in Egypt, but it's more likely just some sicko trying to make a name for himself by painting an ancient name for Satan in blood."

Detective Monti continued, "We need to consider disgruntled coworkers and even students. An academic feud or jealousy seems like a likely motive. As far as what was missing at the university, other than the professor, it is now confirmed that three separate hard drives were removed, all of which were used for cataloging genetics work. Two other larger hard drives used by his students were smashed. We have also discovered that Sisti's flat was broken into and tossed the same night. It's hard to say if anything is missing, as the professor lived alone, but whatever they were looking for, they left most of his obvious valuables."

The two junior detectives sat ready for their orders. Instead of an open collaboration, however, Detective Monti pulled Ruggero over, and they looked to be having a quiet but very pointed discussion. Whatever Monti was directing Ruggero to do, he seemed to be agreeing, as he nodded for a few minutes before the one-way conversation ended, and Ruggero stood and briskly left with his marching orders. That left just Monti and Vivianna in the meeting room.

"Detective Giuseppe," Monti boomed, "you are scheduled to represent the department at the forensics conference in Florence next week, are you not?"

"Yes, but someone else can go. Do you want me to start interviewing Sisti's colleagues at the university? Don't we have anything on CCTV from the cameras there? How about around his flat? Are we looking into his personal life?" She shot questions at Monti in rapid-fire succession. Monti maintained an amused look on his face as the junior detective suggested avenues they should explore.

"Are you done yet? I assure you, we are working every angle. I want you to attend the forensics conference next week as scheduled. We have plenty of people on this case." Before she could protest, Monti held his hand in the air and gave her a look as if to say *don't you even dare question me* before continuing, "The professor had a meeting scheduled tomorrow with an American student from the University of Chicago. They were apparently collaborating on some kind of genealogy project. His secretary said the professor was a very busy man who routinely turned down requests for work, yet he had cleared other things from his schedule to personally work on this project, which is unusual. The lab he developed at Sapienza is one of the best in the world at sequencing genes and pulling genetic information from antique samples. Requests come in daily for work from around the world that he typically turns down.

"His secretary also said he's quiet and mostly keeps to himself, so she has no idea why this project was so important. She only knows that he turned down several other things to take it on. The student's name is Michael Malavolti; he is scheduled to arrive on a flight at LDA at 7:30 tonight. I'd like you to meet him at the airport. Get as much information from him as you can about this project, and bring him into the station tomorrow morning for a statement."

Vivianna objected, "You can't be serious! I'm supposed to babysit an American who wasn't even in the country at the time of the crime just because he was scheduled to meet with Professor Sisti tomorrow to work on a family tree with him?"

Monti just glared at her with that look. Knowing it would be futile to try and get reassigned to something more meaningful, Vivianna relented with a groan and asked, "Fine. What's his flight number?"

CHAPTER SIX

Rome, Italy

Michael shuffled his way off the airplane with his carry-on luggage, excited to be in Rome. He knew that Leonardo da Vinci Airport was near the sea, and he'd have to find transportation for the remaining 15 km or so inland to his hostel near the Coliseum. Lost in thought and post-flight drowsiness, he almost missed the attractive lady standing with the others holding signs to alert passengers to their transportation. Michael did a double take when he saw MALAVOLTI in plain block letters. *Did the university send a driver for me?* This was all too weird; a few hours ago he was having a midflight dream that when he showed up at the university tomorrow, they would have no idea who he was, and no appointment scheduled for him to meet with Professor Sisti. Now it appeared not only were they expecting him, they were also rolling out the red carpet.

He timidly approached the lady holding the sign with his name on it and said in passable Italian, "Hi, I'm Michael Malavolti."

"Good. Follow me, please," replied the pretty driver in English as she turned and started to walk toward the exit.

"Wait. I have a checked bag I need to retrieve."

The woman let out an audible sigh as she stopped and turned toward Michael. Without a word, she began to walk in the direction of the baggage claim area. They stood silently for a moment next to the carousel, waiting for bags to start to appear. Michael broke the awkward silence, saying in English, "So, you were hired by the university to pick me up?"

Her accent was subtle but noticeable. "No. My name is Vivianna Giuseppe. I am a detective with the Rome Police Department."

Michael's face went white. "Is there some kind of problem? What do you want with me?"

"You have a meeting scheduled tomorrow with Professor Federico Sisti, yes?" Vivianna turned her head to look at him. "As of right now, the professor is part of an ongoing investigation, as he is missing. His lab was broken into. Some items were stolen, others vandalized. I will drive you to your hotel tonight, but I will need you to come to my station tomorrow morning. I have some questions regarding your relationship with Professor Sisti and the nature of the research you were collaborating on with him."

"This must be some kind of misunderstanding," he protested. "I've never even met the professor, and we've only corresponded by email. He was going to help me with my PhD thesis project. It's just a genealogy project; I couldn't possibly have anything to do with this."

Vivianna stood stoically, watching the baggage carousel as bags began to pop out. After a long pause and looking visibly frustrated, she replied, "Nevertheless, Signore Malavolti, I will need to talk to you at the station. Once I have what I need, you will be free to go. Besides, you have the day free now as far as I can see, since the professor is missing."

Michael's heart sank. All his fears and trepidations were coming true before his project even got off the ground.

On the way into the city, Michael gave Vivianna a brief description of his thesis project, focusing on the part that involved working on his own family's genealogy and history in Siena. Vivianna kept her eyes on the road at all times, seemingly more intent on weaving through traffic than listening to Michael. When he finished, there was an uncomfortable silence for a few minutes before she finally asked, "What hotel are you staying at?"

"Nero's Palace Hostel," he replied, before adding, "I was able to book my own room there," thinking that sounded more adult. *Why did I say that? Like she cares if I'm staying in a youth hostel.*

"Great, I'll pick you up at 9:00 a.m."

As Michael walked through the police station with Vivianna the next morning, he couldn't help but notice that it wasn't just him she seemed to be angry with, which brought a slight feeling of relief. Michael didn't understand much Italian, but if he had to guess, he figured three different guys had complimented or hit on her while they passed the offices and cubicles. She told all three to go hell in some way or another—that much was clear from her hand gestures.

They arrived at a small conference room where three other people waited. There were two middle-aged women who seemed prepared to write down everything Michael said, Vivianna, and a man who identified himself as Detective Monti. They spoke mostly in English for Michael's convenience.

"Tell us about your relationship with Professor Sisti, and describe what the two of you were working on," Detective Monti ordered after the introductions were out of the way.

Still not really understanding how or why his trip was starting in a Roman police station, explaining his thesis to transcribers, Michael thought, *Oh well, this might be the first captive audience I've had regarding my thesis.* He began nervously, "My name is Michael Malavolti. I'm a student at the University of Chicago in the United States. Next year, I'm beginning to work toward a doctorate of philosophy in Renaissance Studies. The Renaissance is considered a bridge between the Dark Ages and modern times, when human development took a leap forward, generally thought of as the fourteenth to the seventeenth centuries. It's also widely accepted that it began as a cultural movement here in Italy. When people think of the Renaissance in Italy, they typically think of Florence as being the home of the great patrons and birthplace of the humanistic movement."

When he paused, Monti gestured for him to continue.

"My thesis was to focus on the city-state of Siena as the economic and creative engine that helped to drive the birth of the Renaissance. During the Middle Ages, Siena and Florence were natural enemies, always at odds with each other. The culmination of this competition was the Battle of Montaperti, the bloodiest battle of medieval Italy. On September 4, 1260 over 10,000 men died in a great military upset as Sienese forces defeated the much larger contingent from Florence. This victory, along with the newly burgeoning Siena banking industry in the late-thirteenth century, put Siena in a very wealthy and prosperous position. With abundance came a sort of civic self-actualization. The humanistic movement can be seen in the art of the Cathedral of Siena from as early as the thirteenth century. Siena was situated on the road to Rome and was a natural trade center that..."

"Maybe you could just stick to the part of your project that involved Professor Sisti?" Vivianna interrupted, sounding irritated.

"Right, okay...sorry. This is just so interesting to me. As you know, my surname is Malavolti. My ancestors came from the Siena region, and I still have relatives in the area. The Malavolti family of Siena was a noble one with a presence in the city from the beginning of its recorded history up until at least the fall of the Republic of Siena in the mid-1500s. The history of Siena begins to be covered around the time of Charlemagne. There was a small settlement there before then, but after Charlemagne passed through in 796, the area truly began to prosper. Throughout its history, Siena has produced dozens of wealthy noble families, but five families were of utmost importance to the history of the Republic of Siena: the Malavolti, Tolomei, Piccolomini, Saracini, and Salembeni. Of these five, early historical sources have an arrival time sometime after Charlemagne for all of them, except the Malavolti.

Some say the Malavolti family was founded by a knight who came with Charlemagne; other sources imply its origins are lost to history, leaving historians to speculate they were already settled in Siena when Charlemagne came. Regardless, it's generally accepted that their castle in the city is one of the oldest, and their origins in this area are ancient." He paused to gather his thoughts.

"Go on," ordered Monti.

"Right. Various members of the Malavolti family were involved in governing Siena for several centuries, throughout its different forms of government. There was a Phillipo Malavolti who led an army from Siena to the Holy Land for the Crusades in 1150; he returned to be elected as the *podesta* (mayor) of the city. The office of the Bishop of Siena was mostly held by various Malavoltis from 1282 to 1371. The Malavoltis fought in several wars for Siena and led their military company, St. Egidio, in the Battle of Montaperti.

"In time, the patrician families of Siena grew to be some of the wealthiest in all of Europe. Banking collapsed with the fall of the Roman Empire and didn't start again until the 1200s. Siena was instrumental in this. One of the first banks to do business throughout Europe was called the Gran Tavola, run by a gentleman from Siena named Bonsigniori. He was supported by the Malavolti family, many of whom lent money to various popes and kings of Europe. For the 500 years that Siena existed as an independent nation, the Malavoltis were leading power brokers for the state. They were there from its earliest recorded history and in its last hours; it was Orlando Malavolti whom the city sent to plead with the King of Spain. Siena was defeated by Spain in 1555."

"Maybe you could just tell us what you and the professor were planning to do, Mr. Malavolti!" Vivianna interrupted sharply.

"Right, sorry. Professor Sisti had agreed to have his lab run genetic testing for part of my thesis. I was planning to construct a family tree by collecting DNA samples from living male Malavoltis all over Italy and America. We were also going to be testing some ancient Malavolti samples from tombs in and around Tuscany. It was to be a simple family study of the genetic makeup of one of Siena's power-broker families from the Middle Ages. Who were they, where did they come from, and what constituted the family structure? Was there one patriarch who spread the surname or different branches? I was hoping to demonstrate that history is often easily lost. I don't think many of today's Malavoltis know much about the history of the Republic of Siena, a country their family helped establish and run for 500 years."

As Michael spoke, Detective Monti kept checking his phone and texting, even getting up to take a call in the hallway at one point. Vivianna sat silently, looking mostly disinterested. As Michael finished, he felt a sense of relief, as he thought his explanation was boring enough to end this angle of the investigation. It was evident to him that whatever sort of trouble the professor had gotten himself into it had nothing to do with his thesis project.

Detective Monti looked up from his phone as Michael was finishing and asked him to tell them about *Dell'Historia di Siena*.

"Um, it's a history book on Siena? Considered one of the best for its age. It was published in 1574, so it's a good source for information on the early days of Siena. It was written by Orlando Malavolti, the same diplomat Siena sent to plead with the King of Spain in its last days. It's apparently well cited and often considered the most reliable source for early information on Siena. He used various government and legal documents to narrate Siena's history. Why do you ask?" Michael asked timidly.

"It was recently checked out of the Sapienza library by Professor Sisti," replied Monti.

"It was?" Michael smiled before realizing the inappropriate nature of his delight. "I'm sorry; it's just that I wasn't sure the professor would be involved in my project much at all. It's surprising to hear he was taking such an interest in it."

"The professor had two dozen books out on loan from the library," Vivianna interjected to quell his joy. "Do we have all we need?" She directed the question toward Monti, who still seemed more interested in his phone than Michael.

"Yes. Thank you, Mr. Malavolti. If we have any further questions, we will be in touch. Please give Detective Giuseppe your itinerary in Italy and the best way to reach you if we need to." Monti was walking out the door before he even finished his sentence.

Michael sat there dejected, letting the disappointment of his scrapped project set in now that he seemed to be done with the police. He'd planned to spend a few days in Rome and then go on to Siena for several days before heading farther north to his relatives' homes just outside Tuscany in the mountainous region south of Modena in Emilia Romagna. There was a cluster of Malavoltis in that area, and it was going to be the starting point for his DNA collecting endeavor.

"I guess I'll push forward with my itinerary then," he told Vivi. "I mean, I don't have a lab to run my tests, but I could start collecting the samples and worry about testing later. Maybe there's a lab in Chicago that could accommodate me. I'll stay the course and start shipping the samples back to my university. I'll have to make some calls." It was hard to tell if Michael was talking to her or just thinking out loud.

"Look, Michael...I'm sorry about your thesis," she said. "I get lunch every Friday with my uncle. I'm going to meet him at his office in the Vatican now before we get lunch. Do you want to come with? I'm sure he could set you up with a private tour of their museums."

"Seriously?" Michael perked up immediately. "Yeah, that would be great! I was just going to wander around and sightsee today anyway."

CHAPTER SEVEN

Haifa, Israel

Federico Sisti had been awake for what felt like several hours now. He was mentally working through what was happening to him and trying to make sense of it all. His last memory was of working in his lab on Wednesday night. Now he was tied to a chair with both his hands and feet bound and a blindfold over his eyes—with no idea where he was or even what day it was. He only knew that he was on a boat because he could feel the gentle rocking of water, hear a soft creaking, and smell the salt in the air. Or at least the odor of decaying seaweed and plankton that was the smell of the sea. He could also hear the voices of at least two men talking in another room. It was difficult to make out what they were saying, though when he strained, he did catch one phrase that sounded like Hebrew: "מתי אנחנו מגיעים לחקור את הבחורה הזה."

Though he recognized the cadence, Hebrew was a language he did not speak. He feared that this might have something to do with his recent discovery, but how? He hadn't told anyone!

"Hello! Who's there? Help me please!" Sisti yelled out, hoping someone was within earshot. The door suddenly swung open violently. "You've made some kind of mistake. Please! I'm a research scientist. Untie me and we can talk because there must be some kind of misunderstanding." He pleaded with his captor who he could hear walking quickly in his direction.

Then all the air left his lungs as the man punched him in the gut. He lurched forward from the pain and was then pulled quickly backward as a gag was being tied over his mouth. "Keep your mouth shut, and this will all be over soon," his captor sneered before leaving the room and closing the door behind him.

"If this man is such a threat to our people, why don't we just kill him and get it over with, David?" demanded Ishmael as he rejoined him in the ship's galley.

"We are following orders, Ishmael. You know that."

"But whose orders? Can we trust this Egyptian? Is he part of the prophecy?"

"Do you trust Rabbi Bein? Because that's whose orders we're following," snapped David. "There would be no Gideon's Sword without brave men like Rabbi Bein who do what is necessary to protect God's will. If Rabbi Bein says this man is a threat like we have never faced before, then who am I to question him?"

"I would die for Rabbi Bein, you know I would!" replied Ishmael. "It's just that we don't know who the Egyptian really *is*. What is his interest in keeping Israel safe?"

David paused in a moment of frustration before responding, "I'm not happy to be in the dark either, but Rabbi Bein says we should trust this source with our lives and do exactly as he says, so that's exactly what I'm going to do. For now, we are ordered to hold this professor and await further instructions. And that is what we will do."

CHAPTER EIGHT

Vatican City

As Michael walked down a long hall with Vivi, his grief about the professor began to subside. For the past year, he'd been using every free moment to read about ancient Siena. Being inside the Vatican gave him a sense of stepping back into those medieval times. *The collaboration with the professor I was so excited to be working with is apparently not going to happen, but on the flip side, I'm currently walking through the bowels of the Vatican with a gorgeous Italian lady who is setting me up on a private tour. Things could be worse,* he thought.

She reached her uncle's office door a few strides ahead of Michael. "Vivi!" came a bellow from the room; it sounded as if Luciano Pavarotti were excited to see her.

"Uncle Franco!" Vivi replied as she hurried into his office to give him a kiss and hug. Michael reached the office in time to see their embrace. He realized it was the first time since he had met Vivianna at the airport that he had seen her smile. *My God is she beautiful.* Michael caught himself staring as she hugged her uncle, wondering who this woman was. She looked like a different person; gone was the scowl that seemed more of a constant reminder she was an officer of the law.

"Michael Malavolti, this is my uncle, Cardinal Franco Colombi." Vivianna introduced Michael, who was standing in the door with his mouth hanging slightly ajar. Franco, who was still being embraced by Vivi, moved to shake Michael's hand.

"Pleased to meet you, sir," Michael said politely, feeling a bit awed. He'd never met a Catholic cardinal before.

"You as well, you as well. Come in and sit down." Franco, spoke excellent English and motioned to one of the chairs on the other side of his desk.

Cardinal Franco Colombi was a large, gregarious man. He had an enormous presence, both in his physical stature and in the tenor of his booming voice. He shook Michael's hand with two large hands that engulfed his. Everything in his office, from the table and chairs to the art on the walls, looked like it came right out of a museum. Michael didn't know where to focus his eyes next. There were works of art that looked like pieces by the Italian Renaissance masters to his untrained eye. It was due to the use of vermilion, he knew, a shade of red often found in Italian works of art from ancient Rome to Renaissance Florence. There were also maps—lots of maps. Some looked ancient, but it was hard to tell what they were maps of. Michael had noticed a plaque outside the office that answered the question of where he was: it read, "*Pontificia Commissione di Archeologia Sacra*," which Michael knew meant Pontifical Commission of Sacred Archaeology.

"Are these maps of catacombs?" he asked breathlessly as he motioned toward a wall with a half a dozen maps hanging on it.

"Indeed they are! My job involves preserving the labyrinth of tombs under this city," answered the cardinal as he peered over his computer screen.

"Michael is a student from America," Vivianna explained. "He's here to do research on the Renaissance, but the professor he was here to work with went missing two nights ago. A case I'm working on...or was working on, anyway. Is there someone free to give him a tour of the museums?"

"Of course! For my Vivi, the answer is always the same," Franco replied with a warm smile while looking at Michael. "Let me finish up what I am working on, make a call to see who's free to give Michael the grand tour, and then we can go to lunch! I was thinking we would go to the trattoria on Via Cavour, the one with the biscotti you like so much."

Michael couldn't stop looking at Vivianna. She looked ten years younger in the presence of her uncle. "Okay, take your time. I'm in no rush today," she responded while moving around the desk to take a seat near Michael.

"Can *I* call you Vivi?" Michael asked with a grin, then realized how silly he sounded, since he was soon to say good-bye to her.

She rolled her eyes but smiled a bit. "Sure, whatever you like. I have your contact info, and you have my number. If you have any contact with Professor Sisti, make sure you call me right away. I'm actually going to be not too far from you next week. I'll be in Florence for most of the week for a conference."

Cardinal Franco hung up the phone and stood. "What's this business with a missing professor, Vivi?"

"I don't really know. The geneticist at Sapienza who disappeared, his lab was also vandalized."

"Sapienza?" asked Franco with concern. "It's not Federico Sisti, is it?"

They both looked up in shock. "Yes, do you know him?" she asked.

"I've met him at a fundraiser or two for the university. I know a lot of people, Vivi; you know that. Come, let's get going."

Just then, a young man in clerical attire appeared at the door. "Ah yes, Daniel, come in," said Franco as he motioned with his hand. "Michael, this is Daniel Burto, a seminarian also from America. He is an excellent art historian and will give you a fantastic tour. Come, Vivi, I have a busy afternoon." With that, Franco began to move for the door.

"Hi, pleased to meet you. I'm Michael Malavolti." He stood, extending his hand to greet Daniel. As Michael said his last name, he thought he saw Cardinal Franco pause for a moment, as if he were going to say something, before turning away and heading down the hall to catch up with Vivi.

CHAPTER NINE

New York City, New York

General Garret waited in the back of a dark SUV parked near the corner of 68th Street and Park Avenue on the Upper East Side, reading encrypted emails on his cell phone. Soon he'd have to enter the mansion on the corner and lead a meeting of the operational directors of Ordo. The various stars and medals on his chest told the story of a man who had ascended the ladder of the greatest military force the planet had ever seen.

After an eight-year stint serving on the National Security Council, he formally retired from his government position, although he was now as busy as ever. He was a board member of the Council of Foreign Relations (CFR), a think tank founded in 1921 that was headquartered at the mansion he was about to enter. Garret's influence extended to countless other think tanks and policy makers—all thanks to his position as an operational director for Ordo. Most of his time spent and a great deal of his wealth came from his position in Ordo.

Based on a pyramid structure, Ordo was what those at the invisible top of the pyramid (the elite members) called themselves. The larger, more tangible base of the pyramid went by many names, but it all traced back to a fraternal order that began in the late 1800s and attracted a number of wealthy titans of industry in the early 1900s. Ordo Templi Orientis (aka OTO) had grown quickly, attracting powerful members in Europe and America who were lured by its occult religion, the secret society aspect, and the strength it afforded in fraternal bond. The order quickly became powerful, too powerful for those on the outside who felt threatened by that kind of concentration of power. Some of the wealthiest benefactors from the second industrial, or technological, revolution who joined the order quickly formulated a plan that allowed it to continue to grow yet burrow underground and disappear from the public view, while they formed a borderless state and moved slowly toward world domination and control.

Their plan made them the most successful and powerful, little-known fraternal order ever assembled, as they discovered early on the need to stratify their membership and concentrate the crucial influencers at the top. The pyramid base members would be robust and diversified, consisting not only of the fraternal order and external public belief systems, but also they sought—and found—control and sway over other fraternal orders and occult teachings. OTO needed to have influence in as many places as possible, and they used any means necessary to achieve it. Anyone on the outside attempting to study the pyramid's power structure would become lost in a maze of mirrors and conspiracy before ever nearing the most invisible top tier of the pyramid, simply referred to as Ordo.

Ordo consisted of twenty-four operational directors who formulated plans and executed them by exerting pressure downward on the various operatives in the base and utilizing the order's extensive assets. Above the twenty-four operational directors was the "capstone," even more mysterious yet. The capstone was what allowed the order to become the best-funded and most powerful secret society for over a hundred years. The capstone included some of the wealthiest people on the planet who all had the same goal: world domination—the ultimate power. Members of the capstone only dealt with the operational directors, and even they didn't know who all was in the capstone.

Garret himself had only ever corresponded with a few capstone members, who all used aliases anyway. He knew other operational directors had taken directives from different members of the capstone, although the aliases made it hard to determine if that was true or not. He didn't mind; as a military tactician, he found the order's structure and history brilliant. Everything was compartmentalized; no one below the capstone level knew the big picture or the ultimate goals. Only one thing bothered the general about OTO. He had no problem with the religion or occult practices. He knew every state needed a religion, even a borderless state that was everywhere and nowhere. Garret had helped execute countless wars and drafted nation-rebuilding plans during his lengthy military career. He knew religious beliefs and the holy men behind them played an integral role in any properly executed plan for nation building. Citizens needed something to believe in, a higher cause.

Garret had been fast-tracked through the religious occult initiation process, earmarked for a seat among the operational directors, after a long career as an asset of the order in the United States military industrial complex. *A bunch of mystical mumbo jumbo and sexual deviancy*, as far as he was concerned. The occult religion was rarely discussed among the operation directors: As it should be, he thought. They were more concerned with growing the order's control and wealth. He didn't know about the capstone, though, and that bothered him. He knew religious fanatics would act on blind faith and could ignore reason and logic, something he had to work with while planning wars in certain regions.

While serving on the Ordo board of directors something caught his attention, which first created Garret's concern: He noticed some young CEOs of large technology and shipping companies, who were involved in OTO, appeared to be heavily invested in its religion, Thelema. Those members had suddenly seemed to quit the order, and all record of their OTO dealings were expunged from every public forum. Then, mysteriously, all of their companies grew in wealth and influence tenfold. He thought this could only mean one thing: they had paid a fortune to make the leap into the invisible capstone.

General Garret's uneasiness about the capstone's religious beliefs was brought to the forefront when he had recently been given an assignment from a capstone member who called himself the "Relic Hunter." Garret knew nothing about this new contact, of course, but suspected he was old money—like the Ordo directors assumed most of the capstone were—invested in banking or natural resources, such as oil or gold mines. The person was possibly royalty or some combination of all those things. His mission had something to do with holy relics they possessed that allowed them to exert control over various world religions. It involved the extraction of a college professor and some reconnaissance to make sure this professor hadn't shared information that threatened to destabilize OTO's control on a number of the world's religious leaders, who were, in essence, the order's puppets. Having religious leaders in their pocket was invaluable to the order's ends.

Garret had called on a trusted operator in Rome to handle the mission's logistics. Now he was getting some blowback from the Relic Hunter as to how things were handled, and he wondered if it was based on OTO's own religion and occult practices. But he needed to put those thoughts aside as he prepared for his meeting by reading aloud his notes for his upcoming presentation to the Ordo board of directors.

Garrett opened the file titled "Decentralization" and began rehearsing: "For over a century, we have been the steady hand that has guided humanity toward a better tomorrow, ensuring stability, order, and prosperity for mankind to flourish. Slowly, from decade to decade, century to century, we have worked at consolidating power structures. This has made Ordo's mission easier in terms of maintaining control and has brought about several decades of peace and stability to the West after World War II. With the advent of the Information Age, we've increasingly faced new challenges to control. The capstone is concerned, at this time, with the rising tide of populism and now the looming threat of decentralization. Decentralized banking and information sharing has put our future at risk."

Ordo Templi Orientis

"Ordo Templi Orientis (O.T.O.) ('Order of the Temple of the East' or 'Order of Oriental Templars') is an international fraternal and religious organization founded at the beginning of the 20th century by Carl Kellner and Theodor Reuss. English author and occultist Aleister Crowley is the best-known and most influential member of the order.

Originally it was intended to be modeled after and associated with European Freemasonry, such as Masonic Templar organizations, but under the leadership of Aleister Crowley, O.T.O. was reorganized around the Law of Thelema as its central religious principle. This Law—expressed as 'Do what thou wilt shall be the whole of the Law' and 'Love is the law, love under will'—was promulgated in 1904 with the writing of The Book of the Law.

Similar to many secret societies, O.T.O. membership is based on an initiatory system with a series of degree ceremonies that use ritual drama to establish fraternal bonds and impart spiritual and philosophical teachings.

O.T.O. also includes the Ecclesia Gnostica Catholica (EGC), or Gnostic Catholic Church, which is the ecclesiastical arm of the Order. Its central rite, which is public, is called Liber XV, or the Gnostic Mass."[2]

Aeon (Thelema)

"In the religion of Thelema, it is believed that the history of humanity can be divided into a series of aeons (also written æons), each of which was accompanied by its own forms of "magical and religious expression." The first of these was the Aeon of Isis, which Thelemites believed occurred during prehistory and which saw mankind worshipping a Great Goddess, symbolized by the ancient Egyptian deity Isis. In Thelemite beliefs, this was followed by the Aeon of Osiris, a period that took place in the classical and mediaeval centuries, when humanity worshipped a singular male god, symbolized by the Egyptian god

Osiris, and was therefore dominated by patriarchal values. And finally the third aeon, the Aeon of Horus, which was controlled by the child god, symbolized by Horus. In this new aeon, Thelemites believe that humanity will enter a time of self-realization and self-actualization.

Within the Thelemite religion, each of these aeons is believed to be 'characterized by their [own specific] magical formula,' the use of which 'is very important and fundamental to the understanding of Thelemic Magick.'"[3]

CHAPTER TEN

Jerusalem, Israel

It started by looking into the past—then it became an obsession—before his mastery led to a dark vision of the future. Rabbi Isaac Bein was a young charismatic preacher running a synagogue in Toulouse, France when he took his first steps into the mystical world of Kabbalah. His interest in and study of the Jewish population in the area took him back to the Dark Ages, where there were more questions than answers about how such a large Jewish population found themselves in southwestern France in the first place. Researching their regional roots, he learned that the esoteric practice of Judaism known as Kabbalah had begun to take shape in the area during the twelfth century. *Why did members of this particular Jewish community craft and document the discipline over 800 years ago?*

What started as an attempt to understand a branch of his beloved religion became a seductive drug as he ascended the divine ladder of Kabbalah. The prayers and incantations began in earnest as an immersive way to learn about the discipline, and he was often asked questions about it by curious members of his synagogue. As his focus and discipline grew, so did his ability to climb the levels of his soul's existence: Ascending to the Orchard (heaven) as it was known in Kabbalah.

After some time grappling with the practice, it finally became clear. During one of his prayer sessions he felt his soul ascend from Nefesh, the plane of action, to a higher realm of existence, Ruach. Then with more practice and focus, in a trance-like state, he was able to ascend from Ruach to Neshama, an even higher realm of the spirit. In that realm he began to commune directly with Divine Energy, with light. At the Neshama level, there was still darkness that obscured and intermingled with the light, blocking out the clarity he chased.

It took several years of practice and purifying his soul before he was able to ascend to Chaya, the plane of pure Divine Energy, in which he was shown future events that would play out as foretold. Things were good in the life of Rabbi Bein, even if his reputation as a fringe preacher obsessed with the arcane practice of Kabbalah grew. Then one day, while in a trance-like state of prayer, things changed in the Chaya plane: suddenly there was darkness intermingling with him that wasn't supposed to be there. At first he thought he had taken a wrong path on his spiritual journey, reaffirming his previous belief that the practice was dangerous and opened the soul to evil energies. Eventually, after several sessions in deep meditation and prayer, he could see that the evil presence in Chaya was being controlled by the light, which had invited it in to comingle and surround the rabbi. His visions began to become clearer, despite the dark presence; he felt he was being called to surround himself with darkness and evil to serve a higher cause.

Eventually, he was shown a name: Seth.

The rabbi became a shell of his former self. Isolated from his faith and tortured with his visions and beliefs, while living in Jerusalem, he attracted a group of followers interested in his prophecy of the coming time of great strife and upheaval. It was clear to Bein that this was the dark energy he was being called to surround himself with. In time he had a small group of mercenaries, dubbed "Gideon's Sword," who awaited his orders and did his bidding without question.

It all crystallized when a man, who claimed connections to an intelligence report in Egypt that spelled catastrophic danger for Israel, reached out to him. The email had requested an in-person meeting and was signed simply, "Seth." Bein's conscious mind was uncomfortable with the nature of the events unfolding around him; nonetheless, they were happening as he had been shown by the light while in the Chaya plane. He pushed forward, reluctantly, needing to fulfill his divine destiny. Now the leader of his devoted Gideon's Sword followers, David, was providing him an update.

"Rabbi, our mission has been successful up to this point—as directed by 'the Egyptian' you put us in contact with. Ishmael abducted the professor from the university in Rome; we now hold him in captivity and await further orders. The Egyptian also has us shadowing an American student and documenting his movements. It's not clear what the Egyptian wants us to do yet, Rabbi, but I think he's going to ask us to kill these men. Should we?"

Rabbi Bein squeezed the prayer beads in his pocket as David gave him the update. Biting his lip, he nodded in reluctant approval, fighting the urge to break from the path he felt called to follow. *Why is God torturing me so?*

Castel Gandolfo, Italy

Alfonso Carpacci walked a path perched on a cliff along Lake Albano, praying and gazing out on the calm water. His security kept at a distance, allowing him to feel isolated and immersed in nature by the picturesque lake. A phone buzzed under his cassock and interrupted the tranquility of the scene. He began a brisk walk to a bench fifty meters ahead. This phone was reserved for communication with one person, the Grand Master.

"Commander, no leads yet on what they have done with the professor. Recon confirms your suspicion; the student from America has a tail."

"And we still don't know if he is a match?" asked Alfonso.

"No sir. I imagine his tail is trying to ascertain that, as well. Ordo must be worried about what he knows. Do you want us to take him in? It could speed up our timetable and expose us, though. Sir, if I may...the dreams you've been having..."

Alfonso sighed, followed by a long period of silence while he looked out on the lake, thinking about the right path forward before responding. "Soon we will have everything in position to act, but we are not ready yet. I want you to do your best to keep him alive in the meantime. Protect him."

"Yes sir."

"If anything should happen to me, you know what to do. Keep moving forward; you mustn't fail."

"Are you unsatisfied with your security detail, sir?"

"No, no, I'm quite secure here. It's just that at my age it's starting to feel like a small miracle every time I wake up."

"I understand, sir. I'm sure you will see this to the end. I'll have eyes on the American around the clock."

"One more thing," Alfonso replied, as if wavering on the decision, "leave him a clue to the match in the Holy Land. If it's God's will that this man is His messenger, then he will lead him to the truth."

CHAPTER ELEVEN

Rome, Italy

Michael sipped an espresso and watched the throng of tourists mosey through the streets of Rome on a sunny summer day, many with their hands full of shopping bags. *Ah, Rome...the Eternal City, truly a great place to see and get a feel for ancient history mixed with modern convenience.* Everywhere he looked, the stark dichotomy between old and new was present. This once-great empire had done so much to shape Western civilization. Michael's thoughts bounced between anxiety for Professor Sisti and admiration for the lengthy history that was evident all around him as he left the café and joined the tourists.

As he walked, the heat rose up from the dark cobblestoned street; he listened to the constant din of dishes clinking, being changed out by street-side cafes in response to the steady flow of hungry tourists and Romans. Michael scanned his surroundings, trying to identify any ancient structures as he walked, and thought, *Funny how something physicists struggled with can be applied to almost any*

*academic endeavor: the perspective of time. Rome is a beau-
tiful example of man's ancient past, unless you consider the
last few thousand years a drop in the bucket of man's time
here on Earth.*

Via his limited research on Professor Sisti's work, he had
delved into the world of an anthropological geneticist.
Through the use of Y-chromosomes, the sex chromosomes
passed from father to son that make humans male, geneticists were able to track the interconnectedness of every man
on Earth. Every person on the planet has a common paternal grandfather who lived in Africa over 200,000 years ago.
Michael mused about the professor's work as he walked.

Rome is an ancient city by any reasonable standard and
has influenced the world as much as any city, but how much
of our history on Earth is virtually unknown to us now? We
have remnants of advanced civilizations from a few thousand years BC around the Mediterranean, in areas considered the cradle of civilized man. But we know so little
without written language, and even then, history is often
lost. Writing is only 3,000 years old. The Phoenicians are
credited with inventing the alphabet sometime around then;
prior to that, there were more primitive written languages
that relied on symbols around the Mediterranean.

Michael thought, *We don't know what we don't know.
How fun would it be to chat with the professor about his
perspective on mankind, which is certainly broader than
the average tourist marveling at the age of the Pantheon?*

Lamenting his lost opportunity to work with the famed
geneticist, he sauntered through the crowds on the hot
streets of Rome. He had no particular place to be. He knew

he was headed east toward the Spanish Steps as he got farther away from St. Peter's Basilica, which was situated to
face the rising sun. Once he got there, he thought he would
make a right turn and head in the direction of the Coliseum
and his hostel to find a bar and enjoy a slice of real pizza
with a glass of Italian wine.

As he walked, Michael saw a familiar sight—a flag he
had come across in his Renaissance research—so he crossed
the street to investigate. Standing in front of a beautiful old
building, Michael peered through the open doors into a
gated courtyard that looked as if it hadn't changed in centuries, save for the security cameras everywhere. Another
perfect example of Italy's distant past and present right here
on top of each other. On the outside of the building was a
high-end boutique, but behind it was another country, the
third Michael would have visited in the last hour...if he
could only cross the gate and enter the courtyard.

He was standing in front of the lodge of the Sovereign
Order of the Knights of Malta, a 1,000-year-old institution
started by knights in the Holy Land during the Crusades. It
still exists today with United Nations observer status and is
accepted as a sovereign nation by most of the Western
Hemisphere. *It's funny how a twist of fate here or there
means an institution lives on or an event is remembered
forever.*

Michael knew the Knights of Malta were major players
during the timeframe he was focusing his studies on in Italy,
the early pre-Renaissance days. He was also aware that another order of knights from the Holy Land had much more
wealth and political sway in those early days: the Knights

Templar. The Templars had been abolished, accused of crimes, rounded up, and killed by Philip the Fair, the King of France for political and financial reasons in 1307. The same king had been instrumental in bankrupting the Grand Tavola, one of Europe's earliest modern banks—a bank the Malavolti family had helped to start and one often cited as the first modern-day corporation.

Maybe if one or two things had been different, I would have grown up spending summers at one of my family's seasonal villas in Italy instead of camping in Wisconsin.... Nah, I don't think that's how fate works. And besides, camping in Wisconsin is pretty sweet. They probably don't even allow cut-off jean shorts in the grand lodge of the Sovereign Order of the Knights of Malta. He chuckled to himself.

As he admired the façade and pondered the history of this vestige from times gone by, he saw a reflection of an oddly familiar face in the window of the designer boutique. Michael whirled around and stared at a man across the street, who was now reading a newspaper. In the window, he'd seen that man look directly at him just moments earlier.

I'm almost certain I saw that guy on my flight from Chicago. Am I being paranoid? Michael began a brisk walk in the direction of the Spanish Steps.

CHAPTER TWELVE

Rome, Italy

"Vivi, I worry about you. There are many dangerous people in this world." Franco had never been good at saying good-bye to his beloved niece.

"Don't worry, Uncle Franco. I'm a pretty good shot," she responded, patting the small of her back where she kept her gun hidden under her suit coat.

"I know you are. I'll keep praying for you every day. How is your father doing?"

"He's okay. I'll see him tonight. Barbara has some kind of event at her gallery, and I said I'd make an appearance. I'll tell him you said hi," Vivi replied.

"Please do, and Godspeed in locating the professor. Take care, Vivi." Franco gave Vivi a bear hug and kiss on the cheek.

Michael trotted up the Spanish Steps at a brisk pace, then took a seat on a bench in front of the Villa Medici. He waited about a minute before walking back toward the steps to begin his descent. Sure enough, just as he had worried, he could see the big man with the buzz cut ascending on the far right side. Michael made eye contact as the large man quickly looked down at a map, pretending he needed to orientate himself. Okay, time to lose this guy.

As Michael reached the bottom of the steps, he began to run back west in the direction of the Vatican. *I don't want to run directly to my hostel if this guy is actually following me*, he thought. He ran as fast as he could through the crowds for a number of blocks before slowing and checking for a tailing buzz cut, which was nowhere in sight. He then made a left and began to jog in the direction of his hostel.

I think it's time for Operation Slice of Pizza and Glass of Wine with a good vantage point, so I can see that guy coming. Michael soon found a bistro down the street from his hostel where he could grab dinner and keep a lookout for his new friend.

Eating a large slice of pizza and drinking some local wine had a soothing effect on Michael's nerves. Why am I being so paranoid? I'm sure the guy probably recognized me from the flight too. Maybe he just needed some advice from another tourist who speaks English. Whatever the reason, it had been a couple of hours now since he'd seen "Buzz Cut," and it felt like a safe time to head back to his room at Nero's Palace.

Michael entered his hostel to a familiar sight: the same guy behind the desk now was there last night when he checked in and again this morning when he left. Must be the owner, or this guy puts in some serious hours.

"*Buongiorno.*" Michael used his Midwest manners as he greeted the hardworking caretaker, who had his nose in a book. The manager peeked over his book just long enough to nod and acknowledge Michael. *Time for a shower, and then I have to figure out what the hell I'm going to do with my project.*

Michael got back to his room and threw his clothes on the bed, wrapped himself in his towel, and headed down the hall to the community bathroom after locking his door behind him. *For a community bathroom, these shower stalls aren't half bad: private, good water pressure.* Michael took advantage, letting the hot water run on his shoulders for a while, and pondered his next moves.

He'd have to get to work right away on securing another lab to run all his cousins' DNA samples. How was he even going to collect the samples? Professor Sisti was going to get small vials that could be shipped to his lab as he went, so he didn't have to lug a bunch of little jars of spit around. He supposed the first thing to do tomorrow was call his department. Maybe someone from the University of Chicago could run DNA samples, although getting much help at the last minute would be difficult. He sighed. Ugh! *There's no way I'm going to find a lab that can extract and run the old samples! I guess I'll just scrap the ancient genetic component of my thesis. Then what? I have a train ticket and plans to see Italy for the next couple months while collecting samples and conducting interviews. I suppose I could still do the interviews and try to write about forgotten history within my family, even though there will be no hard proof of a link between the ancient Malavoltis and the modern-day ones.*

I have a small problem, Ely texted his boss, David. I think he may have made me. I'm in position near his hostel. He's inside, alone. Please advise; I could take him tonight.

The response came back quickly: *Hold your ground. If he leaves Rome with no further contact with the police, you can let him go. Continue to observe and report back for now. Seth says he needs more time to gather information.*

Michael returned to his room, suddenly feeling exhausted from all the walking he had done that day. The two bags he was going to be dragging around Italy for the next few months greeted him in his otherwise Spartan room. One was a small duffel bag for day trips and carrying around supplies for his thesis; the other was a large suitcase. He tossed his toiletries in his duffel bag sitting on the bed and went to retrieve some clean clothes from his suitcase, which was on the floor at the foot of the bed. He'd left the suitcase unzipped when he dressed that morning. Tossing the top back, he expected to see a pile of clothes; instead, sitting on top of his belongings was a book.

What the heck? Why is there a Bible in my suitcase? Michael lifted the book up to inspect it. It was an old leather-bound Bible. In a moment of panic, Michael quickly took stock of his possessions, but nothing was missing. *I'm going to get to the bottom of this.* He quickly got dressed and headed to talk to the manager at the front desk, Bible in hand. But when the manager claimed no knowledge of the Bible, Michael became even more disturbed by yet another mystery.

CHAPTER THIRTEEN

Rome, Italy

Vivi was just leaving the gallery when her phone rang. Her stepmother ran an art gallery, and there was an opening for a new artist tonight. In an attempt to be a good daughter, she had attended and made the rounds. It was the usual: wine, snacks, and a lot of pretension.

"Hi, Vivi? This is Michael Malavolti."

"This had better be police related, Michael," Vivi responded in her signature tone of mild irritation.

"It is, it is. Well... it's not something I would normally call the police about, but with everything else going on, I just wasn't sure and wanted to run something by you."

"Are you okay, Michael?" she asked, showing the slightest bit of compassion.

"Yeah, I'm fine. Look, I feel dumb calling you now, but here's what happened. After I left the Vatican today—thanks again for hooking me up with the tour, by the way; it was awesome. So anyway, after I left, I was wandering around and stopped over by the Spanish Steps. I thought I saw a guy who was on my flight from Chicago watching me from across the street. Maybe he recognized me or something, I don't know. So I ran toward the steps and then went up them, waited a couple minutes, and then went back down. Sure enough, he was on his way up, following me, when I ran down. Maybe he wasn't *really* following me, but I can't be sure. Maybe I'm being paranoid, but I ran as fast as I could, and I lost him."

"Okay, and you haven't seen him since then?" she interjected.

"No. After I lost him, I got some food and came back to my hotel. The reason I'm calling now is that, um, someone put something in my suitcase...."

"What do you mean, 'put something in your suitcase'?" Vivi interrupted.

"Well...when I got out of the shower and went to get some clean clothes, a Bible was in my suitcase that wasn't there before. My room has been locked the entire time. The same guy's been working here the whole time. I tried to ask him about it, but he acted like he didn't understand my English, and then he just got angry and said that no one had been in my room. It's strange, right? I mean, I debated calling you, but I'm a little weirded out by it."

"Hang on, Michael. I'm nearby. I'll stop by and talk to the hostel manager."

"Okay, thanks, Vivi, and I'm really sorry to trouble you with this," said Michael, before he realized she had already hung up the phone.

He's pacing outside his hostel right now, and that female detective is back. She's in the lobby, and from the looks of it is having a heated discussion with the front desk. You said the boss wanted to know if he had any more police contact. Well, they're here. It looks like some kind of problem with the hotel. Please advise; I'm getting sick of all this recon. I'm a soldier, not a spy. Just say the word, and I'll take them both out, Ely typed into his phone from a dark corner in the bar across the street.

After a moment, the response came back: *Our last orders were to let him go if he had no further contact with the police. I'll report to Seth, but for now, continue your reconnaissance.*

Michael's anxiety over his situation eased as he watched Vivi tear into the hostel manager. *Geez, you do NOT want to get on this woman's bad side.* Vivi exited the hostel, Bible in hand, with a frustrated look on her face. "Did you get any answers?" Mike asked eagerly.

"No, he swears he has not been in your room since he cleaned it two days ago, before you checked in."

"Yeah...they don't make the beds here at Nero's Palace," Mike responded, trying to lighten the mood. "One of the weirdest things about it is the age of the Bible. Look at that binding! I'm no book expert, but I've handled some old and rare books in my University library, and this one has the feel of a book at least a few hundred years old. That could make it valuable. Who would break into my room and leave something like that?" Michael asked, his anxiety level rising again as he voiced his thoughts out loud.

"Was there anything else with it?" asked Vivi.

"No, I don't think so. Oh! There's a dollar bill in it. Look here, an American dollar." Mike leafed through the Bible to find where he had seen the bill. "Here, just one dollar used as a bookmark. I don't know, it doesn't make any sense."

Vivianna spent a minute looking over the Bible under the streetlight outside the hostel. "Look, Michael, I understand you probably don't want to stay here tonight, and it's getting late. You were planning on catching a train tomorrow to make your way to Siena, right? Why don't you sleep on my sofa tonight? Tomorrow I'm driving to Florence, and I'll drop you off where you can catch a short bus ride to Siena."

"Really? That'd be great, thanks! I don't think this guy likes us much," Michael responded, gesturing to the hostel manager, who was now watching them from inside while yelling into the phone, his free hand making a motion like he was screwing in an imaginary light bulb. "Let me get my things. I'll just be a minute."

Fifteen minutes later, Michael lugged his suitcase and briefcase up four flights of stairs to Vivi's flat. There appeared to be an old elevator in the building, but he didn't question when Vivi pointed to the stairs and said, "This way."

"This is a really neat building. Have you lived here long?" Michael asked, trying not to sound out of breath as they reached the top floor.

"Yes, this flat belonged to my father's mother. She passed away fifteen years ago. I'm sorry about the stairs with your luggage, but the lift is broken."

"Oh, no big deal," responded Michael, as he took in some deep breaths and tried to slow his racing heartbeat. "I'm sure it's worth it for the views you have."

"Yes, that's the best part about being on the top floor. I have a small terrace with a view," she responded, while opening the door and pointing out across the main room to the terrace.

Michael hurried across the room and out onto the terrace to take in the view. Even at night, it was something to behold. The moonlight shimmered off the river, and the dome of St. Peter's Basilica was lit up, framing a picturesque backdrop of ancient buildings and creating a view that Michael imagined had looked pretty much the same for several hundred years. He stood in awe, taking it in and wondering what a small flat with a terrace like this might cost in the Eternal City. Vivi appeared, carrying a carafe of wine and two glasses that she set on the table.

"Care for a glass of wine before bed?" She presumptively began to pour.

"Yeah, that would be great, thanks! So...the view looks unreal. What neighborhood is this?" asked Michael, still in a state of disbelief.

"I'm on the edge of Campo de Fiore, the part of the city known as the old Jewish ghetto. In ancient times, it often flooded when the Tiber did, so it was an undesirable area. It was walled in and had a gate under the control of the papacy until the late 1800s. Now it's trendy," she replied, chuckling at the irony and adding, "I hope you are not allergic to cats, Michael?" as two cats came out of the flat and joined them on the terrace. One cat immediately found Michael's leg and began to rub his body up against it as he purred. "That's Dante; I think he likes you. And over there is Niccolo."

"As in Machiavelli?" Vivi nodded her head in confirmation. "I'm not allergic to cats, but I don't know about Florentine writers." Michael picked up Dante, who was loving every moment of the attention. "This guy put a Malavolti in the Sixth Pit of Hell, the one reserved for hypocrites in his *Inferno*."

Vivi gave Michael a look of amusement.

He continued: "The chief political struggle of Central Italy during the Middle Ages was the conflict between Guelfs and Ghibellines. The Guelfs supported the Papal armies, the Ghibellines the Holy Roman Emperor and *his* armies. It's no surprise that Siena, which was filled with old aristocratic families, supported the emperor and was a Ghibelline stronghold to counterbalance Florence's Guelf-leaning politics. In a sense, Siena was old money in those days, and Florence was the up-and-comer. In an attempt to stop the bloodshed and bring some peace, Pope Urban the IV founded the Order of the Blessed Virgin Mary in 1261—an order of ordained knights that was supposed to represent both political factions and help keep the peace. He put leading members of the Guelf and Ghibelline factions in charge of the order to corule. For a brief time, they ruled over Florence. I guess it didn't go too well, since Dante put two 'jovial friars in the Sixth Pit of Hell and condemned them to walk around with shiny cloaks lined with heavy lead. One of them was Catalano de Malavolti." He stroked Dante's back as his purring grew louder.

"I think it's neat that you care so much about history," Vivi said as her other cat jumped on Michael, pushing Dante away in a show of playful jealousy.

"Whoa—easy, guy. I'll give you a neck rub, too."

Michael began to rub the scruff of Niccolo, who seemed more satisfied with getting what Dante had than he did the neck rub itself. "This guy, Machiavelli, tells a story that, in retrospect, is where everything began to go wrong for the Malavoltis. In his *History of Florence,* Machiavelli wrote about an incident involving the Medici and a Malavolti. The Medici political dynasty began with Cosimo in the early 1400s. It was Cosimo's father Giovanni, though, who really should get credit for setting the family on a path that led to them ruling over much of Tuscany throughout the Renaissance. Giovanni started the Medici Bank and pushed hard to grow it. They weren't a noble family though; Giovanni used their modest wealth gained from generations working as apothecaries to start the bank. Medici means *medic*, and their family crest features balls or pills associated with their medicinal cures.

"Eventually, Cosimo ran the bank, and by then it had everyone's attention. Cosimo wielded power due to his wealth, but this rubbed the nobles in the government the wrong way. In their minds, their power was divinely ordained, and they would be damned if they let some commoner take control of their city. Things came to a head when they had Cosimo charged with usury and thrown in jail. During the trial, the entire region was thrown into turmoil, with nobles from far and wide taking sides. At some point, it's written that some of the nobles of Florence gave orders to poison Cosimo in jail and kill him, a surer route than a trial. The lead jailor at the time, to whom Cosimo was entrusted, was Federigo Malavolti. He did *not* poison Cosimo, but he actually ate his meals with him to prove that his food was safe. Cosimo eventually got out and lived in exile for awhile and took his bank with him. Fast-forward 100 years and a few generations later, and Siena had surrendered to Spain, which was acting on behalf of the Medici bank. This led a descendant of Federigo's to open a dojo in California in the 1980s with the slogan 'Strike first, strike hard, no mercy.'"

Vivi sipped her wine and stared off into the night sky.

"Uh, that was a joke about the dojo. That's from the first *Karate Kid* movie," he explained, as Vivi's lack of acknowledgement at the attempt at humor made him nervous.

"I don't think I've seen that one. I don't watch a lot of TV. I read, run, work...that's about it. In my teens, I spent most of my summers traveling with Uncle Franco. He was working in the field as an archeologist back then at digs in Crete, Cyprus, Syria, Israel, Egypt...you name it. It was a really fun way to spend my summers away from school, and it got me out of Rome. I would come back to school not knowing what was going on with pop culture at all, which made me a bit of an oddball and awkward with the other kids. It was a worthwhile tradeoff, though. Instead I'd have learned about the Minoans or Assyrians, or how to make a camel spit."

Vivi got up to leave the terrace. "Michael, there is a pullout bed up in the loft with pillows and a blanket in the chest next to it. I'm going to shower and turn in."

"Thanks for everything, Vivi. Oh, and thanks for the wine. You won't help me finish this off?" he asked, lifting the half-full carafe.

"No, I'm sorry. I've had my fill tonight. I get up early to run, if you hear me leave. I'll be back early, and we'll get on the road sometime in the morning. There's a bar around the corner that serves an American-style breakfast if you are hungry when you get up."

"You run in the morning? I thought that was only an American thing. Hey, can I join you on the run?" He asked.

Now turning and heading into her room, she answered simply, "No," as she shut the door, leaving Michael to enjoy the night air, *vino*, and view all to himself.

Michael put his feet up and sipped his wine. *Hey, things could be worse.* He reflected on his day and the whirlwind of unexpected events. He'd started the day at the police station giving an oral synopsis of his thesis, then he had a private tour of the Vatican museums and gardens, followed by a possible stalker chase and someone going through his things at the hotel and leaving him a Bible. *All's well that ends well,* Michael thought, as he sipped his wine and looked up at the moon, which looked huge. Michael retrieved the Bible from his suitcase and had a seat on the terrace to investigate it under the moonlight while he finished the wine.

I wonder if that dollar is marking a certain passage? Now, where was that thing? Michael flipped through the pages of the old book. *Ah, here it is, the Gospel of Luke Chapter 10, let's see, the dollar was sitting like this...underlining the start of verse 25, maybe? Oh, I know this one, the Good Samaritan parable.*

CHAPTER FOURTEEN

Malta

The general was familiar with the island of Malta, having been there a number of times. It was a favorite meeting place for Ordo's capstone members, on those rare occasions when one of them requested a face-to-face. As his driver accelerated away from the airport and toward the coast, he asked, "Fort St. Angelo?"

Double-checking his encrypted email, General Garret replied with a hint of annoyance, "No—Paolo. I have an appointment in Paolo."

Actually, his meeting was under Paolo. Father Patrick Davies had arranged for them to meet in the Hal-Saflieni Hypogeum, a subterranean temple complex that was over 5,000 years old. It was private yet a totally unnecessary precaution, as the Knights of Malta, which had become a de facto Ordo state, controlled Fort St. Angelo; the rest of the rocky island was a private bastion for Ordo, as much as any other place on Earth. The general didn't protest, though; it was Father Davies' flair for the dramatic that he appreciated and the reason he had delegated this mission to

Patrick Davies in the first place. If he were being honest, the meeting location exhilarated him. He had amassed more money than he could spend in ten lifetimes, but his thirst for power was unquenchable. Power not only over the present and future, but dominion over the past as well, he thought.

Leaving his driver at the entrance, he descended into the subterranean cavern alone and found it lit with torches. The dank air was permeated with the scent of kerosene. "Davies!" His voice echoed throughout the crypts. The flickering light of the torches created dancing shadows that softly illuminated another set of stairs to a lower level. Following the light, Garret descended and found himself in what was once the Hypogeum's main chamber. "Show yourself, Davies!" he shouted as his patience for the theatrics waned.

"I'm in here," came a voice from one of the tunnels off the main chamber. Garret followed the sound and torchlight until he came to a ledge. Standing two meters below him was Father Davies surrounded by a ring of torches.

"Welcome to the snake pit, General." Davies wore his black clerical attire, complete with white collar. His uniform, neatly coifed salt-and-pepper hair, and slight twang of an Appalachian accent when he spoke English tended to put people at ease.

"I should have known this was where I'd find you."

"Why do you need to see me today, General? Is Ordo not pleased with my services?"

"I'm worried—the board is worried—that you have become reckless. Is all this necessary?" General Garret motioned to their surroundings as he spoke.

"Think of all the human capital spent on creating this some 5,000 years ago! The Holy of Holies chamber you just passed through has a porthole that lines up perfectly with the winter solstice. This room would have been filled with serpents." Father Davies held his arms out, showing off the room he had bathed in fire.

"The board of directors is anxious. Are there any loose ends you need to tell me about? Has there been any chatter within the Vatican? Giant bloody hieroglyphs were hardly subtle!"

"Everything is going according to plan. You told me I could leave a message for those in the Vatican who know your organization has the scrolls and might get ideas. Who better to send that message then Set, the ancient god of chaos? I find, General, that when given a choice between chaos and order, people tend to pick order. If anyone is paying attention and thinks the professor's disappearance is connected to the scrolls, believe me, they're too afraid to be talking about it. I know that I'm but one of many sources Ordo uses in Rome; so tell me if this threat is contained. Can it ever be?"

"We're still gathering intel. It would seem that Sisti is the only loose end. The less you know, the better it is for you."

"Spare me, General! If this mission has anything to do with the Copper Scrolls, then it must be true. The bloodline survives to this day, and now science can prove it! But how can that be? The bloodline of Christ, the lineage of King David?" The priest let out a slightly maniacal laugh before continuing, "Oh, that must make some people very uneasy."

"The rabbi you used…I did some checking, and something isn't adding up. He's not an asset and might be compromised."

Davies interrupted, "Oh, you're checking up on me now? Your organization has been asking me for years to cultivate assets. Just because you didn't know about this one doesn't make him any less valuable."

"In the Vatican!" countered Garret.

"Don't worry, General. Rabbi Bein is more motivated to help us than anyone working for money or trying to save their own hides ever could be. You see, he's a true believer!" He let out another chuckle before continuing, "He's the easiest mark to manipulate. I learned of Rabbi Bein's outfit last year while in Jerusalem on business. I reached out to him, pretending to be a man named Seth, who's affiliated with the Mukhabarat, Egypt's intelligence agency."

"You passed yourself off as Egyptian?"

"I can pass for many things, General." Davies turned his palms up, twisting his body to let the light of the fire illuminate his clerical uniform. "Besides, I speak fluent Arabic, and I thought it'd be fun to pass myself off as an Egyptian agent. I first made contact via email, and the rabbi was eating out of my hand in no time at all. I thought his group of men would be perfect for this assignment."

"What sort of 'beliefs' make a rabbi lead a group of bloodthirsty mercenaries?"

"You wouldn't believe me if I told you."

"Humor me!" the general snapped as he glared down at the priest.

"All right then. Bein's an esoteric Kabbalist—and an eccentric one at that. He's convinced God has spoken to him through ancient texts, foretelling of an impending apocalyptic event. He's been prepping for it awhile now, which is why he's on the radar of several intelligence agencies. He's convinced someone will rise from obscurity to reveal the location of the Ark of the Covenant and use it to destroy Rome and Jerusalem, thereby ushering in the End of Days." Father Davies grinned as he looked at the general, knowing that faith and the supernatural were among the few things that made Garrett uncomfortable.

General Garret stared down at Davies for a moment. "Is this rabbi directing the field operation?"

"No, the head of his team of operators is an ex-Israeli naval commando named David. You probably have a file on all his men; they call themselves Gideon's Sword."

Garret replied, "All contact with David comes to me now; your services are no longer needed on this mission."

"I've followed your every directive! They're holding the professor and waiting for my further instructions. The American has been under constant surveillance. What have I done wrong? It's been by the book!" Davies protested.

"This goes up the ladder. One of the members of the capstone is looking to be very hands-on now, and I wish I knew why. Check your account; you were paid in full. I'll be in touch." With that, Garret turned and started his ascent out of the cavern.

CHAPTER FIFTEEN

Rome, Italy

As he watched Vivianna return from her early morning run, Ely tapped into his phone: *He stayed the night at the detective's apartment. I think I spooked him. Please advise, I'm still in position to neutralize.*

The response was immediate: *Seth says the leak is contained. He reports the police are clueless. Hold your ground for now. We don't want more attention on the student.*

Ely angrily punched the keys: *We are CLUELESS! What am I doing here? Tell Seth to call me. I want some answers!*

You're in luck. He's calling right now. Stand by. I'll see if he will speak with you, came the response.

A moment went by before Ely's phone began to vibrate with a call. The voice on the other end was mechanical sounding, as if it were coming through some kind of computer filter. "I was told you men were soldiers. Do soldiers not follow orders?"

"Yes, Seth, I've *been* following orders. Hell, we painted a lab with Egyptian symbols in blood at your request without questioning it! I just want to know what my mission is here. If my target is a threat to us, let me neutralize him," responded Ely.

"This mission is very sensitive, Ely. Rabbi Bein told me your organization specializes in such areas when he put you in touch with me. You are on a need-to-know basis, and you do *not* need to know. There are forces at play here you can't possibly comprehend. I have ears all over Rome, and I am gathering information. Rabbi Bein should have made it perfectly clear that evil forces are at work in preparation for the coming judgment—evil forces that can spawn misconceptions. There is a danger to the entire civilized world. I cannot say more on the phone, but I need you to contain yourself and follow orders to help me solve this problem. Is that clear?"

"Yes sir, of course. Should I continue to follow the student or return to base?"

"You said he saw you yesterday, correct?"

"He did, unfortunately. I believe I spooked him when he saw my reflection in a window, and..."

Seth cut him off. "Excellent. Let him see you again. Scare him. I want him to leave Italy and return home."

"Yes sir, I can do that."

Rome, Italy

Michael looked at Vivi's car as if he had forgotten what she drove. "Um, are we going to drive this all the way to Florence?"

"No, *I* am," she responded. "We may take some more scenic roads, though. I hope you don't mind. I don't like to drive it on the A1. If I take the SR2, we'll pass right by Siena; I could drop you off, and you won't have to take the bus from Florence."

"Sounds good to me." He silently made the sign of the cross and said a prayer for their survival. The car was packed full with Michael's two bags and Vivi's one suitcase as they set off for Tuscany.

It was a beautiful sunny day on the Italian peninsula as they drove north in silence. He tried to make conversation by asking Vivi questions about herself, using different angles about various daily routines or what it was like to be a detective in Rome, but only received short answers or was completely ignored when the questions were possibly too personal. Michael kept on trying. "So...how old is this car anyway?"

"It's a 1966 Fiat 500."

"Wow! Is it hard to maintain a car that old?"

"Not really. Some of it has been rebuilt. I have a good mechanic. It leaks some oil, but I change the oil myself."

"We have this joke back home. That 'Fiat' stands for 'Fix it again, Tony.'"

She looked at him expressionlessly, then suddenly laughed. It transformed her face into something beautiful and much less forbidding. "My mechanic's name is Toni! But she's a girl."

Then, finally, as if Michael had worn down Vivi into a realization that there would be a conversation while they drove, she asked him a question, perhaps just to get him talking about something that interested him, so he would stop peppering *her* with questions: "So: what do you find so interesting about Siena?"

"Well, lots of things, I guess. It's really a fascinating story, in my opinion, but it had its peak more at the tail end of the Middle Ages, so it's not as well known as Florence or Rome. They don't call it the Dark Ages for nothing, I suppose. If Siena had peaked in, say, the 1500s instead of the 1200s, there would be multiple TV shows made about the power struggles that occurred between the nobles of the city. History begins to be better covered with the Renaissance, with the blossoming of the humanities and an emphasis on education and the arts, reading, and writing. But we do know a lot about the early days of Siena, and what we know reads like an HBO show. Kind of like *Game of Thrones*. Do you watch that here?"

He then waited a minute for a response while she focused on the road. Unsure if she had nodded or not, he continued: "When you think of the Middle Ages and feudalism, there's a certain picture the average person conjures up, fair or not. There's a king or queen, and there are nobles. The nobles live in castles and have large tracts of land in their possession. They're the ultimate power on their land, except for the king, who is kind of like the federal power. Just like in *Game of Thrones*. Westeros looks a lot like medieval Europe, actually. You have House Stark in the North in Winterfell castle. Then there's the Houses of Bolton, Tyrell, Tully, Baratheon, Lannister, Frey, and of course, the Targaryens, who have the dragons...I could go on and on; there's a lot of characters. It's all based on the general feudalistic structure of the Middle Ages. Italy, though, was different."

"Is that right?" said a less-than-enthused Vivianna.

Oblivious to the sarcasm and lost in his vision of the past, he said, "Yes! Italy had a more urban concept of feudalism, you see. All the wealthy noble families built their castles huddled close together: multiple castles within a stone's throw of each other, right inside a walled city and mixed in with all the other urban trappings of the time. Due to their brand of feudalism, the cities and their nobles became so wealthy and powerful they were able to become independent states. Now, in the case of Siena, it had been somewhat autonomous before then, but officially became an independent state in the late eleventh century when it began minting its own currency.

"So there were a few wealthy, noble families—and then, of course, all the rest of the citizens—competing for control of the government and fighting for power. It's every bit as interesting as any fiction I have ever read. The power struggles or feuds often ended in murder and mayhem...basically small wars. Remember, those noble families often had their own standing armies. Popes had to step in and end feuds multiple times. There were famous feuds between two of Siena's richest families, the Tolomei and Salembeni, so their disputes often involved lots of troops readying for war. And there were conflicts between the Saracini and Scotti families—even the Malavolti and Piccolomini families had a feud that threw the region into turmoil at times."

"Italians have never really gotten along with each other," she said.

"Yeah, I know. On February 19, 1334, four young men from the Piccolomini family strolled right into the Malavolti castle and found young Niccolo Malavolti playing chess. They slit his throat and then marched back to their castle while singing family songs. Imagine if all the various players in *Game of Thrones* had their castles inside King's Landing. There would be a lot more action, I'd tell you that much—you wouldn't have seasons that dragged on.

"Sometimes, when you study the past, with all its war and fighting and plagues, it's amazing any of us are still here, you know? The Italian peninsula back then was in a state of constant flux, with a constant power struggle among the nobles, the church with their papal armies, and the larger royal powers in Europe. It's no surprise your cat Niccolo's namesake wrote *The Prince* in 1500 about how to seize and maintain power and that it's still read today by millions of college students every year."

"Not so much in Italy," said Vivi.

"It seems like the only thing that made Siena's nobles stop fighting each other was when *outside* forces wanted their wealth and land *or* when other citizens tried to wrangle more power within the Siena Republic. Somehow, in the middle of all this turmoil, really wonderful things happened, too.

"Siena was the first country to write and post a constitution written in the common vernacular of the citizenry so everyone could read it. Did you know there was a large orphanage and hospital in Siena called the Santa Maria della Scala that was run for nearly 1,000 years by the government, caring for the sick and the poor? It just closed in the 1990s. In fact, I'm writing my thesis on how an entire cultural movement that changed the world got its start in this tiny republic. They dreamed big; they patronized the arts; and they were progressive in their governmental structures. Tiny Siena was the banking capital of all of Europe in the 1200s. It's strange to think about the power they once wielded. I guess it wasn't considered so tiny back then."

"Are you going to keep talking about this all the way to Siena?"

"Probably. Anyway, in the 1200s the population rose to around 50,000 people, which is also the current population. That alone is interesting if you think about it. In the 1200s there were, what, a few hundred million people in the entire world? The planet didn't hit a billion people until sometime after 1800, and it's skyrocketed in the last century to a world population of over 7 billion people. During all that time, Siena has remained relatively the same. I mean, it has fluctuated some, of course; the Black Plague is central to any story told about Siena. It decimated the city in the mid-1300s, but still, the city has persevered, and today its population is still around 50,000 people. Pretty neat, right?"

Michael thought it was good Vivi was driving. Otherwise, his talking would have surely put her to sleep by now.

He plowed on. "So, it was only natural that while watching *Game of Thrones* I had to determine which family was closest to the Malavoltis of Siena. Of course, everyone would *want* to be the Starks, the most moral family in Westeros. I talked myself into that for awhile because they did seem kind of cool, but then I read about an incident in the 1300s when a Malavolti bishop took a large piece of land that was left to the church in the countryside and privatized it by signing it over to his nephew. That's a Lannister move if I've ever saw one. Then I was looking at a current map of Siena and realized the entire ancient Malavolti castle is now a *contrada* (district) for the Palio. You know of the Palio, right? The famous horse race in Siena

The Contrada del Drago flag

that began in the 1400s? Well anyway, there's seventeen different *contrade* that can compete in the Palio. Do you know what the mascot is for the *contrada* made up of the old Malavolti land? It's a dragon, which is why it's named *Contrada del Drago*! I guess that ends the debate. The Malavoltis were clearly Targaryens, descended from old Valyria. Dragons were their thing."

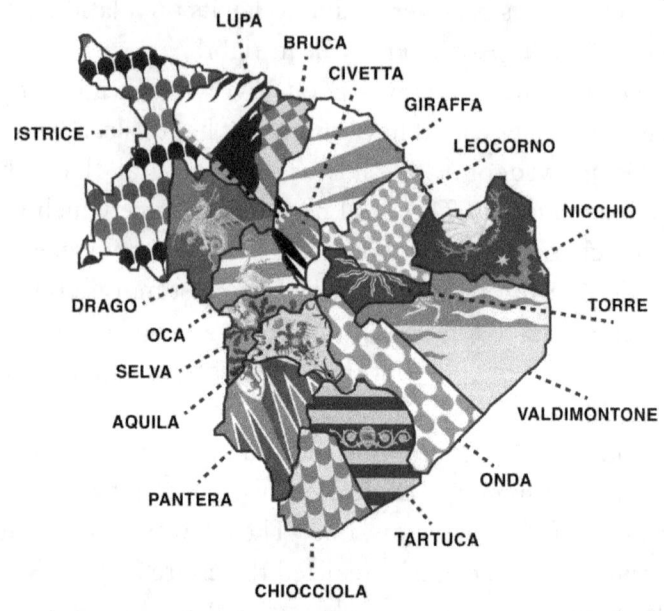

Siena's contrada map

"What the hell is this *Game of Thrones*?" asked Vivi.

"Oh, you've never seen that show? Why didn't you tell me? I'm sure I sounded like an idiot talking about it. It's just a fantasy TV show in a setting that seems a lot like medieval Europe with a long, drawn-out war for the crown of this imaginary kingdom. It's actually really popular—not just some show that physics dorks get together and watch. I'm surprised you haven't heard of it." Vivi sat silently listening, which made Michael feel uneasy. "Reeeally popular."

"Physics dorks? What do you mean?" asked Vivi.

"Oh, sorry, I thought I told you. I was a physics major until last year and had been planning to get my PhD in it. I was hoping to work on this crazy theory involving light and how it can literally create space and time. Then, during my junior year, I was doing some ancestry research and fell in love with the story of Siena. Switching majors that late has been tough, so I haven't done nearly as much research on Siena as I'd like. I had to try and cram a lot of courses into my senior year so I could start the PhD program this year. I even had to quit playing rugby to take a three-hour crash course on Latin two nights a week. To get your PhD in this program, you have to pass a proficiency test in Latin before you can even begin, and I'll have to pass another in Italian before I can graduate."

"Did you play rugby for your school?" Vivi sounded interested now.

"Nah, it was a club sport. It was no big deal, and we weren't very good. I was a better football player—two state championships in high school while I played strong safety." Michael held his hand up as if to say, *please hold your applause.*

Vivi did, but asked, "So you speak Latin now?"

"Not really; no one does...it's a dead language," he answered with a chuckle. "I learned just enough to pass the test, but it should help me learn Italian in the next few years."

"How does light create space and time?" she asked, sounding amused.

"Well, if I could answer that, I would win the Nobel Prize. I don't know; it's just a theory. There are several far-out theories I could've worked on. Everyone's looking for the math that would explain the universe. Light is this really fascinating thing, though, right? We only see a small portion of all possible light; it's called the visual spectrum. If you take the entire electromagnetic spectrum—that's all radiation from radio waves to gamma rays—and lined them up end to end into the same length as the Mississippi River, the part we could actually see would be less than a foot of the river. All these different light waves travel at the same speed, the universal speed limit—the speed of light. As you get closer to the speed of light, strange things happen with space and time. There's a theory that space and time are literally created by electromagnetic energy, which would mean the reality we encounter on a daily basis is made of light."

"That sounds like something someone would say right after I arrested them for doing acid in St. Peter's square."

"Ha ha, yeah, physics can be pretty trippy. Holographic universes, multiverses, it can get pretty strange. You work on the math and work on the math, and the breakthroughs come slowly in such a difficult field. I'm finding medieval Italy to be much less daunting than the nature of reality. I was hoping to show how little we remember the past by interviewing my relatives here in Italy. I doubt that most Malavoltis know much about the history of Siena. It may seem a little silly to some people, caring about something in the distant past. The further you go back, the more we're all related, but still... I do have a few things in common with the Malavoltis who helped found and run Siena: my last name, of course, and my Y-chromosome. It's so fascinating that I could help solve the mystery of the family's origins with something in my blood...one little chromosome that makes me a male. That's all it does."

As Michael spoke, they came upon a freight truck going half the speed limit. Vivianna began tailgating, waiting for an opportunity to pass the truck as he continued: "The mystery of the Malavolti origins is one of the things that drives me, I guess. I know it's only interesting to a handful of people, though. Some of the noble Siena families were related to the other royal houses throughout Europe. Many of the later noble families became wealthy through trade, and Siena created many wealthy merchant families. The Malavoltis are in Siena's recorded beginning, though, seemingly already well-to-do and talking about their ancient origins. The name and family crest add another layer of intrigue for me. Remember, last names were only used by noble families during those years; but who calls themselves 'the evil-doers'? I mean, that's what my last name means, doesn't it?" he asked Vivi, who was more intent on trying to pass the truck as she veered into and out of the passing lane to get a better of view of the oncoming cars than answering him.

"Something like that, I think: evil to the times, to do a bad deed. There are a few different ways you could take it, but it's all menacing. Then there's the family crest." Michael shuffled through the papers he had on his lap to work on during the ride and produced a few sheets with pictures on them, which he realized Vivi couldn't see while driving. "In later years, the crest was always drawn as a black-and-white ladder with some *fleur de lis* above the ladder and sometimes with some stars or a crown above that. The earlier versions, though, usually only featured the ladder like this one on the cover of a *biccherna* from 1473. These were the magistrate or finance books for the city; a number of them were preserved, all the way back to the 1200s when Siena was the banking capital of Europe. They all have art on the covers, some of the work done by now-famous painters. The covers usually featured the crests of the chief magistrates of the year, and the Malavolti ladder can be found on many.

"There's a museum for the surviving 100 or so *biccherna* in Siena that I'm going to have to check out. Most of them were plundered by Napoleon and taken to Paris, but during the Bourbon restoration, they were returned to Siena. While being returned, a cartload of them fell in the Rhone River, and a number of others were sold after they made their way home; those either disappeared forever or are in private collections now. This one from 1473 has what I'm talking about. This crest is how the older Malavolti crests usually looked: just a black-and-white ladder. This one was painted by Sano di Pietro to commemorate a noble wedding.

"Heraldry, or family crests, becomes a lot more popular near the end of the Middle Ages and during the Renaissance, when more and more families started using surnames and titles. If you look up the meaning of a ladder in heraldry,

The gift of the ring, wedding scene between Sienese noble families, 1473[4]

you'll find references to scaling ladders, which were used to storm castles and often put on various knights' crests. But the Malavolti ladder doesn't look like a scaling ladder, which was often drawn with hooks on the top end. The only other thing a ladder symbolizes—and has for thousands of years—is some type of religious expression: the ladder as the means to get to heaven kind of thing.

"When you look at these older versions, some with stars around or at the top, that idea seems to fit better. Why would they call themselves 'evil doers' and have a crest that symbolizes a path to heaven? Just where did their wealth originally come from? Where the original patriarch of the family in Italy came from could be answered through genetics, which is why I was so excited to work with Professor Sisti. My Y-chromosome haplogroup is fairly rare in Italy."

As Michael continued, Vivianna veered all the way into the passing lane and gave the gas all she had to maneuver around the freight truck.

"My Y-chromosome mutation originally occurred and is more commonly found in…" Michael stopped himself as he realized the truck they were passing seemed to be speeding up at the same rate they were. Vivi let out a few choice words in Italian as she raced the freight truck. Realizing the driver wasn't going to let her pass and seeing another truck closing down on them head on, she hit the brakes to swerve back in behind the truck.

As she braked, so did the truck she was attempting to pass.

"What the hell?" Michael braced himself as he swore at the driver, who now forced them to play chicken.

As they decelerated in unison, Michael looked up and caught a glance of the driver, who was looking down at him with a taunting look. It was a familiar face. Michael gasped. Meanwhile, Vivi had to make a split-second decision with the oncoming truck now only meters away. She veered hard left down a shallow embankment, the tiny classic car careening off into an olive grove.

They came to rest with the car's front bumper pressed up against an olive tree and both sprang out to assess the damage. The two front tires were flat, possibly from a bent rim on the left side, and the front bumper had an indentation from the olive tree. Vivi was walking around the car and ranting to herself in Italian. Michael could only imagine what she was saying, but he thought it must involve the best Italian swear words.

"I'm really sorry about your car, Vivi," he said, trying to calm her down.

"It's okay, the car can be fixed. Did you get a look at that guy?"

"I did, and you're not going to believe it, but it was the same person who was following me yesterday. I saw his face for just a second before we went off the road, but I'm almost certain it was him." Michael watched Vivi, unsure how she would respond to this news. To his surprise, she didn't seem fazed and kept pacing around her car to view the damage.

"What does this mean? Do we have to return to Rome to fill out a police report? Should I fly home? Is someone trying to kill me in Italy?" He nervously voiced his near panic.

"Do you want to fly home, Michael?"

"I don't know. I mean...no, I *don't* want to go home. I just don't know what to do. I think that guy was on my flight from Chicago, too; so if he really is following me, I'm not sure whether I'd be any safer going home. But why in the hell is he following *me*? I'm a nobody college student!" Michael's volume rose as he answered her.

"I don't know, but I'm going to find out. I'll call my station and give them a description of the man and also see if we can get any information from the airline if he was on your flight. If there is a connection between the missing professor and this man, then you are in a lot of danger, Michael. If we go back to Rome, I'll be reprimanded for giving you a ride and then sent back to my conference in Florence. They'll take a description from you of our suspect, which will be largely ignored, since the only crime he has committed as far as they're concerned is reckless driving. Detective Monti is already convinced that you have nothing to do with the university case, which is why he assigned me to talk to you in the first place. They'll put you in touch with the U.S. embassy and tell you if you don't feel safe, you should return to your country. No one will take this seriously."

"So what should we do?"

"I'm going to skip the beginning of the forensics conference and come with you to Siena. If we see that guy again, I'm going to arrest him...or kill him; I'm not sure which yet." Vivi reached into her glove box and pulled out a pack of cigarettes, then walked back and sat on the back bumper.

"Does everyone in Italy smoke?"

"I don't usually, it's a nasty habit. I carry these in case of an emergency for when I'm really pissed off." She looked out into the olive grove before continuing, "Three years ago, I was called to a domestic disturbance. When I got there, the husband had already killed his wife and two young daughters with a kitchen knife. After taking their lives, he took his own by stabbing himself in the chest. Twenty-seven times he plunged the knife into himself the coroner said. I got there just in time to see the last three or so plunges. I'll never forget the look on his face. It was pure evil. Since that day, I keep a pack in my car just in case." She lit up and stared into oblivion.

Michael didn't know what to say; he was humbled Vivi had shared that horrific story with him. He felt sorry for her and thought, *What the heck?* as he took a seat on the other side of the back bumper and helped himself to a cigarette, as well. The two sat silently smoking, the quiet hum of traffic drowned out by the noisier buzz of cicadas in the olive grove.

CHAPTER SIXTEEN

Vatican City

Cardinal Franco Colombi was at his desk with his reading glasses on and a stack of papers in front of him. Daniel Burto, his assistant, knocked as he entered with another box of books and papers. "Is that everything?" asked the cardinal.

"Everything that I could access with my clearance, Father," responded Daniel.

"Thanks, this is more than enough to keep me busy for a few hours," replied Franco, while he motioned to the mound of documents and let out a chuckle. He knew he had heard the last name Malavolti before, but couldn't place it while his niece was here, so he'd asked Daniel to pull any documents related to the family in the Vatican archives. Daniel had brought him a number of documents relating to finance, land, and clerical positions during medieval times. Cardinal Colombi was disappointed in himself when he read the document related to the family donating the land for San Domenico Cathedral in Siena.

Of course I knew that! He was, after all, a Dominican priest and an archeologist well versed in Italy's treasure of old churches. The history of the Dominican cathedral in Siena was where his familiarity with the Malavolti family had come from. He didn't know what he was looking for exactly, only that he had an odd feeling his niece was involved in something more dangerous than she knew. He picked the phone up to call an old friend, Detective Monti.

Tuscany, Italy

To Michael's surprise, a tow truck had pulled them out of the olive grove within half an hour of their call and towed them to a small shop a few kilometers down the road. The mechanic thought he could fix the bent rim and get them new tires and back on the road the same day, but it would take him several hours. Vivi was outside pacing, while on the phone with her station, when Michael noticed a pile of old bicycles leaning up against a wall inside the shop.

"Any chance we can rent a couple of those while you work?" Michael asked the mechanic, Luigi, whom he assumed was also the shop owner in this rural setting. Fortunately, Luigi spoke English.

"Go ahead and borrow whichever ones you like. There's a few in rough shape, but I think there's at least two in there that work well. I shouldn't need more than four or five hours to have your car ready."

"Thanks, man," Michael replied as he pulled out his phone and began to search Google Maps.

As she returned, red-faced from the Italian sun, Vivi announced, "I had to call in some favors, but I have someone looking into your flight manifest from your trip over."

"Did you talk to Detective Monti?" Michael asked, now genuinely puzzled and concerned that he could somehow be involved in whatever kind of trouble the professor was in.

"Yes, against my better judgment. I told him what happened."

"And?" Michael asked, dissatisfied with how slowly Vivi was filling him in.

"And...he did exactly what I said he'd do. After he got done yelling at me for offering you a ride and driving an "unsafe" automobile, he told me to drop you off at the nearest train station and proceed to the conference in Florence. He suggested you contact the American embassy if you feel you are in danger, and he laughed when I suggested it may have something to do with Professor Sisti's abduction."

"So does that mean they know who took the professor?" asked Michael, confused by their confidence.

"I doubt it. I've been kept in the dark this whole time, so I only know that I was assigned to question you because they'd already determined you had nothing to do with it. I was only brought in for appearance's sake. Whatever 'real' leads they think they have were never shared with me."

"So what are you going to do?"

"Exactly what I said earlier: go with you to Siena and see the sites for a few days. If we don't see that guy again when you head north later this week, I'll go to Florence and catch the tail end of the conference. I have friends there who can check me in."

"So the mechanic said it would take four or five hours to get us up and running again. Any chance I could talk you into a bike ride to the Castle of Montalcino?" Michael asked, pointing to the pile of bikes. "According to my phone, it's only a few kilometers away, and I really wanted to get there on this trip, but didn't think I'd have time. It's where the story of the Republic of Siena ends."

"That depends," Vivi replied matter-of-factly.

"On what?"

"On how many bottles of wine you can carry back in your backpack on a bike. My favorite wine in all of Italy comes from a vineyard near there."

"Ah yes—even I've heard of the Brunello di Montalcino, and *I* still occasionally buy wine in a box," he responded with a chuckle, happy to see Vivi willing to go on an adventure. "Did you pack anything other than suits and heels?"

"You forget I run every morning. Let me get my bag and find a place to change. Pick us out a couple of bikes in good working order."

Michael waited outside with two bikes he had taken on short test rides while she changed. He had only seen Vivi in her work attire, so when she came out in her formfitting spandex running outfit, he had a hard time hiding his nervous shock. And other reactions. "That will work. I mean... you look nice. Anyway...you get first pick." Michael stumbled through his words as he motioned to the two bikes he had picked out. Vivi rolled her eyes and mounted the bike closest to her.

"Try to keep up," she said as she pedaled away.

It was also the first time he saw the gun that Vivi wore strapped to the small of her back. He found it comforting with Buzz Cut still out there lurking somewhere. They set off for the castle.

Vatican City

Cardinal Colombi hung up the phone with an uneasy feeling. His old friend Monti had said little to calm his sense of dread. He assured him they were doing everything to locate Professor Sisti and that some of his best men were working on it. When he asked if his niece was still working on the case, Monti said she was not due to an obligation to attend a conference on behalf of the department. The normally tight-lipped detective even shared the message left in blood at the crime scene with the cardinal, hoping he might have some insight into its meaning. He did not, but in the Colombi's mind, it reaffirmed the angst he felt in his gut regarding the case. *There is probably more at play here than Rome's P.D. could know if this case involves a discovery made by the world's leading anthropological geneticist.* He rose from his desk and headed to the archives.

CHAPTER SEVENTEEN

Montalcino, Italy

The medieval castle fortress of Montalcino[5]

Michael and Vivi found a place to lock their bikes in front of a café in the tiny hill town of Montalcino. In the distance, looming over the town at the highest local point, was the castle, but it would have to wait. Pedaling a bike through the Tuscan hills had created quite an appetite. "This is the

American vision of an Italian vacation: a panini at a street-side café in a quaint, ancient village; espresso; and gelato for dessert. I could get used to this," he said, clearly enjoying this detour.

"Michael, we need to talk," Vivi said seriously. "I think you are in more danger than you realize if the guy who ran us off the road has anything to do with what happened in Sisti's laboratory. There is something I didn't tell you about the case. The night the lab was vandalized and the professor went missing, a message was left in the lab, a message painted in blood in Egyptian hieroglyphics."

Michael nearly choked on his espresso before she could clarify, "Oh! It wasn't the professor's blood. It wasn't even fresh blood—our lab found a preservative in it. We don't think it came from the university at all, but someone went to great lengths to carry that much blood with them and paint a creepy message for someone to find. And who was it meant for?" Pausing, Vivi could see he was disturbed by this revelation.

"What did it say?" Michael asked when he stopped coughing.

"We were told by experts at the school that it spelled out the name of an ancient Egyptian god named Set in hieroglyphics. My department believes there is some kind of academic dispute going on, since the professor did a lot of work in Egypt, but..." she stopped for a moment, measuring her next thought before voicing it out loud: "It's hard to think this was done by a rival academic. I can't imagine a dispute about genes leading to murder, and I believe this was done by a trained professional."

"Murder? You think Professor Sisti was *murdered*?" His face was white with disbelief.

"I don't know, Michael, but it's been a few days now with no contact from him. At this point, I think we need to assume that the worst is a strong possibility. I just thought you should know. If you decide to stay here, your life may be in danger. It may be in danger, regardless, if this man followed you from Chicago. You should have all the facts."

Michael scowled. "How could my thesis possibly be a threat to anyone? The Malavoltis were quite rich during the Middle Ages, but that shouldn't matter to anyone now, right? I mean, whatever lands and wealth they still had in the 1500s surely would have been wiped out during the long war that was finally ended here in 1559." Michael motioned to the hilltop castle as he spoke.

"Does the name 'Set' mean anything to you?" she asked.

"No. I'm at a loss here. I mean, I've heard of Set before, probably during middle school or high school when I had to study the various gods of ancient Egyptian culture. I actually just read his name a few weeks ago, as well, in relation to something I was studying in Siena. A lot of interesting art is carved into the marble floor of the Siena Cathedral. There are a number of esoteric pre-Christian images that seem out of place in a Catholic church. There's this one of a person or a god, I'm not really sure, named Hermes Trismegistus. He's the supposed author of the *Hermetic Corpus*, an esoteric book they called the 'wisdom texts' in medieval times. It came from ancient Greece, but was thought to be originally from Egypt. In fact, this Hermes is supposed to be a Greek representation of the Egyptian god Thoth, which is why I just read a refresher on Set. Thoth was the bringer of writing and information. He was called the Great Arbitrator because he oversaw the battles between good and evil, making sure neither got an unfair advantage. In ancient Egypt, there were three epic battles of good versus evil, and the last of those was Horus versus Set, if I'm recalling it right." Michael paused, deep in thought, trying to wrack his brain for any possible connection.

"The only thing I can think of is that my Y-chromosome haplogroup is more commonly found in southern Egypt, but I still can't see how this could involve my thesis if the crime has anything to do with the professor's work in Egypt. The Malavoltis have been here in Italy for at least 1,200 years, and I'm guessing even longer than that. Maybe Roman times or even back to the Etruscan era."

"What does it mean that your Y-chromosome haplogroup is more common in Egypt?" Vivi asked curiously.

"It means if you go far enough up my paternal family tree, you'd get to a guy in Egypt. Apparently, my Y-chromosome mutation originated there around 17,000 years ago near Thebes. Way up my family tree, my paternal great-grandfather moved from Egypt to Italy at some point in time. Well, maybe not just like that. My ancestors might have moved up around the Middle East, through modern-day Turkey around the Mediterranean on foot, for a long time before someone settled in Italy. Or they may have come straight here on a boat a long time ago; we don't know. But at some point, my earlier Malavolti ancestors—probably long before they used that last name—came from Egypt, which is one of the reasons I was excited about working with Professor Sisti. He is the world's foremost expert in my Y-chromosome, and I was hoping that, based on certain markers I carry embedded in my DNA, he could actually determine where they moved from and how long ago they had settled in Tuscany."

He sighed. "Whoever the Malavolti predecessors were in Egypt, I just can't comprehend how they could possibly matter to anyone. This has to be some kind of misunderstanding. Maybe the professor had some big gambling debt or was sleeping with the wrong guy's wife or something. Or I've been mistaken for someone else, since I'm here and talking to the police who are investigating his disappearance?"

Vivi glanced at him out of the corner of her eye. "I have no idea, Michael, but if we see that man with the buzz cut again, I intend to find out. Hurry up and finish your espresso, so we can check out the castle. There's a wine shop right in the courtyard that stocks my favorite vineyard."

An hour later they walked along the castle wall, which towered high over the surrounding countryside, giving them panoramic views of Tuscany. "Now *this* is a medieval castle! All it needs is a moat and alligators," Michael joked.

"Perhaps crocodiles imported from Egypt. Alligators are as American as you are." She smiled.

Michael laughed before launching into lecture mode. "This castle was a hotly contested possession in the Middle Ages. It was redesigned and reinforced to what it is now by two Sienese architects in 1361. In 1555, Siena was surrounded by Spanish and Florentine troops and losing that war badly. There was some kind of temporary truce that allowed a number of families to escape Siena; some sources say as many as 700 families and a legion of French troops fighting on behalf of Siena were able to get out of Siena and make their way here. In this reinforced impenetrable castle, made to hold out against the best troops of the day, they continued to run the country of Siena for four more years.

"The Spanish troops surrounded the fort to wait them out. A truce came in 1559, the peace treaty of Cateau-Cambresis, and ended a long struggle between France and Spain for control over parts of the Italian peninsula. The Spanish king was a Hapsburg *and* the Holy Roman Emperor at that time, so Spain came out on top and controlled a number of these areas for the next century. The Republic of Siena was a prize to give to the Medici family for money the Church and the king of Spain owed its bank. When that treaty was signed, Siena was absorbed into the Duchy of Florence, forming a new country, whose borders are now modern-day Tuscany. The pope and the Medicis divided up much of Siena's assets. I guess we better put the Medici and the Hapsburgs on our suspects list if I'm involved," he said sarcastically, "right after the Piccolomini."

"Were the Malavoltis stuck in this castle during those four years?" asked Vivi without acknowledging his attempt at humor.

"I assume so, but, regardless, I have a theory. My great-grandfather emigrated from Emilia Romagna, just north of Tuscany, and there's a pocket of surviving Malavoltis there. According to baptismal records from the local parish, they seem to have a history in that area dating back to shortly after that war. Emilia Romagna borders Tuscany now, but back then it would have been right outside of the Duchy of Florence and, therefore, outside the reach of the Medici. The area is mountainous and was part of the Duchy

The Peace of Cateau-Cambresis, Tablet by Biccherna, preserved by the state archives of Siena (1559)[6]

of Modena in that time. The House of Este controlled it, and they were no friends of the Medici. I'm thinking my Malavolti ancestors who settled there may have been deliberately trying to escape the Medici by taking the higher, safer ground that was controlled by an old ally nearby so they could plot their return."

Vivi nodded thoughtfully. "We should start plotting our return to the automotive shop. Are you ready to load that bag with some wine?" she asked, pointing to the wine shop below them.

"I'm fine carrying all your wine back, but we're not racing." Michael had had a hard time keeping up with her on the Tuscan hills while they biked there.

"Don't be a wimp. It's mostly downhill on the way back anyway."

Michael couldn't help but laugh. The mild insult was the most personable thing Vivi had said to him since they'd met. "Okay. Then you know the wine will add weight and make me faster!"

CHAPTER EIGHTEEN

Castel Gandalfo

"Commander, the student, Michael Malavolti, is traveling north with a detective from Rome, Vivianna Giuseppe. They were run off the road near Montalcino, but appear to be okay." Alfonso read the update text he had just received from the Grand Master.

"I assume this was no accident? Ordo is trying to scare him away," he replied.

"Unconfirmed, Sir. We had a man nearby, but he did not see the incident."

"That detective is Cardinal Colombi's niece," replied Alfonso.

"I know, Sir. We have eyes on them still."

"They don't want to draw attention to the student if he is a match, but that won't stop Ordo from killing him if they think he knows. Please put another man on this if you have one to spare."

"Yes sir, I already have. I also left him a clue to the match in Samaria as you requested."

Alfonso let out a long sigh before texting, "Very well, keep me updated."

The Relic Hunter was at his desk; the many phones he used to run his business empire and Ordo operations were quiet. The resources he had requested about Siena sat in a neat pile, all except one book. A picture book on the Cathedral of Siena lay open on the center of his desk. He stared down at an image and description of Hermes Trismegistus, rhythmically tapping his fingers on his desk obsessively. *Thrice-greatest Hermes! Did they know as recently as the construction of this church? How could that be?*

Siena, Italy

As Vivi and Michael arrived at Siena, the sun was low in the sky and cast the golden hue that Tuscany was famous for over the countryside. She found a parking space outside the walled city, as cars are strictly regulated within it. As they walked up a steep hill toward a gate, it dawned on her that she didn't have a hotel reservation and surely didn't plan to stay in a communal youth hostel like Michael. "Where is your reservation?" she asked. "I don't want to stay too far away from you in case we run into any problems. But I'm not sure where to get a room. It's high season for tourists."

"You can stay with me. I have a reservation at a small bed and breakfast, so I'm not sure there will be any available rooms. I'm sure I can get a rollout bed or a cot, and you can take the bed. I made this reservation months ago, when I found the place online doing family research. It's called Poggio Malavolti, which means Malavolti Hill, right?"

"Yes, of course you booked there. If they don't have a room, I'll see what else might be nearby. I've stayed in Siena a few times; everything is so close, so I won't be too far either way."

"The proprietor of Poggio Malavolti sounds like a real nice guy. He was really excited when I told him I was coming to do research on the Malavoltis. I'm sure he could make a recommendation if they are booked. Giorgio is his name; hopefully he's there this evening. We talked for awhile about my thesis—he's a bit of a history buff himself, so I'm looking forward to meeting him."

Arriving at the hilltop, they were greeted by a large gothic, arched gate welcoming them into the walled city. From the outside of the gate, Siena looked like one giant medieval fortress. Above the entrance was a black-and-white shield, the coat of arms for Siena.

"Your family crest is a black-and-white ladder, and the crest of Siena is a black-and-white shield. Is there any connection? What is the relevance of the black and white?" she asked as they passed through the portal into a city filled with narrow cobblestone streets shaded by ancient buildings.

Michael was smiling from ear to ear as he set foot inside the city. He was also shocked to hear Vivi ask about the crest because he didn't think she'd been listening to his history "lesson." "Yeah, you noticed that, huh? I had the same thought and tried to do some research on it, but couldn't find much other than legends. All I can do is speculate. Often, black and white are used together to show contrast or dichotomy, kind of like the different forces in the world: the yin and yang, masculine and feminine, Apollonian versus Dionysian—or the duality of man as in good versus evil."

"What does that mean to you, 'the duality of man'? In my experience, there is far more darkness in man than light."

"Well..." he began, "I guess that's the sort of metaphysical question that requires a profound answer, but I'm not sure I have one. There's a story about the duality of man that I like. It goes something like this:

"There was an old Native American chief talking to his grandson by the fire one night. He says, 'Son, there is a battle between two wolves going on inside all of us, and they will fight to the death. One of the wolves is evil and represents everything you don't like in the world. The other wolf is good and full of everything that is beautiful and right in the world.' The boy thinks about two wolves fighting inside him for a moment before looking up with concern and asking his grandfather, 'Papaw, which wolf wins the fight?' The grandfather looks down and simply replies, 'Whichever one you feed.'"

She responded with a slight smile. "I like that."

Michael's eyes were as big as saucers as he walked through the streets of the old city in which he had invested so much time and thought recently.

"Do you know where you're going?" she asked, as their suitcases rumbled over the stone streets behind them.

"Yes! I've walked these streets dozens of times. Pretty soon we'll get to the northwest corner of the *Drago*. The hotel isn't too much further."

"I thought you said this was your first time in Italy?"

"It is. I meant using Google Maps' Street View, I've walked these streets. A virtual vacation!"

"Physics dorks. Is that the expression?"

"Ha ha, well, in this case it's history dork or Siena dork." he corrected her before pointing up at the street sign that read Via Malavolti. "We're in the old Malavolti castle now, though, so I'd prefer Count Dork. Or just Michael."

"Okay, Michael it is. Michael, the dork." It made him feel at ease that she had let her guard down and was poking fun at his enthusiasm for Siena. They walked along Via Malavolti until they came to a piazza.

"This is Piazza Matteotti; it was created in the early 1900s. Siena is one of the best preserved cities in all of Italy. Much of its center is now a UNESCO World Heritage Site, but in the early 1900s, for some reason, they knocked down some ancient buildings here to make room for this piazza and that post office. The ancient church of St. Egidio stood somewhere around here." Michael explained as he pointed at the post office. "Follow me, we're almost to the hotel," he said as he crossed the piazza and started the gentle descent down what was known as Malavolti Hill.

They arrived at the address, which featured only a small placard pointing to some external stairs. Climbing the stairs, Vivi was already on her phone searching for what other options might be nearby. At the top they were greeted with a pleasant surprise: the bed and breakfast was small, but had a charming lobby with a large terrace that featured a sweeping view of Siena.

The owner enthusiastically welcomed them in to his hotel and home. "*Ciao*, you must be Michael; welcome home! I am Giorgio. We spoke on the phone."

"Nice to meet you in person, Giorgio. Your place is beautiful—hard to beat this view." He fished his passport out of his bag and handed it over to Giorgio, who was punching away at a computer behind the small front desk.

"I have you down for three nights, Michael. Does that still work? Will it be the two of you?" Giorgio asked, looking over at Vivi, who was inspecting the common area as if it were a crime scene.

"Vivianna Giuseppe, Rome P.D. Do you have another room available?" She curtly introduced herself while laying her police credentials on the counter. Giorgio gave Michael a look of shock; he responded with a half shrug and a raise of his eyebrows, as if to say: *Yeah, sorry; she's kind of a bitch*.

"You're in luck! I am normally booked up at this time of year, but I had a cancellation just two days ago from someone who had booked a room for the entire week. How many nights would you like to reserve a room for?" responded Giorgio with a large smile.

Vivi looked at Michael and seemed to think about it for a minute before responding, "*Due,*" (two).

Giorgio gave them a tour that ended on the terrace and said, "There's an espresso machine and a cooler with bottled water just inside the lobby. Normally I charge one euro for each, but for a Malavolti it's on the house! Have as much as you like."

Michael gave Vivi a look, as if he was bragging in jest. "Thanks very much, Giorgio. You're a gracious host," he said, as the proprietor left them on the terrace.

"I see you get the VIP treatment," she teased.

"I told you: the Malavoltis are still a big deal in certain circles. Even if those circles are limited to small B&B owners who named their place after the medieval family," he joked.

After getting a rather pleasant dinner at a nearby restaurant, they sat on the B&B's terrace and enjoyed the view and a bottle of the wine they had purchased in Montalcino. "Wow, this really *is* great wine." Michael stated, as if he didn't think he'd be able to tell the difference between it and the cheap Chianti he was known to buy in Chicago. "You booked your room for two nights. So you'll go to Florence sometime Monday, then?"

"Yes, I'll stay here with you tomorrow and most of Monday. Then I'll drive to Florence that evening. You plan to travel up north to see your relatives on Tuesday, yes?"

"That's the plan. They're expecting me Tuesday. I'd like to go to Mass tomorrow early in San Domenico—there's a 7:30 a.m. service, so you could come with, or I could meet you back here afterward if you want. There's a few things I'd like to see while I'm here, so I hope you don't mind me dragging you all over the city tomorrow."

"I'm going to run in the morning. I'll meet you right here before Mass, and we'll go together. I'm hoping we get a chance to see your stalker again," said Vivi, as she got up from her seat and started to move inside.

"Okay. Good night, Vivi. Thanks for staying here with me for a couple days. I feel a lot safer with you around."

CHAPTER NINETEEN

Haifa, Israel

Ely boarded the yacht to find David and Ishmael smoking cigarettes and playing cards in the galley. "What the hell are we doing? This guy's still breathing?" Ely protested while motioning toward the bedroom.

"Relax. Seth said he needs a little more time. And besides, once he's done gathering intel, he may need your expertise to extract some info from this guy," replied David.

"About time I got my hands dirty. This cat-and-mouse crap is *not* for me."

A phone on the table began to ring. "Speak of the devil. Maybe he's ready to let you go to work," David said to Ely before answering the call.

"Your work is not done in Italy," came their master's voice. "It appears this student doesn't scare easy. I need you to send a man to Siena tonight. The police officer and the guy from America just checked into the same hotel there. I need eyes on them by morning; there is a jet waiting now. Send the man who took care of business at the university. I need him ready to make them disappear at a moment's notice if this situation is not contained. Is that understood?"

"Understood." David hung up, as Ely and Ishmael eagerly awaited an update. "Looks like your stunt on the highway didn't work," he told Ely. "The student and the cop are still together. Seth wants eyes on them ASAP in Siena."

Ely looked furious as he opened a cabinet and began to load weapons into a duffel bag. "Not you, Ely; your cover is blown."

Ely slammed his fist on the counter as Ishmael got up and snatched the bag full of weapons. "I'll show you how it's done," Ishmael taunted Ely as he took inventory of the weaponry.

"This one is all mine!" Ely replied, pointing to the bedroom with the restrained professor.

"Sit down," David snapped. "You're not doing anything until we get the go-ahead." Ishmael hurried off the boat as a frustrated Ely sat and poured himself a full glass of whiskey.

CHAPTER TWENTY

Siena, Italy

After attending Mass, Michael and Vivi strolled around the nave of the Basilica of San Domenico. The large cathedral was nearly empty and, though impressive, it was plainer than a number of other Italian basilicas, in keeping with its original function as a home of a pious religious order.

"The story goes that St. Dominic passed through here and met a member of the Malavolti family in the 1200s," Michael said. "They were so impressed by him that they donated this land and resources to build this church for his start-up religious order. I'd say the Dominicans have had a good run. There's so much I want to learn about this church, but I just haven't had the time or resources to do so yet. I know it's built in the shape of an Egyptian cross, unlike the main Cathedral of Siena, which was built around the same time in the shape of the Latin cross. Maybe that's a clue."

Vivi raised her eyebrows. "What do you mean 'Egyptian cross'? An ankh?"

"No, just this versus that," Michael said as he held his hands in the shape of a T and then slid the top hand down in the shape of a cross. "I was only kidding about the clue; I don't see any altars to Horus or Set in here. But one of these chapels is the Capella Malavolti, which was built for the family. I'm not sure which one it is, although I've found art scattered throughout the world that was originally commissioned for it. The Baltimore Art Museum has pieces I've seen that were painted by Giovanni di Paola for the Capella Malavolti altar. A number of Malavolti bishops are buried here, too. Professor Sisti was working his connections to get the local government and church's permission to open some of the male Malavolti tombs, so we could retrieve DNA samples for the study."

"Why do you only care about the Malavolti men? What about the women?"

"I don't only 'care' about the men—I'm sure there were some amazing Malavolti women. In fact, arguably the most important, and certainly the most famous inhabitant ever of this city, was a woman." Just then, they arrived at an alcove chapel that had an altar with a shrine containing the head of St. Catherine.

Motioning to the chapel, he continued, "St. Catherine is the patron saint of Italy—heck, she's one of the patron saints of all of Europe. She wrote, or I should say she *dictated* because she couldn't write, several letters in her short life. Two of the surviving letters I'm aware of were written to Malavolti women. I have no doubt that the women of my ancient family were instrumental in the history of this city. It's just that, well, think of it this way..." He paused, thinking about how to explain this part of genetics.

"You have two parents, four grandparents, eight great-grandparents, etc. It doubles every generation back.

By the time you get back to, say, the 1300s, there are hypothetically over a million 'grandparents' in your family tree. We're all related if you go far enough back—you, me, and everyone in here. Now, there's not really a million different people in your family tree at that point, because there's a lot of doubling up—most marriages throughout history were to close cousins, and people were geographically isolated for long periods of time."

Michael could tell he was losing Vivi's attention as she peered at St Catherine's head while he rambled on about family trees.

"To the point: in a patriarchal society, last names are passed down from father to son. So is one little piece of genetic information that helps us track people due to its stability throughout time, the Y-chromosome. It would be hard to tell, given the genetics of a woman in my family from 800 years ago and my genetics, if we were part of the same family. Given the Y- chromosome of a male, though, it should match my Y-chromosome if we come from the same patrilineage, the same male line. So, in theory, the last name and the Y-chromosome should have traveled together over the last millennium. As far back as nearly 1,000 years ago, there was already talk of three branches of the Malavolti: the Orlandi, the Egidi, and the Fortebracci. With Y-chromosome analysis of men from each branch, you could tell if they all descended from the same man."

Michael hoped he was making some sense, but got little indication from Vivi as she walked away and, to his surprise, knelt in front of the head of St. Catherine and began to pray. Sensing she might be a minute, he continued to walk around the church for the next ten minutes until he was rejoined by Vivi, who looked as if she had been crying. Michael wanted to ask her if everything was okay and give her a hug, but he didn't think either would be welcomed. So he just said, "Do you want to get some fresh air? I could go for an espresso and breakfast."

They exited San Domenico to a sunny morning. "C'mon, let's make our way over to the main square, Il Campo. It's considered one of the best medieval public squares in all of Europe. I can't wait to see it with my own eyes!"

As they walked, Vivi remained silent, so he nervously talked to fill the void. "We're in the *Contrada del Oca* (District of the Goose), which is where St. Catherine was born. She spent most of her life in the church and convent we just left, though, so both *Drago* and *Oca* claim her. Her father was a wool dyer. Wool dying and banking were Siena's two biggest industries. Life was hard back then. When Catherine was born, the town was in the throes of the Black Plague. Her mother had already given birth to over twenty children, but about half of them died at birth or very young. Catherine was a twin, but the story goes that she was nursed by her mother while her twin was given to a wet nurse, and the twin didn't make it. Catherine's mother had a few more children after her, and lived to be eighty-nine. Catherine died young, in Rome as I assume you know, which is why the rest of her body is still there."

As they walked, the flags on the buildings changed from green and yellow to red and black, and he continued to share his knowledge of the various *contradas*.

"We've entered the *Contrada del Civetta* (the Little Owl) now. This is Piazza Tolomei, and that church there is

Chiesa di San Cristoforo. It's nearly 1,000 years old. The meeting with diplomats from Florence took place there before the battle of Monteparti. Obviously, diplomacy didn't work out that day; the Florentine demands involved opening Siena's gates and swearing allegiance to Florence."

Michael looked at Vivi, who seemed to be lost in thought and was still glassy eyed. He wondered if he should stop talking. In the center of Piazza Tolomei was a sight that can be seen all over Siena: the Capitoline Wolf. This she-wolf statue is made of carved marble and supported on a large pedestal. Vivi, pointing at the she-wolf, said, "That one is Romulus, the legendary founder of Rome. Why is this image associated with Siena?"

"Yes, that's right; the two infants suckling from the wolf are Romulus and Remus. Hey, come to think of it, this legend and the legend of Horus and Set have some similarities! Romulus and Remus were said to be the twin sons of the daughter of the king of Alba Longa, the kingdom that preceded Rome in Central Italy. Their mother's name was Rhea Silvia, and their grandfather the king's name was Numitor. Legend has it that he was a descendant of Aeneas of Trojan War fame. Numitor's brother murdered him and all other male heirs to become king of Alba Longa. He made Numitor's daughter, Rhea Silvia, take a vow of chastity, but she was impregnated by the god Mars.

"When the twin babies were born, she put them in a basket that was sent down the River Tiber to be hidden. Sounds familiar, right? Later they were rescued and nursed by a she-wolf. Eventually, human shepherds found them and raised them to be shepherds themselves. Both Romulus

and Remus gain a large following, as they're natural charismatic leaders, even though they're ignorant of their past.
At some point, they discover their true identities and take
revenge by killing the evil king. They decide they don't
want to rule over Alba Longa with the same capital, so they
found a new city for their kingdom, Rome."

"Yes, I know the story, but why is this wolf all over
Siena?"

"There's more to the story. There are various versions
of this legend, but they all end with Romulus killing Remus
over some kind of dispute. Remus had two sons, Senius and
Aschius, who feared for their lives after their father was
killed, so they fled Rome. They took the statue of the Capitoline Wolf with them and founded the city of Siena, thus
appropriating the symbol for this city.

Ancient Capitoline Wolf statue in Siena[7]

"So I guess whether it's the Horus and Set story or the Romulus and Remus story, the moral is the same: if you're a king, keep a close eye on your brother; and if you need to hide your newborn baby, throwing them in a river is the way to go." He had hoped to cheer Vivi up, but his dark humor didn't seem to faze her.

They arrived at Piazza Del Campo, the grand public space at the center of Siena, which fanned out like a seashell and was surrounded by numerous options for them to sit and get a bite to eat. Vivi had a preference, as she passed a few options before sitting down at an outside table with a good vantage point of the large piazza. As they ate breakfast, she seemed distant. Michael wanted to talk about the history of the piazza; he especially wanted to tell her about the large tower on the other side of the public space, the Torre del Mangi. The tower was built in 1338, and at just under 300 feet, it was built to the exact same height as the Siena Cathedral to show the equal power of the church and state—something he felt was truly forward thinking in the early 1300s.

Siena was once a city of towers. *In the 1200s and 1300s, it must have looked like Manhattan in comparison to other cities,* Michael thought. As the number of wealthy families grew, so did the number of towers, a status symbol for the newly wealthy and old aristocrats alike. Eventually, the city passed a law to bring down all the towers. He not only wanted to talk about what he knew about the piazza and the towers, but also to ask Vivi why she seemed so sad. He felt it was best to give her a moment of silence, though; so instead of talking, he ate and continued to survey the crowd, looking for any sign of the guy with the buzz cut.

For once, the palpable silence was broken by Vivianna.

"My mother died when I was ten." She paused, collecting her thoughts while sipping an espresso. "Her name was Catherine. She was named after Catherine of Siena. I grew up going to Mass on Sundays at St. Maria Sopra Minerva, where St. Catherine's tomb is in Rome; we lived around the corner. Sometimes, after Mass, my mother and I would kneel at the altar where St. Catherine's body is and pray to her. My mother died of cancer when she was thirty-three—the same age as Catherine of Siena was when she died.

"As a ten-year-old girl who had just lost her mother, I hated St. Catherine. I thought she took my mother from me. I got over it with time, though, and felt Catherine comfort me whenever I was in that church. I still stop in occasionally and kneel at her tomb to talk to my mother. When I saw St. Catherine's head in San Domenico this morning, I felt like I was seeing a ghost."

Vivi paused again, as if she needed to stop talking in order to control her emotions. Michael reached out and squeezed her hand. "I'm so sorry, Vivi."

Using her napkin to dab her eyes, she continued eating. Michael sat attentively, hoping she would go on, but knew that was probably all he was going to hear regarding her past.

"What else do you want to see today?" she asked.

"We don't have to do anything. I'd be content if we sat here and drank wine all day. I'm not going to be doing as much traveling to meet Malavotis around Italy now as I had thought, so I'll probably come back here and spend a few days exploring before I have to fly back home."

"Nonsense! How long have you been dreaming about being in this place? I'm sure you have a long list of things to see for your thesis research. Besides, I think it's best we move around if someone is still tracking us. I'm hoping I get a chance to meet the man responsible for that dent in my bumper."

"Okay, if you insist. Why don't we try and see the Biccherna Museum today, and—oh! you know what I really want to see? It's probably tiny and we'll only be there a few moments, but most of the individual contrade have their own museums. I'd really like to see if the Drago Museum is open today. They might have some neat history of the neighborhood, which is basically the entirety of the old Malavolti castle. They even put out a newspaper with happenings for Contrada del Drago named The Malavolti. Obviously, I need a copy of that as a souvenir. Then there's no rush. I think I need to see the main cathedral today. It's going to be hard to wait any longer to see that beauty. In a country with breathtaking churches everywhere, the Siena Cathedral is considered by many to be one of the most beautiful. I'm really looking forward to it. It's full of works by Renaissance masters."

Ishmael sat in Il Campo with his windbreaker's hood up over his long scruffy hair. He had a pocket full of birdseed he was scattering about. The pigeons hopped around at his feet, pecking at the ancient burnt-red bricks.

The tranquil scene was interrupted by a vibration of his phone. *I want updates every 30 minutes while those two are together in Siena*, read the text from Seth. *Be ready to eliminate them if needed.*

He replied: *They were at the church called San Domenico earlier. Now they are eating breakfast. I'm in position to act.*

Ishmael was tempted to ask Seth what he should be watching out for, but he knew he was on a need-to-know basis. He was tired, too, but the feel of the various weapons strapped to his torso under his jacket exhilarated him. He set a timer for thirty minutes on his phone, put his sunglasses on, and went back to feeding the pigeons.

Vivianna got up from the table first, "Come on, you're finally here. Where should we go first?"

"Okay, if you insist. The Biccherna Museum is just a block off the Campo, over there by the university. It's actually in the old Piccolomini palace; it should be open now. Why don't we stop in there?"

CHAPTER TWENTY-ONE

Castel Gandolfo, Italy

From the kitchen window, Sister Mary could see that the early morning guests were leaving now; more of those serious-looking men in suits. She glanced at the clock on the wall and thought: *He hasn't eaten anything yet today and already one meeting done.* Mary shook her head in disapproval as she worried about what was going on. Her old friend had sought her out for support for some reason, and she was beginning to sense it was something bigger than just familiarity. She picked up the prepared breakfast tray and hurried off to catch him between meetings.

Knocking on the open office door and entering cautiously, she found him clutching his rosary in prayer. "Forgive me for interrupting, Your Holiness. I've prepared some breakfast for you." Receiving a warm smile in return, she almost left the man alone to pray before thinking better of it and taking a seat across from him. "I'm honored that you requested my presence here this summer, but I have to wonder why. Certainly you have assigned staff that could be here, and who are all these men with guns?"

"Please, Mary, call me Alfie like you did when we were children. They are Swiss guards—retired Swiss special forces. All good men I trust and have known for a long time. No need to be alarmed," answered Alfonso Carpacci.

"And so I can assume that's why you requested my presence as well? Because I've known you since you were a young man, running around Spoletto with my older brother and roughing up any boy who hurt my feelings? But then I have to ask what is going on inside the Vatican that has made you take refuge here? Forgive me. I know it's not my place, but I'm worried about you. You've barely eaten in days, and I thought you were supposed to be resting and focusing on your health, yet you seem to be burdened by an enormous weight."

"Sister Mary Margarita, you are a better friend and caretaker than I deserve. My work is taking my every waking moment these days."

"You have too many waking moments then! You need to be getting more rest, or you will be no good to anyone."

Father Alfonso reached out and embraced Mary's hand. He looked deeply into her eyes, pausing as if to assess how much he was willing to share his burden with this lifelong friend, then said, "Imagine you stand at a fork in the road, Mary, with two possible paths to choose from. One of those paths starts off dark with lies and deceit, but may lead to preserving a greater good. Temporary bad things must be done with the right intentions in the hope that it will lead to a benefit for all mankind. The other path starts off light with honest yet difficult truths. These truths, however, may lead humanity to a place where it finds itself lost and suffering from despair. A complete loss of purpose and direction."

Mary held Alfonso's hand, probing his anguished eyes before she spoke, as if the answer might be found in his pain. The long pause was not awkward, not for these two old souls who were as familiar as family. Finally, she said, "The light of truth dispels the darkness in which lies the stronghold of evil. Sin is the bondage of powers of the soul, and this bondage is willed because the soul does not see its fearful evil. When it perceives the truth, there comes to it a power that rouses it from its stupor and strengthens it to break the fetters by which it has been bound."

Sister Mary did not wait for a response. She could see from the glint in Alfie's eye that the passage from the Book of John was something His Holiness had needed to hear. She left a tray with tea and food in hopes that the Pope Emeritus, the first retired pope in over 600 years, might have more of an appetite today.

CHAPTER TWENTY-TWO

Siena, Italy

As Michael and Vivi left the Museo delle Tavolette di Biccherna, the University of Siena campus was within sight. "Today the university makes up a large portion of the population of Siena. I think it has an enrollment around 20,000 students." He continued to play tour guide just in case it helped Vivi take her mind off her mother.

"Is there anything you'd like to see here on our Malavolti tour?" she asked.

He appreciated how enthusiastic Vivi was when her head was clearly somewhere else. "I don't think so, not today. I'm sure a number of Malavoltis were educated here. It's one of the oldest publicly funded universities in Italy, probably the world. It first opened in 1240. As always, the age of things in Italy blows my mind as an American. Our oldest university is Harvard, which was founded in 1636. Meanwhile, Siena had already set up a school for higher education 400 years earlier with public monies.

"I know of one Malavolti connection with the university that's pretty interesting. One of the many Malavolti bishops,

Azzolino Malavolti, was able to get the university accreditation throughout the Holy Roman Empire in 1357. I think it was Charles IV of France who granted the title of *Studium Generale* at the request of Azzolino. This meant the university was no longer just recognized locally, but all over Christendom. The Malavoltis seem to have a long-running positive relationship with the French crown. Except for Philip the Fair in the late thirteenth century, I guess. I don't think anyone got along with him."

"What did he do?" Vivi either enjoyed his history lessons or simply liked the time when her mind could wander while he spoke.

"He fought a lot of people and always needed more money. War is expensive. He levied impossibly high taxes on the clergy, causing a rift with Rome. He kicked all the Jews out of France so he could collect on their loans. He famously brought an end to the wealthy and powerful order of the Knights Templar just so he could confiscate their wealth. Philip was all about the money.

"I don't know how it went down, but he was also at least partially responsible for ending the Gran Tavola, Europe's first international bank. It's often credited with being the first modern-day corporation due to the way it was structured. Apparently, Philip the Fair bankrupted a number of noble houses at the time of the bank's collapse, including the Malavoltis. That was in the late 1200s, and many of the family remained wealthy and powerful for some time, so I'm not sure how big their financial hit really was.

"Actually, Vatican records on medieval finance are where most of the details about that would be found. Maybe I'll reach out to your uncle or his assistant, Daniel, if I get into a bind with my research later." As they walked toward the main square again, they passed another bank, which he pointed at, and said, "Did you know this is the oldest continuously operating bank in the world?" Vivi shook her head. "Banca Monti Dei Paschi di Siena first opened in 1472 and has been in business ever since, making it the oldest still in operation. 'The Mount of Piety' is a funny name for a bank, in my opinion. It was started by the magistrate's office of Siena as an answer to the noble families growing rich off interest and running their own banking schemes. It's been in the international finance news a lot lately. Overleveraged, bad debt...I guess some things remain the same when it comes to humans and money, power, greed, and corruption. The bank is a great benefactor to the city, though. I hope for the sake of Siena it's able to right itself and be here for another 500 years."

"How do you keep all these dates straight?" Vivi asked, curious.

"There's an old trick I use. It helps to use three-dimensional visuals in your thinking. So when I'm studying history, say Siena from 1000–1500, I picture a timeline in my mind, but I try to see it in three dimensions. I put various things I know on the timeline, like a mental picture of the cathedral when its construction started or a vision of St. Catherine on the day she was born.

"By creating visual images and seeing it in my mind's eye as a big three-dimensional timeline versus something linear, I can remember points and dates better. As I learn new things that fit into that timeline, I can visualize where I'm sticking them between other mental pictures already on it. It's actually a technique that's been around since ancient

Roman or Greek times. It's called the 'method of loci,' or the memory palace technique. It works because the brain is best at recalling memories related to spatial memory. So if there's anything you need to remember and you can visualize it in some type of organized three-dimensional space in your head, it will become easier to recall."

"Anything in your memory palace telling you why someone might not want you to work on a family tree? Don't forget to keep a lookout for the man who ran us off the road," Vivi reminded him.

"Oh! Yeah, I'm so excited to be in this city I almost forgot about the professor. I've been scanning faces everywhere we go, but no sign of Buzz Cut yet. I still think this has to be some kind of misunderstanding. This city had its heyday in the thirteenth and fourteenth centuries. Back then it was as big as Paris and much richer. Look around. It's a living museum; I love it!

"My point is that this is all ancient history. I don't think your case has anything to do with Siena or the Malavolti. Besides, the perpetrator left that message about Set for someone in particular, right? And it couldn't be the professor because they took him, so what's *that* about? Talk about ancient history. I was reading as much as I could about Set in the car yesterday after Montalcino, and he goes waaaaay back. He first appears in pictures from over 5,500 years ago. We're talking before 3500 BCE. Seems to me that either had to be a message for someone else, or your boss is right, and it's some psycho trying to be scary by invoking an old name for Satan. "

As they walked back along the edge of Il Campo, Ishmael had barely moved all morning; he was able to keep tabs on them from the edge of the main square, away from the tourists, where he was still feeding the pigeons.

"Have you ever been in this square for a Palio, Vivi?" asked Michael.

She smiled faintly. "Ah, yes, I've been to the Palio twice. It's really crazy—the people here are so passionate about their *contrada*! I think you would love it, Michael, and of course, you'd have to root for *Drago*."

"Yeah, of course! I'm trying to picture this square packed with people waving their neighborhood's scarf or flag. It's a funny juxtaposition next to my thesis. Siena has this reputation for being stuck in the past, kind of backwater. To understand that, though, you have to understand the city's past and how great it was. In some ways, it is still coming to terms with surrendering to Florence 500 years ago. The genetic portion of my thesis was going to help me show how social amnesia works, how descendants of this great city don't know much about its history. Now that I'm here, though, you can feel how Siena's modern inhabitants cling to its glory days through things like the Palio. All the pageantry and traditions that go along with the race date back centuries. I think my favorite tradition is that each horse racing that day gets a blessing in the official church of its *contrada* early on the race day, and if the horse leaves a pile of manure on the church floor during the ceremony, it's considered a very good omen for that *contrada*."

That surprised a laugh out of Vivi.

"I know, right? Also, when babies are born in Siena, it's not unusual for the parents to bring a little dirt from their *contrada* into the birthing room and put it on the floor, so the baby can be born into their neighborhood. From an outsider's perspective they seem fanatical and stuck in the past, but I get it. Maybe I should put a little dirt from *Drago* in my suitcase in case I ever have kids." Michael chuckled at the thought.

"So where to next?" asked Vivi.

"I'd really like to see the Drago Museum, now that you mention it. Why don't we walk back there? I'd like to get some pictures of some of the older buildings that belonged to the Malavoltis and then go to that museum. Then we could get a snack and end the day with a tour of the cathedral. Sound good?"

She agreed, so they walked along Via Banchi di Sopra back toward the *Contrada del Drago*. Medieval stone buildings rose four to five stories high, towering above the narrow cobblestone streets filled with pedestrians.

"Coming from a country where a hundred-year-old building is considered ancient, so much of Italy feels surreal," Michael said thoughtfully, "but I have to say that walking these streets feels like a dream. Even like coming home. The beautiful, centuries-old buildings gives the illusion that you're inside a castle almost everywhere you go in this city, even when you're outside. Then, on top of that, you have all these modern boutiques and cafes, and it seems like I should be in some kind of medieval Disney theme park—but this is the real deal. Sorry, I know I'm rambling, but I just thought that since you've lived here your whole life, you probably don't realize how alien it feels for me to walk down a street that's lined with towering architecture much older than the United States."

"No, I'm glad you are enjoying it. I was also thinking about how the lack of open spaces is not ideal for tracking someone, though. I'm constantly assessing our environment, and all the narrow openings make it difficult. If someone were to attack us, we might not see them until they were right on top of us. Please be vigilant, Michael— these tight spaces are not the smartest place for us to be right now."

"The perspective of a police officer—I can appreciate that. Trust me; I'm still looking for Buzz Cut every chance I get."

They passed an open space created from Palazzo Salembeni before reentering the narrow confines of the cobblestone path, eventually arriving at an area where three streets came together, creating a slightly more open landscape where the sun's beams could reach the ground without being directly overhead.

"I *think* this is the edge of the old Malavolti castle. See the age of the bricks on that tower right there? That's still called the Torre dei Malavolti, and if it's what I think it is, then it's roughly 800 years old. Almost four times older than the United States!"

Even with the age of the surrounding buildings being centuries old, the stone tower at the corner where the streets Banchi di Sopra and Giuseppe Pianigiani met looked out of place. Its weathered stones, which rose five stories up, looked much older. "When do you think that was built?" she asked.

"Well, Phillipo Malavolti led troops in a number of battles in the late twelfth century. He fought here at home and even sailed to Acre in the Holy Land, leading a group of 500 Sienese men in the Crusades. He returned from there to be elected *podesta*, the head of the government at that time, and fought in more wars after that. He even led an attack at Montalcino later in his life. Siena was a city of towers, but few were built with public money. Phillipo was so loved that the city voted to erect a tower in his memory, and I think this is it—the bottom five or so stories of it anyway. Built right on the edge of Malavolti Hill."

Michael was busy snapping pictures; everywhere he looked seemed like it would make a worthy postcard. He especially wanted to document the *Contrada del Drago*, as it took up residence entirely in grounds once belonging to the Malavolti family. They walked along the cobblestone path a little further, until they came to a tiny, ancient church, Santa Maria delle Nevi. Running along its southern side was Via dell'Arco Malavolti.

"This is where the entrance into the Malavolti castle used to be. I've seen drawings of what it looked like. It stood until the late 1700s. It was this big gothic arched door; the Malavolti ladder could be seen stamped on the wall on either side of the entrance." Michael paused to take a picture of the street sign. "C'mon...this way to the museum."

CHAPTER TWENTY-THREE

Siena, Italy

Ishmael kept a distance and blended in with the crowds as his targets slowly walked through the cobblestone streets. Every thirty minutes he sent a text to Seth about exactly where his marks were in the city. So far he had received back only short one-word answers confirming the receipt of his updates. The latest update was no different: *Back near the hotel, entering the museum for Drago on Via del Paradiso.*

The response was the same every time: *Copy.*

As Michael opened the Drago Museum door, it rang a small bell to alert the elderly gentleman reading a paper behind a display case that guests were present. The *contrada* had clearly outgrown its current museum space. The room was cluttered, bursting at the seams with Palio paraphernalia spanning centuries.

The room was an explosion of *Drago* colors: red, green, and gold. It was filled with various jockey uniforms, trophies, religious artifacts, and pictures of famous jockeys and politicians; the chaos of the room made it difficult to focus on any one thing. Michael walked around, taking it all in, keeping an eye out for the newspaper named *The Malavolti*. After a few minutes with no luck, he asked the gray-haired man working the museum, in broken Italian, if they had any copies of *The Malavolti*. The gentlemen moved his stack of newspapers, revealing a small pile of the latest printings of *The Malavolti*. A delighted Michael asked if he could take two, explaining it was his last name and he was doing research on the family. The man behind the counter continued reading his paper with indifference, so he snagged a few and stuck them in his bag.

There was a small architecture book published in the 1960s on the castle of the Malavolti in Siena that Michael owned. It featured a number of pictures of the area from the mid-1900s. The museum had a wall with a number of black-and-white pictures that looked to be from the same era. "Do you mind if I take some photographs in here? I'd like to get a picture of all these old black-and-white neighborhood photos," he asked the attendant, holding up his camera as he spoke.

The gentleman shrugged with indifference again, not letting on if he understood a word Michael had said yet. He began working his way down the wall, taking a picture of each building photo on the wall.

"These photos are great, Vivi! At one time, my family controlled everything in this neighborhood. There was one main lodge they lived in during the Middle Ages, and all Malavoltis had an equal ownership in it—but the other buildings were rented out to citizens and were owned by various individuals in the family. The tax records in the *biccherna* will be a good source for sorting out some of those ownership questions. Man, I'd love to see what the buildings they tore down in the early 1900s were like!"

Vivi stood silently in the middle of the room, looking as if she were afraid to touch anything. As he leaned over the display case to center up a photo he was taking, he got to within inches of the man reading his newspaper. To Michael's surprise, the gentlemen closed his paper and asked him a question: "So, you are a Malavolti?"

"Yes sir, I am, from America. I'm doing a research project on Siena and trying to write a bit about my family's history within that history."

The gentlemen spoke to Michael in a hushed, measured manner, although he and Vivi were the only other people in the museum. "My grandfather told me a story about the time they tore those buildings down in 1903." He leaned in even closer, as if he didn't already have his attention; his next words were, "He says they were also digging and looking for something under the church."

"Under the Church of St. Egidio? Who was digging? What were they looking for?" a wide-eyed Michael asked him questions in rapid-fire succession.

The older gentlemen picked up his paper again as if he might just ignore the questions before continuing, "Nobody knew. My grandfather worked on the demolition and on building the post office. He says after they tore down the old buildings, a big fence was put up so no one could see in the area. Another group came in and dug there for three months. The whole neighborhood was abuzz, but they had no real information. The workers came in by bus, he said, and they had guards. If they were government employees, they weren't local."

Michael stood staring at the man with the expression of a child hearing a ghost story, hoping he would continue. After he went back to reading his paper, Michael offered, "Maybe they were looking for another Lysippos?"

The man chuckled, "Ha ha... maybe, crazy fascists."

As they exited the museum, they didn't notice the man sitting on a bench in Piazza Matteotti who was keenly watching their every move.

"It's a damn shame, isn't it? Tearing down parts of what might have been the oldest castle in this city just 100 years ago to make way for *this*," Michael said while motioning to the post office and some of the surrounding buildings. "It is a nice-looking post office, though, I'll give them that. We don't make them like that in the States."

"You want to tell me what that was about? What is this about Lysippos?" Vivi asked.

"Oh, that was just an old man telling stories. The mystery around the Malavoltis does keep getting weirder and weirder, though. Let's find a café near the cathedral, and I'll tell you everything I know about the Lysippos legend... which isn't much. We need to update our suspect list to include international art thieves, I guess."

Michael continued taking pictures as they walked.

Vivi led the way as they passed through the *Contrada del Selva* (Forest) and entered their destination *Contrada del Aquila* (Eagle). She found a café with good sight lines and they took a seat to eat.

"I'm glad you picked a place in *Aquila*. You know, it's the only official ally *contrada* of *Drago*." Michael had a knack for pointing out trivial minutia, and Vivi had a knack for ignoring it.

"So what do you think they were looking for, digging under your family's old home and church 100 years ago? What is this about Lysippos?" asked Vivi.

"I have no idea who was digging or what they were looking for. I assume, like most 100-year-old oral lore stories, it's lacking in facts. Who knows? I still don't understand why they would have knocked down some of the oldest buildings in a city so well preserved, so maybe there *is* something to it. Maybe someone was looking for something? Lysippos was a fourth century BCE Greek sculptor. Considered one of the best from ancient Greece."

"I know who he is. What does he have to do with the Malavoltis?" She was clearly growing impatient with the history lesson.

"There's a story about a Venus sculpture carved by none other than Lysippos himself that was found under the Malavolti castle. They unearthed the marble statue during the 1300s. Some sources say it was hidden under floorboards, others say it was found when digging a new foundation, but either way it was under the Malavolti home. There was some kind of inscription on it that led everyone to believe it was a genuine Lysippos. The town found it so beautiful that they put it in a prominent position on a fountain in the main *campo* for a while.

"A plague or famine or war or something hit the town, and the pagan statue was blamed for their misfortune. What did the Sienese do with a pagan idol statue that brought them a curse? Why, naturally they used it against Florence. They broke the statue up into a few pieces and buried it around the city of Florence in an attempt to transfer the statue's bad juju onto them. Later on, when the Renaissance was in full swing, the Medici learned there was a broken-up Lysippos from the Malavolti castle buried around Florence. They had the pieces dug up and set to having their best sculptors imitate the design. The only problem was that we now know Lysippos only worked in bronze—or at least we *think* he did. If it was a marble Venus, it was probably a Roman-era copy of a bronze Aphrodite that had been done in Lysippos' studio. I guess it's one more thing that adds to the mystery of the origins of the family and how far back in history their wealth went. Do you know anything about St. Egidio, Vivi?"

She thought for a moment before answering, "No, I'm sorry to say I know nothing, despite my Catholic education. Who was he?"

"Yeah, don't feel bad. I also went to Catholic schools my whole life, and I'd never heard of him either. In studying the Malavoltis, I became curious about who he was, since their church and military company was named for him. I learned that Egidio is Italian for Giles, but that didn't help much, because I'd never heard of St. Giles either; he's an obscure saint. There *is* one weird thing about his history though, another strange legend.

"St. Giles lived in the late 600s in the south of France, but he was believed to be from Athens. He lived as a hermit, but was commonly thought to be Greek royalty. Sometime shortly after the year 1000, a story associated with St. Giles appeared in Latin and French texts in different parts of Europe. The legend holds that he was saying Mass when a bird landed on the altar, carrying a piece of paper with a message for him. The message contained a sin committed by Charlemagne that was so great he was unable to confess it to him directly. It was referred to as 'the unspeakable sin of Charlemagne' or 'the great sin of Charlemagne.' Miraculously, St. Giles was able to absolve this sin in absentia. Of course, in the Middle Ages, it was hot gossip to speculate on what that sin was. The strangest part of the story, though, is that it's thought now that St. Giles lived his entire life before Charlemagne was even born."

"That's interesting, but what do you think it has to do with the church here or the Malavoltis?" Vivi asked.

"Oh, I doubt it has anything to do with them. Just pointing out that Charlemagne is associated with St. Giles because of this bizarre story, which doesn't even fit chronologically, and Charlemagne is also associated with the Malavolti origin story. There's not much to go on, which is why I was so looking forward to working with an anthropological geneticist. The story, or maybe I should say *legend*, of the family origin is that they were founded by a knight who accompanied Charlemagne when he passed through here on his way to liberate Rome and form the first unified Holy Roman Empire."

"When do *you* think the Malavoltis first settled here?" Vivi asked, while sipping her espresso and watching the street.

"Usually the simplest answer is the best. I'd guess, based on their established presence in Siena's earliest recorded history, they were here already when Charlemagne passed through. As I mentioned before, my Y-chromosome comes from Egypt; it's in the E grouping.

"Charlemagne was king of the Franks. The Franks and all the other early European tribes carried Y-chromosomes predominately from the R group, or a few other haplogroups.

It's a long-winded explanation about Y-DNA analysis and early human migrations, but most of the people who settled Europe came from East Asia several thousand years ago in a few different waves. My paternal ancestor, though, came from Egypt. It's certainly possible—but unlikely, in my opinion—that a Frankish knight was the first Malavolti."

Michael and Vivi ate their lunch at a leisurely pace, both feeling mentally drained from the day's events. There would be no siesta, but at least they could have a long lunch with wine and espresso while things slowed during the sunny midafternoon hours.

As the two sat sipping their drinks, Michael began reading something on his phone. "Hmm, that's interesting. I've tried to research the origin of the dragon mascot and emblem. Why did they pick a dragon for the mascot of that *contrada*, a dragon with a crown on it? Like so many things, there are various theories. The dragon dates back to at least the 1400s. One theory is that it has something to do with the Borghese family, as they came from Siena and have a dragon on their family seal. Another is it comes from the Benincasa family—that's St. Catherine's family. There are other theories, of course, but none ever seemed convincing to me. They just don't make much sense, since *Drago's* borders are exactly the outer edge of the old Malavolti castle, and the family would have surely had some presence if the name and emblem came about in the 1400s. I'd think they would have had some say in it, but maybe not. What do you think of when you think of Catholic saints and dragons?"

"St. George," she immediately replied.

"Yeah...for some reason I never had that thought until right now and was reading up on St. George on my phone. As you know, he's famous for being depicted slaying a dragon." He read from his phone to Vivi as she finished his desert: "He was a Roman soldier of Greek origin who's said to have served under the guard of Roman Emperor Diocletian. Read this part on his Wikipedia page." Michael passed Vivi his phone.

She read: "The episode of St. George and the dragon was a legend brought back to Europe from the Crusades. Some evidence links the legend back to very old Egyptian and Phoenician sources in a late antique statue of Horus fighting a 'dragon.' This ties the legendary George and, to some extent, the historical George, to various ancient sources using mythological and linguistic arguments. In Egyptian mythology, the god Setekh (or Set) murdered his brother Osiris. Horus, the son of Osiris, avenged his father's death by killing Setekh. This iconography of the horseman with spear overcoming evil was widespread throughout the Christian period."[8]

"Interesting, right? There's an ancient statue, and it appears now that this image or statue has been found in multiple places around Egypt; apparently, it was fairly common in ancient Egypt. It's a depiction of a man on horseback killing a huge crocodile (which can look a bit dragonish) with a spear. The man is thought to be Horus, and the beast is meant to represent Set. So the image of a dragon and St. George was a retelling of that story, where the dragon is Set, or Satan." Michael paused, looking down at his empty espresso glass, his mind lost in thought.

Vivi said, "Your last name means 'to do an evil deed,' which Set came to represent. Your ancestral home is now represented by a dragon, Set's icon. And someone painted his name in blood in the lab of a professor you were working with." She looked at him seriously. "Do you *still* think that has nothing to do with you, Michael Malavolti?"

"It just doesn't make any sense, though. Maybe we're seeing a bunch of interesting coincidences because we're looking for them, or is there something to it? It does seem odd that I've twice read the name Set while researching Siena in the last week, but all legends come from somewhere—and ancient Egypt was a birthplace of many things."

CHAPTER TWENTY-FOUR

Siena, Italy

After lunch, Michael and Vivi walked a short distance over to the cathedral. As they approached from the front, a group of pigeons that had been sitting near the base of yet another pedestal featuring a sculpture of the Capitoline Wolf took flight. They both paused at the foot of the stairs leading up to the cathedral to take in the amazing façade, which had enough ornate artwork and sculptures to gaze at all day.

"Every time I come here I marvel at the outside of this church. Do you know when it was built?" she asked.

"Tell me about it. You could spend days just studying the art on the front side of the outside of this building, and there are beautiful sculptures all over it. On the inside, there are works by Bernini, Raphael, Donatello, Michelangelo...it's a 'Who's Who' of Renaissance sculptors. Obviously, something this grand wasn't built in a short period of time, but most of the general structure you see now was built in the early to mid-1200s. That wall extending to its side was to be another huge extension on to this church in the 1300s, but then the Black Plague hit and killed over half the town, putting an end to *that* lofty goal. There has been a church here for much longer than that, though. Records indicate a church and bishop's residence back to the 800s at least. The Catholic Church actually had a synod here in 1058, so it must have been important at the time, but obviously nothing like this."

Michael motioned to the façade as he spoke. "They've even found remains of an ancient temple to Minerva under this church. It was fairly common to build churches on sites of previous religious importance. This has probably been a place of worship since pre-Roman Etruscan times."

Romulus and Remus with she-wolf statue at the Siena Cathedral[9]

Ishmael had changed his appearance a few times throughout the day. He was starting to understand why Ely grew impatient when doing this kind of reconnaissance work. He had done recon as a soldier, but he always knew more about the enemy back then. Blindly following around a couple of tourists hardly seemed like worthy work. Every time he texted Seth a detailed update of their activities, he got back the same text: *Copy.*

That is, until now. He'd texted, *At the cathedral,* and in an instant received, *Follow them inside, watch them closely...be ready to act.* Ishmael felt his pulse quicken.

Michael and Vivi entered the cathedral through the middle of three large doors. "Wow!" He could feel the hair on his arm rising upon finally setting his eyes on the inside. They slowly walked down the middle of the nave, taking it all in.

"I can't imagine how hard it would be to create something like this now, much less with the tools they had at their disposal 800 years ago. You could say that about a lot of things in Italy, though. Oh, and I don't want to miss any of the floor mosaics. They keep them covered for most of the year to protect them, only uncovering them for viewing during special times, so I'm happy we came when they're on display. I may make it back here before my thesis is done, but I might never see all these mosaics in person again. We need a plan," he said, while he pulled out his phone and brought up a map of the cathedral floor.

"Let's go in here first and get it over with, then we can work our way around the floor. This is the Piccolomini Library, built to honor a Piccolomini who had become pope, commissioned by his nephew who was a cardinal at the time. The nephew went on to become a pope, too. They were popes Pius II and III." They entered the library room to an explosion of color. Every inch of the walls and vaulted ceiling were painted in beautifully preserved pastel colors.

"Now, this is gorgeous!" exclaimed Vivi.

"Yeah, those Piccolomini assholes had good taste," Michael quipped, then received a quizzical look from Vivi. "Hey, just trying to keep the rivalry alive; it's the Sienese way."

"Did any Malavoltis become pope?" she asked.

"No, only lots of cardinals and bishops as far as I know. Hey, wait a minute—are you on Team Piccolomini?"

"I'm not sure yet. What *contrada* did they live in again?"

"I think their palace was in the *Contrada del Giraffa* (Giraffe)."

"Hmmm, red and white, right? I think I'm a *Contrada del Onda* (Wave) girl. I like the blue and white." Vivi clearly enjoyed teasing him. "What is this statue called? I know I've seen it in Rome a few places as well?" she asked, referring to the sculpture of three women embracing in the middle of the room.

"You *would* root for water," answered Mike, unhappy with her *contrada* preference. "Anyway, the statue is called the Three Graces. It was popular in Rome, but goes back to ancient Greece. They're supposed to be the three daughters of Zeus. Not sure why they were chosen for this library, but the number three was always important to the Sienese. Siena is built on three hills, and they tried to incorporate that number or its multiples into everything they created."

As they left the library, Michael looked at his phone again, referencing the few links on the cathedral he had open. "Let's move back toward the entrance along this wall. I want to get pictures of all the floor mosaics. It's interesting that they would feature so many images of sibyls (ancient priestesses) along this wall. I think it speaks to the openmindedness of the Renaissance; there was a real thirst for knowledge from any and all sources. Anything considered old or esoteric was even more in vogue. That's why, I'm guessing, there's that picture of the god Hermes I was telling you about." He clicked a picture of every sibyl as they made their way along the wall back toward the front door. "Here he is. Wow! I didn't realize he was right inside the front door, the first image you see as you enter through the main entrance.

"This is the image I was telling you about in Montalcino. It's Hermes Trismegistus, or Thrice Great Hermes because he was said to be the best philosopher, priest, and king ever. The Roman god Mercury was based on Hermes, and *this* Hermes was thought to be the same as Thoth from Egypt. Perhaps he was given such a prominent position due to his connection with ancient secret knowledge. There are bits and pieces from books labeled *Hermetic Corpus* written in the second and third centuries AD. These Egyptian-Greek wisdom texts were thought to be much older, though, during the Renaissance, dating back to the times of pharaohs.

Whether it was Hermes or Thoth, he was thought to have authored books containing the secrets of the universe.

"Thoth was thought to be the creator of language and a prodigious author, supposedly writing thousands of books that have been lost with time, yet enough to have filled the earliest libraries in ancient Egypt. These libraries were called 'Houses of Life,' and were contained in the early temple complexes of Egypt."

Michael scrolled through some links he had opened earlier on his phone to refresh his memory about Thoth. He read aloud from a page he had last been studying: "Near the end of ancient Egypt's history, during the Ptolemaic period, there appears a work of fiction called *The Book of Thoth*, a dialogue between someone called 'the one who loves knowledge' and Thoth himself."

"But why would that be connected to the professor's genetic work in Egypt or you, for that matter?" Vivi asked.

"I have *no* idea. I've tried to think of anything, even farfetched, and I just can't think of anything that would cause someone to wish harm on the professor, but I don't know about his Egyptian work. There were three epics of good versus evil way back in ancient Egypt: the first of these battles was between Ra and Apep, the second was between Heru-Bekhutet and Set, and the third and probably most famous now is the battle between Horus and Set from the Osiris and Isis legend. Thoth was the mediator between good and evil in all these epics, and he healed the injured.

"Egypt was once split into Upper and Lower Egypt, two separate lands that were united to form one country around 3,000 BCE. Some scholars think Horus and Set are based on real kings from Egypt's distant past: a king of the north and a king of the south. Obviously, the further back in time, the less accurate an historical account."

Michael continued to flip through the open links on his phone as they stood next to Thrice Great Hermes. "I'm just thinking out loud here, Vivi, but let me throw out a really crazy outside-the-box scenario: The professor's lab is one of the best in the world at sequencing genes from really old samples. No doubt he's tested many samples from ancient Egypt at the country's request. What if he had a sample of a king he thought might be the historical Set? Maybe some king from the Upper or Lower Kingdom. Okay, so let's say this sample might even show that the Malavoltis are descendants of this king."

"You could tell that from several thousand years ago?" Vivi's curiosity was piqued.

"It depends. I think so...well, it's possible. The Y-chromosome is quite stable over time. It also sometimes carries unique mutations that can link patrilineage over long periods of time. Did you know that one in every 200 males on Earth are direct descendants of Genghis Khan?"

"Genghis Khan? How could he relate to any of this?" Vivi tried to wrap her head around Mike's genetic trivia.

"Nothing. My point is that we all come from *somewhere*. My Y-chromosome comes from Egypt, and the professor's work demonstrates it originated from a major mutation that created my haplogroup in the vicinity of Thebes roughly 17,000 years ago. Let's just say, hypothetically, the professor discovered I was a living descendant of some previously unknown ancient Egyptian king. Who would really care that much? It would be interesting, maybe late-night-history-channel interesting, but not worth killing over. Kings were known to spread their seed, if you know what I mean, some more than others. Obviously, Genghis Khan is an extreme example—I think they have his picture next to 'raping and pillaging' in the dictionary, which is why his genes became so dominant. He had four royal sons who did the same, helping to spread a rare family mutation carried in his DNA.

"My point is, would a discovery like that warrant Professor Sisti's abduction? If an unbroken string of males were born from some ancient Egyptian king with a rare mutation, there would be, at the very least, thousands of men or more carrying that Y-chromosome marker. For instance, if I carried it, then at least hundreds of my living male Malavolti relatives would too, and surely others. Do you think we could start a class action lawsuit to ask for the throne of Egypt back from several thousand years ago? I thought the Siena wealth from hundreds of years ago was ancient history. I just don't get it."

"What does it say here? Let's see how good your Latin is," she said, pointing to the tablet Hermes was holding.

Michael pulled up a translation on his phone just in case. "Take the letters and the laws of the Egyptians, right on the stove, which kept a sphinx/God, the creator of all things, with God himself created the visible and created the first and only person who was glad, and very loved his own son, who is called the Holy Word."

"What do you think that means? And why is 'Contemporary of Moses' written underneath his picture?" she asked.

"Ummm, good question. I'd speculate that since they sought out old sources of knowledge, even if not canonical or accepted by the church. Perhaps this character best represented that desire for knowledge from ancient sources. But the Moses quote? You got me. Since this is in a cathedral, they were probably trying to link this ancient wisdom with the church through two characters that came from Egypt's past."

Ishmael had already sent one message from within the church that was met with the same *Copy* response. Now he texted, *They've been at some picture on the floor talking for the last 20 minutes*, which he thought was a mundane update.

He immediately received, *Which picture?* from Seth.

"Is this guy serious?" he muttered. He responded, *Stand by for picture when they move.* He had a hard time believing it mattered to Seth which piece of art the marks were discussing, but then again, this mission had made little sense from the beginning.

Michael and Vivi worked their way down the center of the cathedral, stopping at each mosaic. The next mosaic on the floor featured the Capitoline Wolf at its center in a circle representing Siena. Orbiting it were twelve other smaller circles with various animals and city names. "It will be interesting to research why they picked each animal for their rival cities," Michael said. "It speaks to the history and the politics of the time. This might make a good cover photo for my thesis: Siena at the center of the Italian peninsula's universe."

As they continued their way down the center of the church, they eventually arrived under the dome. A hexagon of mosaics on the floor gave Michael a lot to photograph, but it was hard for him to keep his eyes on the floor. "I'm going to have to spend a few days in this church," he announced. "There's so much art and history. Look at that pulpit carved out of marble and granite—the detail is incredible!" He pointed at the pulpit created by Nicola Pisano in the 1260s. It was an octagonal structure with detailed ornate carvings covering its hulking body at every

Hermes Trismegistus, Thrice Great Hermes floor mosaic in the Siena Cathedral[10]

angle. Vivi had wandered a short distance away and was gazing up at the pulpit's carvings.

Meanwhile, Ishmael stood at the feet of Hermes Trismegistus and took a picture for Seth. He hit send as his annoyance with this mission grew by the minute.

A response was immediate and unexpected: *Where are they now?* He could almost feel Seth's excitement.

In the church still, taking pictures near the altar.

The response came back right away: *Kill them both. Do it now. Make it loud.*

Ishmael's adrenaline surged as he received the orders he had been waiting for. He double-checked his map and went over his exit plan in his head. He had enough firepower on him that shooting his way out of the church shouldn't be hard. Then it was a short distance to the outer wall of the city, where he could climb out and escape on foot to a waiting car.

Michael was taking pictures of the altar when he turned around to find Vivi still standing near the pulpit, trying to decipher the various Bible stories in its carvings. He felt a wave of appreciation that she was with him. As he took a step in her direction, his admiration was interrupted by a man he noticed out of the corner of his eye, but something was off. Maybe it was the angle of the guy's approach; he walked with an intense purpose not usually seen in tourists. When he cleared a column that brought him into Michael's sight line, the man made a slight turn and headed directly toward Vivi. Michael took a few more steps in her direction as the man unzipped his baggy windbreaker and reached inside it; the look in his eyes gave away his intention.

"Vivi!" Michael screamed as he bore down on her, eyes fixed on the man heading right at them. While still a few steps away, he could see the man pull out a large handgun. She began to turn toward Michael at the sound of his scream, so he made a quick decision: they could use one of the many large black-and-white marble columns for cover, but the column was a few meters away from Vivi. He would have to hit her as hard as he had ever hit anyone. He took one more step, lowered his shoulder, and drove it into her rib cage, launching them into the air. It felt like they were airborne for an eternity. As Ishmael raised his arm to fire, he suddenly collapsed to the ground, errantly spraying rounds from his automatic weapon in the process. The sound of gunfire echoed throughout the church.

When Michael and Vivi came crashing to the floor, he thought he could feel her ribs crack from the impact on the marble pavement before they came to a skidding stop behind the pillar. But before Michael could even assess whether he had been shot, Vivi was already up on one knee with her gun drawn. It was less than a second, but the next moment would be the only clear memory Michael would ever have from the chaotic scene—one in which time stood still. There were sounds of screaming tourists, but they didn't completely register in his brain.

The shooter was silent. In an instant of complete shock, Michael looked up at Vivi, unsure if he could feel his body. The moment he made eye contact with her, he snapped out of his shock and realized he was okay. Her reassuring gaze quickly refocused on the shooter. She led with her gun while peering from behind the pillar, screaming orders in English

Interior duomo *of the Siena Cathedral*[11]

and Italian. She got to her feet, and to his surprised horror, began walking toward the shooter, screaming, "Stay down! Don't move!"

Michael stood and peeked out to see a man lying face down in the center of the cathedral, blood running from the base of his neck onto the mosaic floor. Vivi screamed orders and trained her gun both on the downed man and up into the dome of the cathedral. An Uzi lay on the marble next to the shooter. Vivi was screaming orders still in multiple languages. "Stay where you are!" she yelled as she trained her gun up into the dome. She also yelled at Michael to stay where he was, but those commands fell on deaf ears as he stood near the gun in shock, looking up into the dome to see what Vivi was searching for.

The cathedral dome was a rich blue and covered in golden stars. At the top, the evening sun poured in and radiated off a ring of golden angels that framed the opening. The bright sunlight made it difficult to gaze directly up into the dome for too long. Michael tried, squinting his eyes. The adrenaline and shock mixed with the dizzying view was surreal. A *ping ping ping* could be heard as a single shell casing fell from the dome down onto the marble floor below. Vivi again yelled for Michael to get back. He looked down at the shell casing just a few meters away and then directly back up into the light.

The attacker's blood had created a larger pool now and ran onto the mosaic of Moses drawing water from the rock. As he looked back up into the starry light, then back to the floor, Michael suddenly had an idea what this was all about.

CHAPTER TWENTY-FIVE

*"Faith and reason are like two wings on which
the human spirit rises to the contemplation of
truth; and God has placed in the human heart a
desire to know the truth—in a word, to know
himself—so that, by knowing and loving God,
men and women may also come to the fullness
of truth about themselves."*

—Pope John Paul II

Siena, Italy

Michael Malavolti sat on the edge of a chair on the terrace
of his B&B, his body curled up into a ball with his knees in
his chest and his feet on the railing. He rocked back and
forth, trying to stay warm as the sun peeked over Il Campo
and Siena's historic skyline. His eyes were puffy and beet
red; a wastebasket with vomit in it sat next to his chair. The
previous evening had been a bureaucratic blur after the
shooting. He gave statement after statement and waited

around while Vivi did the same, as well as take phone call after phone call. In the end, Vivi told him they could stay in their small hotel, where an extra guard would be placed; they would travel back to Rome the next day, where he would be put in touch with the American embassy and give further statements to her boss.

"Michael?" Vivi sounded startled to find him on the terrace at sunrise as she returned from a run. His computer was on, showing what looked like dozens of open links. Papers were strewn about the table; sitting on top of the mess was the Bible he'd found in Rome. His trance-like state was broken by the sound of her voice.

"Vivi? You went for a run? I'm pretty sure I broke your ribs yesterday, and you're jogging the next morning?"

"Yeah, I think you did too!" she groused as she moved her right arm over her head gingerly, wincing as she palpated her chest with her left hand. "It's not the first time I've broken ribs, and besides, I don't run for my cardiovascular health, I run for my mental health, and today I needed to run. What *is* all this?" She motioned to the messy workstation he'd set up on the terrace. Before he could answer, she leaned in closer to get a good look at his face in the early morning light.

"Wait, Michael, you look terrible. Have you been throwing up? Have you even been to bed?"

"I'm fine. Well, to be honest, I *was* fine until I started throwing up a few hours ago, then I got cold. I'm okay, though, I just had too much espresso and carbonated water." He turned his attention to the door, where a concerned Giorgio stood, trying not to appear he was eavesdropping;

but clearly he was also shaken by the recent events. Michael gave him a smile and a thumbs-up, which Giorgio returned in a forced fashion before walking away.

"I've been up working on something all night. I didn't have an opportunity to talk to you in private, but I wanted to do some research first anyway. Vivi, I had an epiphany last night in the cathedral about what Professor Sisti may have discovered and why people are trying to kill us."

Vivi turned and walked back into the hotel from the outdoor terrace. Michael sighed, fearing he must sound as crazed as he probably looked at the moment. She returned moments later, however, with a blanket she put around him and a bottle of flat water. Then she got herself an espresso and pulled a chair in close. "Michael, that shell casing from the church came from a sniper's rifle. It had an Egyptian symbol stamped on the bottom of it. Obviously, someone thinks you are connected to whatever the professor is involved in."

"Let me guess: the Eye of Horus?" he asked.

Vivi's eyes bulged in shock as she turned her phone around to show Michael an image of the eye stamped on the bottom of the shell casing. "Okay, you have my attention."

CHAPTER TWENTY-SIX

Castel Gandolfo, Italy

Alfonso Carpacci didn't know how much time he had left. He had dealt with his fair share of scandals and stress as a bishop, a cardinal, and finally as pope. His eighty-four-year-old body now reminded him of that accumulated stress daily and that his earthly days were finite. He had made a fire to warm his old bones on this early summer morning and was doing what he filled his every free moment now doing, praying for forgiveness and guidance, when the head of his security detail interrupted by knocking on his open door.

"Forgive me, Your Holiness, but there is a Vatican official here who is demanding to see you. He says it is urgent. A Father Patrick Davies."

Alfonso did not speak or rise from his knees. He merely gave his guard a warm smile and nodded his head in the affirmative to let him know it was okay. Within moments, his security detail had returned with Father Davies.

"It's okay. Close the door, please, and leave us," Alfonso said to his security. Once alone, Patrick walked over to Alfonso and knelt beside him on his kneeler near the fire. The room was silent, save for the crackling of the burning wood, until Alfonso said, "Are you here to kill me?"

"Please, Alfonso! I am many things I am not proud of, but a killer is not one of them. I don't suppose you know anything about what happened in the Siena Cathedral last night?"

"I heard there was a shooting," answered Alfonso as his fingers moved down a bead on the rosary he clutched.

"I want you to know I had nothing to do with it," said Patrick, who watched the face of Alfonso for a reaction. None came as Alfonso stared into the fire, shuffling his prayer beads. "I think they have some really big things planned. They're fearful that they're losing control. Forcing your resignation was a part of something bigger—much bigger, I'm afraid. You weren't the first pope to challenge the U.N. or their Ordo handlers. I'm afraid they want to guarantee Church support at this time because a series of events has been planned to achieve their goal of one world government in the near future. In order to generate the kind of transparent control they seek, they must have some very bloody plans in the works."

Patrick looked for some emotion from Alfonso. Concern, anger, regret...something. Instead the former pope just stared into the fire, occasionally shuffling one more bead through his fingers. After what felt like an eternity, Alfonso finally looked at the priest and asked, "Why are you here? What do you seek from me?"

"Absolution," answered Patrick.

CHAPTER TWENTY-SEVEN

Siena, Italy

Michael paced as he spoke in a near-manic state: "The University of Chicago has a center for interdisciplinary study on the ancient civilizations of the Near East called the Oriental Institute. It was founded by a man who was actually born in my hometown in the 1800s, James Henry Breasted."

"I'm familiar with him." Vivi didn't know whether to interrupt and try to calm Michael down or let him go on. Her worry over his physical and mental state was outweighed by her desire to learn what he thought he had discovered.

"Breasted was actually a Hebrew major and got a Masters in Hebrew after studying at Yale before he went on to study Egypt and its hieroglyphics at a Berlin university. He was the first American to receive a PhD in Egyptology. He became fascinated by the age of the culture and was one of the first people to point out that much of the wisdom found in the Bible, originally written in Hebrew and Greek in those early days of written language, had actually come from earlier hieroglyphs found in Egypt. I've studied

Breasted's life and know he had a great influence on Sigmund Freud, which is why I was familiar with a theory that hit me like a ton of bricks last night in the cathedral."

"Freud? What does this have to do with psychology, Michael?"

"Psychology? Nothing. Well…nothing or everything. If I'm right, it has to do with the greatest story and cover-up ever told. I think I know what the 'great sin of Charlemagne' was, Vivi!"

"I'm all ears," she replied, dryly, the way a sane person might while trying to pacify the delusional.

"I've been stuck on this mystery of the Malavolti origins here in Siena, but something about it never made sense. Of the five most notable noble families written about in the Republic of Siena's history, sources show four of them arrived after Charlemagne passed through just before 800 AD. Not to mention some back story about where they came from. For the Malavoltis, there's a legend the family was founded by a knight Charlemagne made a count of this territory."

"Yes, you told me yesterday that theory was unlikely, based on your genetics from Egypt," Vivi interrupted Michael, reminding him of his opinion when he was less sleep deprived.

"I know! That's because I was trying to use logic and Church-approved history from the Dark Ages. In Italy, today, my haplogroup's highest concentration is logically in the south as you get closer to Egypt—and even there, it's only carried by less than 2% of men. In Tuscany, it's more like one-half of 1%, and it becomes rarer the farther away from Egypt one looks.

"So as I said yesterday, not only would some man have had to make his way that far north—which is entirely possible, of course—but he would have had to ingratiate himself somehow with Charlemagne to be made nobility and put in charge of this most important strategic area. Remember that Charlemagne has just entered into a revolutionary and tenuous relationship with the Catholic Church as he formed the first unified Europe since the collapse of the Roman Empire. With Catholicism as the official religion, he'd provide stability for his kingdom and have divine backing for the right to rule.

"Think of the Guelphs and Ghibellines, Vivi, the political struggle that would persist for centuries between factions whose allegiances were with either the Pope's troops of Rome or the Holy Roman Emperor's armies. Why was Siena a stronghold of nobles who supported the Holy Roman Emperor and thus the separation between church and state? Because Charlemagne, the first Holy Roman Emperor, made sure to plant nobles there he could trust. And which noble family in Siena's history is the only one purported to have come with Charlemagne? The Malavolti!

"But something has been gnawing at me since I first stumbled upon the story. Using the more likely DNA dispersion and basic logic, the Malavolti should have been here before Charlemagne arrived, so how could they convince him to allow them continual rule in this area? History is brutal; mankind is brutal, and it was always illogical to me that it was just a case of 'dibs.' Charlemagne would have needed to have a most trusted noble family here—his own family, you'd think."

"Okay, still not getting it," Vivi said.

"It's highly unlikely any of the other old royal lines in Europe at that time would have had my Y-DNA. Yet sources imply Charlemagne's family *did* intertwine with the feudal nobility in the area of Siena at that time, and the Malavolti family seems to be an extension of the feudal nobility already around in those early days of Siena's recorded history.

"There are tax documents from this period between the pope and Charlemagne that divide up territories for taxes—some taxes going to the Church, others going to the king. However, Siena is conspicuously missing from various tax agreements. This omission has led historians to speculate that Siena was left to be somewhat autonomous even in those early days of the first Holy Roman Empire, before they begin to mint their own currency and gained official statehood in the 1100s. You'd think that kind of power and prestige bestowed upon a territory would be reserved for an area ruled by close relatives of the Holy Roman Emperor. I could see Charlemagne giving his child or a close relative castles and lands in Siena to rule, but why someone with my Y-DNA?"

"I don't know, Michael. Why don't you tell me what you're thinking?" she asked, now a bit frustrated.

"I was always stuck on this conundrum of my family's origins, which is one of the reasons I was so excited to get to work with Federico Sisti. I couldn't think of a logical solution because my historical sources made no mention of the Jewish kingdom of Septimania that Charlemagne and his father Pepin III founded in southwest France."

"The *what*?" Vivi replied, still uneasy about Michael's mental state.

"In 1972, a professor named Arthur Zuckerman published a book through Columbia University titled: *Jewish Princedom in Feudal France, 768–900*. Any history from the European Dark Ages involves a great deal of supposition, of course, since little documentation survived. Through an extraordinary scholarly effort, Professor Zuckerman dug up and translated Islamic sources from their original Arabic. He also found and translated medieval sources in German, Latin, and Hebrew to corroborate a fascinating story that had been lost to history. His book, although well researched and logical, has been widely ignored or disputed by other historians. The story he tells might be the missing link I was looking for to help understand where the Malavolti came from."

"How so? Are you saying that the Malavolti origins were Jewish?"

"More than that. Zuckerman explains that Charlemagne's father, Pepin III, was leading a charge to drive the Moors out of southern France and parts of Spain. For reasons that have been lost to history, there was a large Jewish community on and near the coast in the southwest region of France named Septimania at that time, particularly in the coastal city of Narbonne. Narbonne was an important port city, and it was surrounded by a fortified wall that Pepin couldn't breach. So the king of the Franks asked the Jews of Narbonne to open the gates and help him expel the Moors from Narbonne. They refused because of the risk; if the king wasn't successful on his quest to rid Europe of the Moors, the retribution would be severe. He offered to pay them a great deal of money, and they still refused to open the gates of Narbonne. So Pepin made them an offer they couldn't refuse: 'Open your gates, fight with me to drive the Moors out, and I'll give you Narbonne to rule by yourselves—your own Jewish principality.' But Pepin put one stipulation in writing: the Jews of Narbonne would have to find a king to rule them who was a legitimate descendant of King David, the royal line of ancient Israel and Judah.

"They took the deal. A Jewish ambassador was sent to Babylonia, modern-day Baghdad and the center of Jewish scholarship at that time, to tell them of the need of a king in the line of David to rule their own Jewish kingdom in Europe. A man named Natronai ben Zabinai, a Jewish royal with a Persian name, came back to take the job. Natronai was a legend in his own time; he supposedly spoke eight languages and was an impressive warrior as well as scholar. He was named exilarch, a title that meant 'King of the Jews in Exile," in his twenties—apparently an incredibly young age for an exilarch. Most importantly to Charlemagne, though, was that this exilarch was a reputed descendant of King David."

Vivi's espresso momentarily forgotten, she demanded, "Are you saying what I think you're saying?"

"Maybe. Natronai, now living in Europe and leading his own Jewish principality of Narbonne, ruled under the Hebrew name Makhir. He's known as Makhir of Narbonne, and it quickly became apparent why Pepin made the deal in the first place. The Carolingian kings (of whom Charlemagne was the greatest) wanted to legitimize their right to rule by linking their family with the oldest and most important royal line on Earth: the line of King David, also Jesus's lineage. Charlemagne married his Aunt Alda to

Makhir, although sources offer no explanation as to how this happened, as it would have been incredibly taboo at the time since Alda was Catholic and Makhir was Jewish; presumably, neither was willing to convert.

"Makhir and Charlemagne became fast friends and allies as they fought together, achieving several victories. The Jews fought valiantly for Makhir, whose banner and nickname was the Lion of Judah. Some Jews proclaimed he was the messiah promised them in a prophecy to appear 700 years after the fall of the temple in Jerusalem. Charlemagne even expanded the territory promised to the Jewish community beyond the port city of Narbonne. The principality now surrounded Narbonne and included at least two other substantial cities in its vicinity in France, giving them a sizable and important principality that existed for five kings and nearly 140 years, from AD 768–900, according to the research provided by Arthur Zuckerman."

"So you think *this* was the 'great sin of Charlemagne'? And that the Malavoltis are tied into this story?" she asked, while calmly sipping her espresso and watching Michael pace.

"Think about it, Vivi! Siena was the first territory north of Rome and the Papal States. As I said, it was in a very strategic and important position for a French king entering into an alliance with the Church. In exchange for his protection, the Church recognized the king of the Carolingian line as the rightful ruler of all of Christendom. Charlemagne knelt at the altar in Rome and was crowned Holy Roman Emperor on Christmas Day in the year 800 by Pope Leo I. Who was he going to put in charge of Siena, the territory immediately to the north of the Papal States? I would have said only family, which is why I didn't understand how that man could have had a Y-chromosome from the Ev12 haplogroup! But that was before I knew about the king's quest to link his family to the line of David to legitimize their right to rule, which they had usurped from the previous Merovingian kings!"

"So you *do* think your family was originally Jewish, then?" asked a confused Vivi, trying to put the pieces together.

"Yes! I think they were royal Jews who were turned into European nobility by Charlemagne when he married various family members into this important paternal line. The 'great sin of Charlemagne' was that he seeded strategic points in Europe with nobility that was part Jewish. He was forming the first Holy Roman Empire with nobles whose beliefs contradicted the very beliefs of the now-official state religion. Back then, that would be viewed as sacrilegious. Catholicism was the law of the land, and if the Carolingians wanted to rule, they would have needed to go with the flow. Something that taboo would have needed to remain a secret, and that secret was probably lost to time relatively quickly. It would certainly explain a lot about my family's mysterious origins and why they were given such an important area to help rule. It would also explain why Charlemagne had his family intermarry with them and how my Y-DNA could have come with a knight held in high regard traveling alongside Charlemagne."

"So you think the Malavoltis would have identified as Jewish around the time of Charlemagne and hidden that fact?" asked a suspicious-sounding Vivi.

"It's possible, yeah, but I also think it likely they would have converted to Christianity in short order if they were ruling Siena during that historical time. Think about the differences in beliefs when a new Europe was forming, united behind a king and religion that said Jesus was the Son of God, born divine. The royal Jews, in turn, believed that Jesus was an important prophet, but he was *not* born by divine Immaculate Conception, rather their distant cousin Joseph of the House of David was his father. He was their ancestor and relative through his father."

"But wait—even if that were true, and your family was founded here in Siena by a knight Charlemagne thought was of the line of the biblical King David, why would that cause someone to want you or Professor Sisti dead? And how did you learn about this Makhir of Narbonne last night in the cathedral?" Vivi was attempting to connect the dots Michael had presented.

"I didn't learn of Arthur Zuckerman's book last night. In fact, I found his book by typing some different word combos into search engines just an hour or so ago, and it was the last major puzzle piece I needed. If I'm right, this story goes back further in time—2,000 years before Charlemagne—and it's *much* more scandalous than a Jewish principality in Europe. No, in the cathedral last night, it was something Freud wrote that hit me."

CHAPTER TWENTY-EIGHT

Castel Gandolfo, Italy

Father Patrick Davies normally appeared cool and collected, but gone was his air of supreme confidence as he stood directing questions at Alfonso, trying to grasp the game he was caught up in. "Have you seen the scrolls and artifacts from Qumran that Ordo holds over the Church with your own eyes? Surely they must have had more leverage than that? You've always struck me as a fighter. The Church will survive doctrine-challenging relics from the past!" Patrick said to Alfonso, who stared into the fire, praying. After reaching the last bead of his rosary, Alfonso rose from his knees and sat down.

"Have a seat, Patrick." Alfonso motioned to a chair as he continued to gaze into the fire. "I've seen pictures and various translations; Ordo also has a thick file on me and enough dirt from my past to bring a great deal of negative attention to the papacy and the Church. And, of course, it wouldn't stop with me. Yes, they possess Qumran scrolls and artifacts that would cause an uproar if made public, but that's the least of their power; they probably have a warehouse full of dirt on the Church going back centuries.

"Ordo has files on everyone important, and they control enough politicians to seemingly have the world in its pocket. Their hands can be found in everything, from intelligence agencies to the media and banks. They have technologies you couldn't dream of and stand unopposed to whatever ends they desire." Alfonso paused before shifting the conversation to Patrick, who was still pacing. "How about you, Patrick? How many pieces of silver did *you* sell your soul for?"

Patrick looked as if he were about to object to the question, before he paused and took a seat for a moment to reflect. Then he said slowly, "I sold my soul long, long ago to escape hell. I grew up in a shack in Appalachia with a father who had a temper and a drinking problem. We would occasionally go to a Sunday service that was held in an old RV the preacher lived in with his pet snakes. When I was a teenager, I met the nearest parish priest at a clothing drive where the Catholic Church was providing warm clothing to poor mountain people like me. He drove a nice new Buick that priest. He spoke fluent Spanish and English as he administered clothing to those who showed up. I got to talking to him that day and learned he had lived on three continents before he found himself in Booneville, Kentucky, helping out at that parish. I knew that day that the Catholic Church could offer me salvation—not in the afterlife, but from my current hell on Earth. He seemed so regal, so cosmopolitan. I thought if I could become a Catholic Priest I'd be treated like a prince; I thought I *would* be a prince. I found salvation that day, or so I thought.

"Once in, I was a quick study and fast riser. I ran from my past and recreated myself over and over again, as necessary. My ability to be a chameleon allowed me to rise all the way to the Vatican. I guess Ordo has a knack for finding the morally flexible; I never thought that by helping them I was doing anything that wouldn't happen anyway. As you know, their power is impressive. 'Ain't no hill for a climber,' we used to say where I grew up, and I was a climber. I'm not sure why I came here today, to tell you the truth, but I know something is going on—and I can't shake this feeling of existential dread. Faith is a funny thing, isn't it, Alfonso? Able to make certain in man's mind the most implausible of scenarios. Perhaps I'm sensing my own lack of faith for the first time, and I'm afraid."

Patrick sighed. "Ordo was behind that shooting in Siena, but I assume you know that. The potential shooter who was killed was a follower of a fanatical Jewish rabbi. I know because I arranged the meeting. Do you know about Rabbi Bein or his doomsday prophecy? That he has a militant occult following?" Alfonso shook his head.

"This Rabbi Bein has been preparing his followers for an apocalyptic event," Patrick continued. "He preached that his followers would play a role in preventing the triumph of evil in the coming war. He was an easy mark; all I had to do was feed his fantasies: 'An evildoer from the house of Judah will rise from darkness to reveal great secrets of the Ark of the Covenant and carry with him the vengeance of God.'" Patrick chuckled as he reiterated Rabbi Bein's teaching. Alfonso, who had taken his eyes off the fire for the first time, was looking directly at him, nodding in agreement.

"So you *have* heard of Rabbi Bein?"

"I don't believe I have."

"But you have heard of his end-times prophecy?"

Alfonso stared at Patrick for a moment, as if resisting his urge to share more. Patrick looked back with the same uncertainty before Alfonso said, "No. I have foreseen it too."

CHAPTER TWENTY-NINE

Siena, Italy

"I need to take you back to the beginning of our family tree." Michael rifled through some papers he had spread around the table.

"*Our* family?" asked Vivi with her eyebrows raised, still teetering on whether or not Michael was making some kind of breakthrough or experiencing a stress-induced anxiety attack.

"Yes, *our* family. *Homo sapiens*! Every man alive today has a common male ancestor who lived in Africa around 200,000 years ago. It's not that he was the only man alive then, but he was the only man alive to have any male offspring still living. His genes won out when Africa was sparsely populated with humans. This first guy is often referred to as 'Y-chromosome Adam.' As in Adam and Eve, because in a way, he's like the biblical Adam. Every man alive descends from him and, therefore, has traces of his Y-chromosome.

"Like I told you, the Y-chromosome is very stable and rarely has any major mutations, so we can use it to track our human history. When a major mutation does occur, it creates what's called a new haplogroup. So every haplogroup today flowed from this original Y chromosome, haplogroup A, which was carried by Y-DNA Adam. This is called a haplogroup tree." Michael handed Vivi one of the papers he was shuffling about the table.

A B C D E F G H I J K L M N O P Q R R1a R1ab

"For most of mankind's history, we lived as hunter-gatherers. The earliest tribes of people would have been nomads, largely made up of familial groups that only moved in order to provide food and safety for their tribes. Of course, things happen over long periods of time, creating the need for some groups to move farther, such as food shortages, climate change, wars, etc.

"Look at this map with the various Y-DNA haplogroups and their dominant distributions. We can see when and where different tribes of people moved out of Africa and populated all the lands on Earth. Using the Y-chromosome, because of its stable signature, we can piece together our distant past and see the flow of our ancestors out of Africa, which didn't start to happen until roughly 60,000 years ago.

Vivi looked at the global map, completely lost.

World Map of Y-DNA Haplogroups
Dominart Haplogroups in Native Populations
with Possible Migration Routes

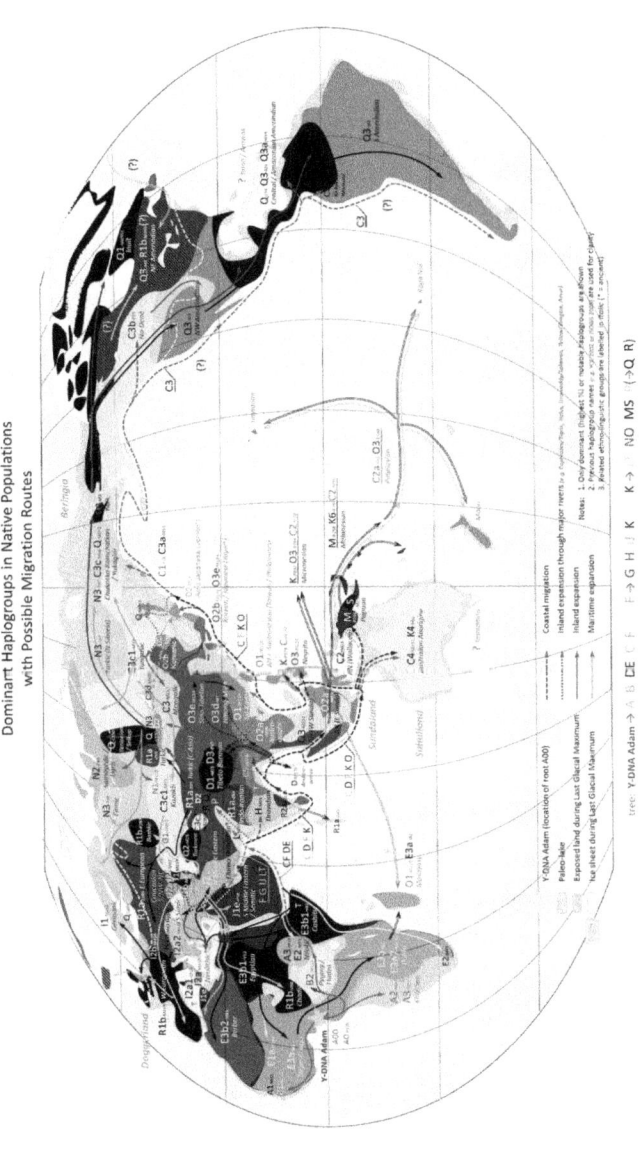

World map of Y-DNA haplogroups[12]

He went on inexorably: "Sometime around 10,000 years ago, give or take a few thousand, some tribes began to form communities along the Nile Valley and in Mesopotamia along the Tigris and Euphrates rivers. This was made possible by advances in farming. The fertile land around these rivers' flood plains caused ancient man to put down roots and grow food. The food supply controlled human behavior for hundreds of thousands of years, but with the advent of farming, people began to live together in larger tribes and formed more sophisticated societies. With an abundance of food, there could be a division of labor and specialization: warriors, architects, bakers, priests, etc. Which is why, in terms of the Western world anyway, this area of the Middle East and northeast Africa is often referred to as the cradle of civilization.

"When I got back here last night, I started my research by rereading something written by James Henry Breasted in his book *The Dawn of Conscience*[13] about the giant leap forward that humankind took in forming societies and then cities. Of course, farming was the key that drove these early societies, but what followed fascinated him the most. In his estimation, when humans began to gather in larger tribes and formed fixed farming societies, they created something we take for granted today: a societal morality with laws that govern us and allow us all to achieve more through cooperation. In Egypt the fertile flood plain of the Nile allowed farming as well as protection from other tribes due to the geography of the deserts and bodies of water surrounding them. It's no wonder this was where mankind first evolved into one of the most advanced ancient civilizations."

Michael pulled up different pages on his laptop before finding the one he was looking for. "Now here is the kind of thing that was a real eye opener for Breasted, who was a biblical Hebrew scholar before he was an Egyptologist. *The Egyptian Book of the Dead*[14] is a funerary text that deals with their beliefs about death and the afterlife. Before 2000 BCE, the Egyptians already thought that if you lived your life accordingly, anyone could live in a paradise in the afterlife. And not just royals—a concept of heaven was attainable for anyone. This book contains something called the 'weighing of the heart' seen as a post-death judgment. Here is how the hieroglyphs read when a man pleads his case in the afterlife:

'I have not reviled the God.
I have not laid violent hands on an orphan.
I have not done what the God abominates...
I have not killed; I have not turned anyone over
    to a killer.
I have not caused anyone's suffering...
I have not copulated (illicitly); I have not been
    unchaste.
I have not increased nor diminished the measure, I
    have not diminished the palm; I have not
    encroached upon the fields.
I have not added to the balance weights; I have not
    tempered with the plumb bob of the balance.
I have not taken milk from a child's mouth; I have not
    driven small cattle from their herbage...
I have not stopped (the flow of) water in its seasons; I
    have not built a dam against flowing water.

I have not quenched a fire in its time...
I have not kept cattle away from the God's property.
I have not blocked the God at his processions.'"

"Interesting," Vivi mused.

"Yes! Doesn't that sound a lot like commandments for living a good life that the newly deceased is pleading he hasn't broken? That comes from a 1700 BCE funerary text, which is long before the Old Testament was written in Hebrew and Greek. The first hieroglyphic writings from Egypt date to around 3500 BCE, and cuneiform writing was established in nearby Mesopotamia shortly after that.

"It isn't until the concept of an alphabet, though, that written language really took off. That was first invented or used by the Phoenicians around modern-day Lebanon, only around 3,000 years ago. Hebrew, Greek, Latin...all the early languages stem from this concept of an alphabet that wasn't even invented until around 1000 BCE."

"Michael, I like history too. I think it's important, but can you tell me what you think this is all about, please?"

"Yes, I'm getting there; please bear with me. Let me walk you through my train of thought last night. As I was saying about Egypt: The first king of a unified Egypt is thought to have ruled around 3100 BCE, creating the First Dynasty of Egypt. Keep in mind that hieroglyph writing was invented just a short time earlier, so anything further back in history is even more speculative. What we know from recorded history is that a king, Narmer, unified Upper and Lower Egypt to rule over the whole country a little before 3000 BCE. By then, though, the god Set was already a well-established god; a drawing of what is believed to be a representation of Set was found in a tomb from around 3700 BCE, so other gods were mostly likely worshipped as well.

"Okay, so how did you know the bullet casing had the Eye of Horus on it?" Vivi was trying to follow him, but hoped he would just skip to his epiphany.

"I'm getting to that, I promise. There's much more to this story of Egypt." Michael tried to organize his thoughts, shuffling through papers on the table and clicking through open links on his computer. "After Narmer unified Upper and Lower Egypt around 3000 BCE, the Pharaoh Khufu was thought to have built the Great Pyramid around 2594 BCE. The pyramid's burial chambers were looted by robbers in short order, but I'll get to a point about his tomb again in a second.

"Moving right along through the centuries to around 1800 BCE, Egypt was in a dark period, not quite as strong as it had been during the previous millennium. That created a power vacuum, in addition to an influx of Canaanite peoples who move down around the Nile. Remember that genetic map I showed you?" Michael flipped the map down in front of Vivi that showed the dominant haplogroup dispersions. "The Canaanites were from the land of Canaan right next door to Egypt; along with the rest of the Semitic tribes from the western side of the Asian continent, the Canaanites would have had men who carried Y-DNA predominately from the J1 haplogroup. So with weak leaders and foreigners moving in to poach prime farming areas around the Nile, the country became destabilized.

"Around 1650 BCE, a group of foreign invaders— thought to also have been made up of Semitic tribes from the Near East called the Hyksos—conquered northern

Egypt. They introduced the chariot to the Egyptians when they used it to conquer them. This is mankind's story over and over again—whenever a tribe or group of people made an advancement in technology, they used it to conquer their neighbors. The Hyksos conquered and ruled over parts of Egypt inhabited by native Egyptians, the Canaanites, and their own people who moved to the Nile. Set was a popular god in Egypt during the Hyksos period, worshiped by the invaders and Egyptians alike. The Hyksos, as the new rulers of Egypt, saw Set as a representation of their old god Baal, their god of storms and chaos. The worship of Set by these foreign invaders is thought, by some, to have contributed to his eventual resentment among Egyptians; Set was gradually viewed as an outsider's deity, leading to him being vilified years later.

"The Hyksos period lasted roughly 100 years and was brought to an end around 1550 BCE when a leader named Ahmose I led the Egyptian armies to fight back the Hyksos invaders and once again united all of Upper and Lower Egypt under the rule of a native Egyptian. This began the Eighteenth Dynasty. Ahmose's son, the second king of the Eighteenth Dynasty, was Amenhotep I; his son, the next ruler, was Thutmose I. He was the first king to be buried in the Valley of the Kings. Tomb raiding had already been a problem for 1,000 years, so Thutmose built his tomb underground in an out-of-the-way valley, so he could be at peace for eternity. Did you know that Thut is a form of Thoth, and Mose means 'from' or 'child of'?"

"No, I didn't know that, but why is that important?" She was clearly getting agitated and worried.

"Because Mose or Mosis or Moses is an Egyptian word for 'from' or 'child of,' and it was a common suffix for a king's name. The king was believed to be the living embodiment of a god on Earth: both god and man. Sound familiar? So Thutmose would be translated as 'child of Thoth.' Nine pharaohs are listed in the Eighteenth Dynasty before one earns the nickname "the magnificent king." After 200 years of the Eighteenth Dynasty, Egypt was back to being the regional powerhouse. Amenhotep III used his military to expand Egypt's territory and trade routes in every direction."

Michael showed her a chart listing the kings of the Eighteenth Dynasty:

Eighteenth Dynasty of Egypt

Ahmose I

Amenhotep I

Thutmose I

Thutmose II

Hatshepsut

Thutmose III

Amenhotep II

Thutmose IV

Amenhotep III—"the magnificent king"

"Now, here is where things get *really* interesting, and if my theory is right, the course of the world for the next several thousand years was drastically altered by what comes next."

CHAPTER THIRTY

Rome, Italy

General Garret's secure line was ringing; he knew an unhappy member of the capstone was on the other end.

"Garret speaking."

"Someone has been watching us, General! They were waiting and ready when I gave the order to take out those two yesterday. I don't like being played for a fool." The Relic Hunter spoke softly yet in an authoritative tone.

"Yes sir. I've been getting updates all morning from Siena. I'm in Rome trying to sort this out, exhausting all resources to find out who was behind it."

"Then I suppose you know that the sniper who took out your man left a shell casing with the Eye of Horus engraved in it. They are taunting us, General!"

"I know, sir. How do you want me to proceed with the student? There is certainly a spotlight on him now, but we have several capable assets in the area."

"No, things have changed. The student, Michael Malavolti, is no longer your concern. Finding whoever helped him is your sole mission now."

The Relic Hunter hung up the phone and tapped his fingers on his desk rhythmically for a few tense moments while contemplating his next move. Then he rose from his desk and walked down a long curved hallway before reaching a vault door. He placed his right palm and left eye on scanners, and a mechanical groan followed as the vault door slowly rumbled open. He moved through a series of museum-style display cases before stopping in front of one that contained a number of copper scrolls. Standing over them, he tapped his fingers on the glass case, while staring down at them for several moments before moving on to the next case, which contained a number of yellowing sheets of paper. The Relic Hunter opened the case and removed the one he was looking for. His mood shifted from contemplative to giddy as he read the sheet aloud to himself: "There will come a time when the progeny of the patriarch will reveal himself. This man will make manifest the lineage of the patriarch and founder of the Aeon of Osiris. Follow the rituals laid down before you, and spill his blood in the Kings Chamber. So begins the Aeon of Horus."

He carefully placed the sheet of paper back in the display case that contained various other unpublished prophecies from Aleister Crowley's diary and rushed back to his desk. His office was perched over 300 feet in the air in a giant golden orb in Astana, the capital of Kazakhstan. Looking out from his desk, his gaze passed through two golden glass towers, representing the Masonic pillars of Boaz and Jachin. His eyes then moved onto the Presidential Palace—which was positioned where the Grand Master's seat would belong in Masonic rituals—to the pyramid beyond it. The top of the Pyramid of Peace and Reconciliation was the primary focus of his gaze and where he would soon call an emergency meeting of the capstone.

But first he would need to consult with the goddess Nuit. The Relic Hunter picked up the phone and placed a call: "This is client #33. I need someone special for tonight. She may not be able to work for several days. I'll cover any extra expenses." He hung up the phone and continued rhythmically tapping his fingers on his desk, lost in thought. *Tonight will be a long ritual; I need some sexual magick to guide me.*

Siena, Italy

"Why are you telling me about ancient history from 3,500 years ago? I'm still not following how it relates to you and your research," Vivi complained.

"I'm *getting* to that; it's a complex scenario. Patience, my friend! So Amenhotep III, the magnificent king, put Egypt in a really dominant position in the ancient world as a military and economic powerhouse. Taking a closer look at his family, we know his wife's name was Tiye, and that he loved her very much. We know this because she is seen in statuary reliefs created to honor her all over the country. He built several temples for her in Egypt and even in foreign lands that they controlled. An interesting thing about Tiye is where she came from. Pharaohs often married close family, sometimes a half or even a full sister to maintain the royal bloodline. But Tiye's father was a man named Yuya, and he was not a royal; he was a wealthy noble from the city of

Akhmin. He was probably a priest, government official, and overall rich important guy, but not a royal. He was, however, married to a member of the Egyptian royal family named Thuya. The most interesting thing about Yuya is that many Egyptologists speculate he was a foreigner.

"Remember, this is only a few hundred years after the Hyksos period and a large influx of Semitic people into Egypt. It's been speculated that Yuya's family may have originally been from Canaan, so he was a Semite. In ancient Egypt, the royal line was carried by the females just as much as the males, so it's noteworthy that Tiye may have been the daughter of a foreigner. It's been speculated that some of the priests who wielded great power in ancient Egypt may have resented her and considered her unworthy of the Egyptian throne, even if her mother was an Egyptian royal.

"Amenhotep III and Tiye's first born son, Thutmose, died young, and the circumstances around the death are unclear. One theory is there was friction between the high priests of the god Amun and the royal family about Yuya's lineage. It's hard to say, but this tension may have caused the royal couple to raise their second son, Amenhotep IV, in isolation from the high priests." He pointed at the next page of the chart, which began:

Amenhotep III—"the magnificent king"

Amenhotep IV

"There were numerous temples and priest cults in Egypt at this time," Michael continued, "and many of them were dedicated to gods that had been around for thousands of years. The highest god of the day and the most powerful and wealthiest set of priests would have been found at the temple of Amun-Ra. Amun was a relatively new god compared to some of Egypt's older gods like Set, but once he became connected to the sun god, Ra, he grew in popularity and power until becoming the official state god during the Eighteenth Dynasty. Amenhotep means 'Amun is satisfied.'"

"If my epiphany in the cathedral last night is right, it would rewrite history. There is a great deal of debate and speculation surrounding the series of events that took place under Amenhotep IV. Here's what we know from records that have survived from ancient Egypt: He was married to the famously beautiful Nefertiti, and the records show they had six daughters. Nefertiti was his chief or first wife, but it was common for pharaohs to have other minor wives.

"When Amenhotep IV ascended to the throne after his father, the very popular and powerful 'magnificent king,' he began to implement religious reforms. At first, he allowed all the gods of Egypt to be worshipped, but proclaimed that he would worship only one supreme god he called Aten. By the fifth year of his reign, Amenhotep IV had even changed his name to Akhenaten, meaning 'the glory of Aten.' Akhenaten built a new capital city to honor his god and moved thousands of people there. This new city was located at Amarna (now an archeological site) on the Nile, a short trip north from Thebes, Egypt's capital at the time. Eventually, he forbade the worship of any other god but Aten, sending troops into the other temples, like those of Amun-Ra, to shut them down, even to the point of trying to remove their names from the walls. This was not a popular move and stirred great discontent throughout Egypt. His religious reformation was so total that he tried to have any reference to 'gods' removed from temples, because in his mind there was only one true god, Aten.

"Sounds ahead of his time," muttered Vivi.

"I know! To say that Akhenaten was a revolutionary would be an understatement. Not only did he attempt to drastically alter the ancient polytheistic practices of Egypt, but he took on the highest and richest class of Egyptians outside of the royal family, the high priests, who were corrupt. These events happened on the heels of a prosperous time for the Egyptians. He was clearly a thinker, and his thoughts were radical. Akhenaten even changed the way art was created in Egypt. His family is the only royal family in Egypt's long history to be shown in natural scenes, sometimes in mid-action or showing affection for one another. The bodies were also uniquely stylized, having long heads and thin, spindly limbs. He himself is often depicted with feminine hips and breasts. Remember, the pharaoh was the living embodiment of a god, both human and a god himself. In this case, he believed he was the son of Aten, who was the god of all things. Aten was referred to as the father *and* mother of all in temple reliefs.

"He had the rays of the sun depicted as hands or arms extending down from a sun disc, the symbol of Aten, which was how people could see this new god and know that his power gave life to all things. There's been much confusion and debate about Akhenaten's god, but it was clearly revolutionary, *not* just an emphasis on sun worship. Ra, the original sun god, had been around already for a long time. In fact, Akhenaten even forbade others to depict the Aten; depiction was under his sole control.

"He seemingly had everything, but for him, it was not enough. He had this firm belief in a singular supreme being and upended centuries-old traditions and practices in order to honor that god. Did you know that the Old Testament story of the Exodus is estimated to have occurred around that time?"

"What?" Vivi asked, looking up. "I thought the Moses story happened under Ramses?" She was trying to follow along, but was beginning to be more convinced Michael was sleep deprived and delusional at the moment.

"That's what most people think, because that's what Hollywood went for in the most famous *Ten Commandments* movie. The truth is, the Bible doesn't say exactly when it happened or name the pharaoh. There *is* one reference to the Israelites building the supply cities of Pithon and Rameses in Exodus, which is why Ramses is often thought of as the pharaoh of the biblical Moses story. Ramses II is maybe the best known and documented pharaoh of the distant past, because like Akhenaten's father, he expanded Egypt's power and influence and built a great number of monuments. We know a great deal about the Nineteenth Dynasty of Egypt and Ramses I and II, but have no record or mention of any Hebrew exile.

"But in a different part of the Bible, 1Kings 6:6 says the temple of Solomon was built 480 years after the Exodus. The temple is thought to have been built a little after 1000 BCE, which would put the Exodus around 1480 BCE—a hundred or so years before Akhenaten, during the Eighteenth Dynasty, but again, there is no record of anything like that. Some Orthodox rabbis today date the Exodus to 1312 BCE, which would place it shortly after the known reign of Akhenaten and during the reigns of Ay and Horem-heb, two rulers who followed Akhenaten at the end of the Eighteenth Dynasty, but there's no historical proof. If any-one left for religious reasons, it would have been the fol-lowers of Atenism, who sound much like the Israelites of the Old Testament who also worshipped one God. Canaan, the modern day Holy Land, was under Egypt's control, so a group of slaves couldn't escape Egypt and then set up a country in an Egyptian territory."

Vivi frowned. "What are you saying, Michael? That this religious revolution of Akhenaten directly relates to the Bible and may even upend accepted beliefs? And because of what you suspect and might be able to prove genetically, someone is trying to kill you?"

"Maybe. And I know it sounds farfetched, but I'm be-coming more and more convinced." Michael shuffled through some timelines he had quickly constructed the night before, and handed her a piece of paper with hand-writing on it.

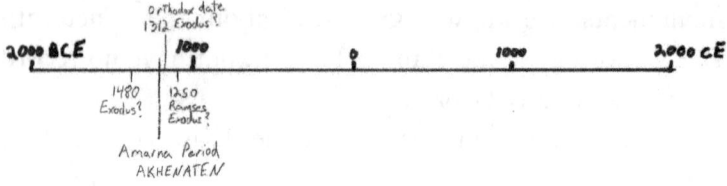

"Let me walk you through my entire night, and then you can call me crazy. That period in Egypt's history is called the 'Amarna Period' because that's where the pha-raoh Akhenaten moved the capital to honor the new sole god of Egypt, Aten. It's well documented and recorded in history, even though later rulers tried to erase any evidence of it. You can imagine all the logistical problems Akhenaten created for his faith. He inherited the kingdom when it was in a position of power and prosperity, then ordered his subjects to worship differently now, which created a revolt. The cast of characters and family tree is important to my theory." He showed Vivi another lineage chart.

Amenhotep III—Tiye

Two sons; the first dies young, the second becomes pharaoh

Amenhotep IV (Akhenaten)—Nefertiti

Six daughters

Akhenaten—Kiya (minor wife)

Possibly two sons, Semenkare—Tutankaten (later Tutankhamun)

"Records show Akhenaten and Nefertiti had six daughters, but make no mention of a son. Akhenaten fathers the next king of Egypt, King Tut, with one of his minor wives named Kiya, and her origins are mysterious.

"There *is* one other person who shows up in the records as a coregent near the end of Akhenaten's reign. He or she is listed as Semenkare. I say he or she, because there are various theories as to who this person was. Some believe it was just another name for Nefertiti as she coruled alongside her husband. Others believe it was a young man who helped rule for a time before dying young and disappearing from the records—possibly a son of Akhenaten with the same Kiya or a close relative.

"Next is King Tut, who was born named Tutankaten, which means 'living image of the Aten.' He would later change his name to Tutankhamun to honor the god Amun when he ascended to the throne. He was married to his half-sister from Akhenaten and Nefertiti, born with the name Ankhesenpaaten and later changed to Ankhesenamun. King Tut died violently while in his teens with no heir (just two stillborn daughters). Following Tut are two interesting characters central to unraveling this mysterious time in Egypt. Ay, who was a chief advisor to Amenhotep III, Akhenaten, and then Tut, took the throne. Historians believe Ay married Tut's wife Ankhesenamun after he was killed to legitimize his right to the throne. They birthed no heirs during his short run as pharaoh, as Ay was an already old man when he usurped the throne.

"After Ay died, Horemheb, the commander of the army since the reign of Amenhotep III, became the last ruler of the Eighteenth Dynasty."

Amenhotep III (the magnificent king)

Amenhotep IV (Akhenaten)

Tutankaten (Tutankhamun)

Ay (Top advisor for three previous kings)

Horemheb (Top military commander
for four previous kings)

"This historical period is mysterious not just because it was roughly 3,400 years ago, but also because several pharaohs after the Amarna period, starting with Horemheb, tried to erase any record of Akhenaten or his ideas of religion. They scraped his name off anything they could find and referred to him as 'Akhenaten the Heretic.' Even hundreds of years later, any reference to him was forbidden, and he was referred to as the 'great sinner' or 'evil doer' or 'heretic.'

"Do you see what I'm getting at, Vivi?" he asked, but she seemed unimpressed.

"Think about what Malavolti translates to in Italian! Add to this the fact that there is little-to-no archeological or historical evidence to support the Exodus story in the Bible, which is actually the case with much of the Old Testament. Many people now speculate that this time in history is the genesis for the biblical story of Moses.

"Even Sigmund Freud wrote a book on it, *Moses and Monotheism*,[15] which is why it hit me last night in the cathedral when the shooter died on the Moses mosaic. It was the last book Freud wrote. I only read a quick synopsis, but he postulated that at some point while Egypt regressed under Akhenaten's radical changes, there was a revolt against his new religion. Freud theorized that after Akhenaten died and the new religion was squelched, one of the high priests of Aten (called Moses in the Bible) might have led the remaining ardent followers of the movement, possibly including groups of Semites from Canaan who still made their home around the Nile, and moved north up into what is now the Holy Land—beginning a movement that would go on to spawn Judaism and eventually Christianity and Islam. There *is* circumstantial evidence to support what Freud claimed came to him through meditative visions.

"Like I said: we don't know much about Akhenaten because later pharaohs tried to erase any record of him from Egypt's history. One piece of writing about his new religion did survive, however, and is called the 'Great Hymn to Aten,' a lengthy hymn giving praise to the one god, Aten and thought to have been written by Akhenaten himself. It was found etched into walls of tombs from the Amarna period. Take a look at this, Vivi! When you lay the 'Great Hymn to Aten' lines next to the lines of Psalm 104 from the Book of Psalms in the Old Testament, you can see the amazing similarities—too close to be mere coincidence for texts that survived millennia." Michael clicked an open link and brought up the hymn transposed next to Psalm 104:

"O Sole God beside whom there is none! (Aten)

O Yahweh my God you are very great. (Yahweh)

How many are your deeds...You made the earth as you wished, you alone, All peoples, herds, and flocks. (Aten)

O Yahweh, how manifold are your works! In wisdom you have made them all; the earth is full of your creatures. (Yahweh)

When you set in western lightland, Earth is in darkness as if in death (Aten)

You make darkness, and it is night, when all the animals of the forest come creeping out. (Yahweh)

Every lion comes from its den (Aten)

The young lions roar for their prey...when the sun rises, they withdraw, and lie down in their dens. (Yahweh)

When you have dawned they live, When you set they die; (Aten)

When you hide your face, they are dismayed; when you take away their breath, they die (Yahweh)

You set every man in his place, You supply their needs; Everyone has his food. (Aten)

These all look to you to give them their food in due season. (Yahweh)

The entire land sets out to work (Aten)

People go out to their work and to their labor until the evening (Yahweh)

The fish in the river dart before you, Your rays are in the midst of the sea. (Aten)

Yonder is the sea, great and wide, creeping things innumerable are there (Yahweh)

Birds fly from their nests, Their wings greeting your ka (Aten)

By the streams the birds of the air have their habitation; they sing among the branches (Yahweh)

He makes waves on the mountain like the sea, to drench their fields and their towns (Aten)

—You make springs gush forth in the valleys; they flow between the hills…The trees of Yahweh are watered abundantly (Yahweh)."[16]

He looked at Vivianna, excited. "And that's not the only bit of writing from this time that's found almost word for word in the Bible. There was a royal vizier under Amenhotep III who also served under Akhenaten as the top vizier or advisor in all of Egypt, holding the title of Director of Lower and Upper Egypt. He was possibly the most powerful and well-known vizier Egypt had ever had. Archeologists have found that this vizier was even worshiped as a god long after his death, and many monuments were built in his honor. His name was also Amenhotep or Imhotep; he's known as Amenhotep-Huy or Amenhotep son of Hapu. In 1935 a fresco was found in a memorial temple dedicated to him with the following text written in hieroglyphs about the day he was installed as vizier of Egypt."

Michael scrolled down the same web page to show Vivi the fresco's translated text:

> "He received ornaments in gold and all kinds of precious minerals; his body was dressed of delicate fabric and first quality linen. A collar in pure gold and all kinds of materials spent on his neck... Year XXX...The great royal scribe, Amenophis, bowed before her Majesty."[17]

Michael flipped through the open web page on his computer. "Now compare that text to the Bible's version of Joseph being installed as a great vizier of Egypt from Genesis 41:42 and 46:

> [42] Then Pharaoh took off his signet ring from his hand and put it on Joseph's hand, and clothed

him in garments of fine linen and put the gold
necklace around his neck.

[46]Now Joseph was thirty years old when he stood
before Pharaoh, king of Egypt. And Joseph went
out from the presence of Pharaoh and went
through all the land of Egypt.

"So history has left us some clues, and there are countless books and conspiracy websites on this subject. There's
even a theory that the kings David and Solomon, whom
archeologists can find no traces of, might have been meta-
phors for earlier Egyptian rulers!

"The problem with all this information, though, and
probably why you have never heard that theory of the birth
of Judaism and all other monotheistic religions is because
it's all conjecture. Those events took place so long ago that
it's impossible to prove. So what if there are similarities
between ancient Egyptian practices and what the Hebrews
eventually wrote down as the Word of God? There was a
cultural influence, right? And we'll never know for sure, so
you can always fall back on 'faith.' It's a matter of faith that
the Bible comes to us through divine dictation. But you
know what isn't conjecture? What could be the smoking
gun to prove that much of the Bible is political fiction?"

"You lost me, Michael. Where is the proof?" Vivi asked,
confused.

"Genes, Vivi! What if Akhenaten and Nefertiti didn't
die in Egypt? What if it wasn't a high priest of the Aten
temple who took followers to the land of Canaan to start a

new religion as Sigmund Freud suggested? What if it was the king of Egypt himself, the 'living son of the Aten'?"

She stared at him, openmouthed, as he continued, "Imagine a scenario in which Akhenaten found his kingdom and influence collapsing around him. He wouldn't be the first or last pharaoh to rightfully fear assassination. He'd made many enemies during his tumultuous reign from his dramatic reformations. What if he and Nefertiti and a group of their followers picked up and left? Neither of their bodies has been definitively found, after all.

"It's not hard to imagine that Ay and Horemheb might have decided they'd had enough of his changes and raised a revolt to put his son, Tut, on the throne for awhile when he was young and they could control him. Then, he was eventually murdered in his teens, and Ay took the throne for a short period late in his life before he died heirless. After that Horemheb finally got what he thought he'd earned through his military might, the throne of Egypt. He quickly began erasing any reference to Akhenaten or his move to Amarna, which was immediately abandoned.

"Now imagine Akhenaten, Nefertiti, and a band of their followers and high priests of the Aten temple escaped into the Holy Land. Remember, Canaan was still a vassal of Egypt at this time with military outposts in Gaza, Yaffo, and Beit She'an, according to letters from the Amarna period. So where would this group on the lam from Egypt go for safety in the Holy Land?"

"To the mountains? To high ground in the wilderness to hide out and plot their return?" Vivi answered Michael, following his logic.

"That's right! At least, that's what I would do. What if once they were established there, Akhenaten had more children? Specifically, more boys..."

"They would be heirs to the throne after Tut," Vivi said.

"Correct, but more important to my theory, they would have a Y-chromosome that looked exactly like Tut's since they had the same father, Akhenaten. Now, at a little before 1300 BCE, a new religion appeared in the Holy Land. Its leader and chief prophet was believed to be both God and man. If that person was, indeed, Akhenaten on the run, he was also the rightful king of the most powerful nation on Earth at that time, but he gave it up for his faith in one all-powerful God. As time went on, his followers grew the beliefs into a new religion. Of course, the true identity of Akhenaten and Nefertiti, as well as any of their offspring, would need to remain a secret to all outsiders, as their mere presence would be a threat to the current Egyptian pharaohs. A circle of trusted insiders would have to be formed quickly.

"Have you ever played the telephone game, Vivi?"

"No, what's that?"

"Just a childhood game where you line up people and a secret is told at one end in a whisper. The secret gets passed along a chain of people, until the last person says the whispered secret out loud, which is usually very different than the original whisper, due to human error."

"Oh, we play that game here too! We call it *telefono roto*, broken telephone," she said, laughing.

"Okay, now imagine playing the game over hundreds of years with wars, politics, and exiles mixed in for good measure. The original writings of the Old Testament/Torah were written in Greek and Hebrew, offshoot languages of the first alphabet, a concept that wasn't even around until roughly 1000 BCE, hundreds of years after Judaism began."

"So even if your theory is correct, explain how could you prove it with genetics?"

"My idea is based on the premise that Akhenaten had other boys than just Tut, and those boys had more boys, creating a patrilineage or string of male heirs that still exists today. I got the idea in the cathedral yesterday. I had just told you, as we were standing over Hermes Trismegistus, that it would be interesting, but no big deal, if the Malavoltis had descended from some ancient Egyptian king. Then, as I watched the attacker's blood pool on a mosaic of Moses, it just hit me like a ton of bricks: there's one king/pharaoh who, if he had descendants in certain places, could rewrite a lot of sacred history. When I got back here last night, I began to scour the Internet for anything related to this theory.

"I didn't know if King Tut's genetics had been published, so I first searched for that information and found an article published several years ago in an archeology magazine about the importance of King Tut's genetics to a number of different organizations."

Vivi scanned the article, which touched on some of the genetic research that had been done on King Tut's mummy and noted that interest in his genetic makeup was coming from a wide range of people. Everyone from the Mormons to the Muslim Brotherhood seemed to want to know the boy king's genetics. It also discussed the denied requests for samples and the starts and stops the research on Tut had experienced, including the fact that, curiously, Egypt seemed to block attempts at sequencing the young pharaoh's DNA. Eventually, in 2010, Egypt finally announced that they had sequenced all of Tut's genes and were ready to publicize some of Tut's genetic findings, as well as those of other mummies from the Amarna period. The article stated they had not and did not intend to publish all of Tut's genetic makeup, however. "Here, read this sentence a couple times, and think about my Y-chromosome theory."

Michael scrolled to a specific paragraph in the article for Vivi, who paraphrased, "An anonymous source at the Egyptian Ministry of Antiquities reported that the full genetic results will never be published because Egypt is afraid it will strengthen the notion that the pharaohs were Jewish."[18] She glanced at Michael. "Why would they say that? How could a pharaoh be Jewish in 1300 BCE before the Torah was even written?"

"I know, right? But look again at the map of Y-DNA migrations. The western side of the Middle East was filled with the J1 marker; that's what predominately made up the Semitic tribes. It's still the most common Y-haplogroup of men who identify as Jewish; but of course, lots and lots of men descend from this Y-haplogroup who are not Jewish, and none of their ancestors were either. So merely being a member of a Semitic Y-DNA group is not enough to assume someone is Jewish. So how could DNA denote someone as Jewish 3,300 years ago?"

"If they still have living ancestors and those people are Jewish?" Vivi answered with a look on her face that said she wasn't sure she understood what she'd just said.

"Exactly!" Michael exclaimed. "Remember, the Y-chromosome is very stable, so over long periods of time it can be used to track human ancestry. If we go back 3,400 years, almost anybody in the Middle East or North Africa, or heck, most of the world, could probably claim to be related to that person from 3,400 years ago. No big deal. But if there's an unbroken string of males ranging from Akhenaten through various male lines of Jewish priests and kings, it could prove that Akhenaten had more boys than just Tut, and that those children were born in the Holy Land, where he was founding a new religion—one that would spawn Judaism, Christianity, and Islam."

"So you think that you carry this genetic marker? The same Y-chromosome markers as King Tut—and that someone is afraid that this information will get out?" Vivi was still trying to wrap her head around Michael's theory.

"If my theory is right, then yes, I do—as would all of my biological Malavolti cousins. But so would others, and some of them carrying this Y-chromosome would still identify as Jewish today."

"Okay, but even if you're right and your family comes from a line of males extending back to Akhenaten, how could science use your genes to prove your theory that a self-exiled group, including the king and queen, moved from Egypt to the Holy Land and started a religious movement that later became the basis for the biblical Old Testament? And how did you know the shooter's bullet had the Eye of Horus on it, Michael?"

CHAPTER THIRTY-ONE

Castel Gandolfo, Italy

"Alfonso, if you're involved with people pushing back against Ordo, let me help. If we make everything we know public, your voice would certainly still carry a great deal of weight!" Father Patrick Davies was now moving about nervously as he talked to the former pope, who remained seated near the fire. The calm indifference offered by Alfonso only made Patrick more agitated. "They're going to start a bloody world war, Alfonso! I foresee a future with a small ruling class controlled by Ordo and a disposable population that feeds the beast—because it is already happening, and I'm ashamed to say I've helped."

Patrick ceased ranting and waited for Alfonso to respond, but he seemed more content to gaze into the fire, seemingly lost in thought. Patrick continued, "Okay, okay, let me be frank. I'm sure you already know this, but I've helped Ordo a number of times over the last decade. For my services I've been paid nicely, gained their trust, and was promoted several times within the Vatican. They contacted me and said that a professor at Sapienza and a college student from America were working on a project that jeopardized exposing information that could destabilize the Catholic Church and the world.

"They told me the professor might need to disappear, and some reconnaissance was necessary within the Vatican and on the student. My Ordo contact asked me to listen for Vatican chatter about the Qumran artifacts they possess, specifically some copper scrolls. Of course, I've never seen those scrolls, but I've heard whispers that the rumored scrolls clearly lay out the genealogy of Christ and the House of David. I posed as Egyptian intelligence to feed bad intel to Rabbi Bein, and his mercenaries did the rest. Okay?

"Believe me, I was as shocked as anyone when I heard they were going to execute the American kid, and in a church no less! Somebody was ready for them, though. None of this is adding up for me. What could be so dangerous to cause Ordo to behave so recklessly? What exactly do these scrolls say?"

"They fear losing control," replied Alfonso before offering more. "It's not just Christian doctrine their scrolls would challenge. It's the entire foundation of the Abrahamic story, Judaism, Christianity, and Islam would all be affected. They've probably leveraged their scrolls all over the Middle East. And now science is ready to clarify things even further."

"I'm under the impression most of the deep pockets involved with Ordo are devotees of Thelema. Certainly they would welcome such news?" asked a perplexed Patrick.

"You're probably right, but they aren't done using it to their advantage. Right now the information is more valuable to them as leverage to control various religious and state leaders. You're right about their ultimate goal, as well: they want to establish one state, one world government and then implement their brand of 'religion.' First they give the people the state, the promise of stability and peace... then the religion."

"We have to stop them, Alfonso! If you're involved with people who are ready to take on Ordo then I pledge you my sincere allegiance and support in any way I can." Patrick knelt at the side of the former pope's chair.

"Rise, Patrick, and go back to Rome. The head of my security will give you a number to call should you learn anything new. When the time is right, we may call upon you."

"Thank you, Your Holiness. I will not betray your trust."

Alfonso chuckled before responding, "I don't trust you Patrick! I finally trust the path that is being laid before me by our Heavenly Father, and He has placed you before me for a reason. No man is beyond redemption with the power of His love. Go now and pray for guidance."

CHAPTER THIRTY-TWO

Siena, Italy

"Vivi, do you know who the Samaritans are?"

"Umm, like the 'Good Samaritan' parable in the New Testament?"

"Yes, that's them. Samaria is a remote mountainous area in the Holy Land. In biblical times it divided the more densely populated areas of Galilee in the north and Judea in the south. The Samaritans were the inhabitants of this area. To understand them, it helps to know a little about geography and the tumultuous history of the Holy Land.

"In the early days of Judaism, there are two documented exile periods when large numbers of Jews were forced to leave the Holy Land or live in captivity. The Assyrian Exile took place in the 700s BCE and the Babylonian Exile from 598 to 538 BCE. It's thought that much of the Torah, the Old Testament, was actually written by exiled Jews during the time of the Babylonian Exile.

"Around the historical time of Christ, Samaritans were treated as lowly foreigners. The politically elite Jews of the south thought of them as if they were the foreigners brought in to live there during the exile periods. The Samaritans always said they were part of the original tribes of Israel and lived their faith as it was originally meant to be practiced by maintaining ancient customs. They had many of the same religious beliefs and practices as their Israeli neighbors to the south and north, with some minor differences. The Samaritans claimed that their remote, protected habitat in the mountains had allowed them to escape the two forced exiles—although their records show that during those exiles, their numbers dwindled to the point that some men had to take foreign wives.

"Today the Samaritans still exist as one of the most isolated religious sects on earth. At certain points in the past, their numbers were in the millions. Today, less than 1,000 Samaritans are left in their community. In recent years, and thanks to genetic testing, the Samaritans' ancient oral history has been proven correct. The males carry certain markers found only among their Jewish neighbors, while the female Samaritans are more diverse in their genetic makeup, so that supports their claim that they were indigenous to the area before Judaism and were not foreigners brought in during the exiles.

"Here, take a look at the parable of the Good Samaritan, which is only told in one gospel, Luke." Michael pulled the parable up on his laptop.

Luke 10:25-37

The Parable of the Good Samaritan

²⁵ On one occasion an expert in the law stood up to test Jesus. "Teacher," he asked, "what must I do to inherit eternal life?"

²⁶ "What is written in the Law?" he replied. "How do you read it?"

²⁷ He answered, "'Love the Lord your God with all your heart and with all your soul and with all your strength and with all your mind'; and, 'Love your neighbor as yourself.'"

²⁸ "You have answered correctly," Jesus replied. "Do this and you will live."

²⁹ But he wanted to justify himself, so he asked Jesus, "And who is my neighbor?"

³⁰ In reply, Jesus said: "A man was going down from Jerusalem to Jericho when he was attacked by robbers. They stripped him of his clothes, beat him, and went away, leaving him half dead. ³¹ A priest happened to be going down the same road, and when he saw the man, he passed by on the other side.

³² So too, a Levite, when he came to the place and saw him, passed by on the other side.

³³ But a Samaritan, as he traveled, came where the man was; and when he saw him, he took pity on him.

³⁴He went to him and bandaged his wounds,
   pouring on oil and wine. Then he put the man on
   his own donkey, brought him to an inn and took
   care of him.

³⁵ The next day he took out two denarii and gave
   them to the innkeeper. 'Look after him,' he said,
   'and when I return, I will reimburse you for any
   extra expense you may have.'

³⁶ "Which of these three do you think was a
   neighbor to the man who fell into the hands of
   robbers?"

³⁷The expert in the law replied, "The one who had
   mercy on him."

Jesus told him, "Go and do likewise."

After Vivi finished reading the parable, she asked about
its significance.

"It's thought this parable includes a Samaritan because
to most Jews they were considered lowly outsiders, and they
were obviously unimportant to the Roman occupiers because they weren't Roman. Jesus used them as an example to
show how even groups of people without common heritage
or beliefs can and should still help each other out in times of
need. Jesus also used two politically elite groups in this parable—a Levite and a priest. According to the Old Testament,
the Levites carried special favor with God and are the only
one of the twelve tribes allowed to carry the Ark of the Covenant during the exile. Jewish priests are from a class of Lev-

ites they call *kohen*. Oral history maintained that the *kohen* were descended from Aaron, the brother of Moses, both Levites. The parable, then, uses two people from groups generally held in high regard, a *kohen* and Levite, and another generally held in low regard, a Samaritan."

"Enough already with the biblical history lessons, Michael! *How* did you know the bullet bore the Eye of Horus?" Vivi was anxious for any kind of meaningful break in this case.

The Bible that had been left in Michael's hostel room in Rome sat on the table among the strewn papers. Michael grabbed it and opened it to a dollar bill marking a page. "Look at the dollar in that Bible mysteriously left in my room. Look closely *here*." Michael pointed to the pyramid on the Great Seal of the United States. "Now let's compare it to another dollar bill." Michael handed her a different bill from his wallet. The seal featured a pyramid that was unfinished; thirteen rows of stone made up the foundation of the pyramid, representing the thirteen original states.

The unfinished pyramid was capped with a triangle surrounding an all-seeing eye known as the Eye of Providence. From behind the triangle, rays of light shone out in all directions. Underneath the pyramid was a ribbon with the Latin words *NOVUS ORDO SECLORUM* (a New Order of the Ages). Above the pyramid were the Latin words *ANNUIT COEPTIS* (Favor Our Undertakings). The dollar bill left in Michael's Bible was the nearly identical to the one from his wallet, except it appeared to be printed with the Eye of Horus rather than the standard Eye of Providence.

"This bill looks like a good forgery," Vivi said, holding it up to the light as she felt the paper and inspected the rest of it. "How did you notice this small difference?"

"When I got back here last night, I searched for anything related to Tut's DNA, which is how I found that article I showed you and how I realized the Y-DNA of Tut isn't public information. I also searched for anything related to Jewish Y-DNA, and the top hits included the study done on Jewish priests, or *kohanim*—the *kohen* class I was telling you about. The study has been updated a few times by various universities in Israel; it's colloquially named the 'Y-Chromosome Aaron' study. Remember, the oral tradition is that all *kohanim* descend from Aaron, the brother of Moses. If that were really true, it would be evident by looking at the Y-chromosome of all living male Jews with the last name of Kohen or Cohen. They would all come from the same Y-haplogroup, for starters, and share many of the same deeper markers."

Michael clicked through some pages on his computer, pulling up the Wikipedia page on the Y-Chromosome Aaron study. "Look at these results. No surprise, but Kohens from around the world come from various Y haplogroups, so they couldn't really all be descended from the same male in the last several thousand years. J1 is the most common haplogroup, but again, that's no surprise, since it is the most common haplogroup among men who identify as Jewish. Although, read this." Michael scrolled down to a paragraph near the end of the page, which summarized the Samaritans' genetics.

"The Samaritan community in the Middle East survives as a distinct religious and cultural sect. It constitutes one of the oldest and smallest ethnic minorities in the world, numbering slightly less than 700 members. As a religious sect, reportedly the Samaritans broke away from the mainstream Jews around the fifth century BCE. According to Samaritan accounts, it was the other, southern tribes who left the original worship as set forth by Joshua. The Samaritans have maintained their religion and history to this day. Samaritans claim to descend from the Biblical Israelite tribes of Ephraim, Menashe, and Levi.

Since the Samaritans have maintained extensive and detailed genealogical records for the past 13–15 generations (approximately 400 years) and farther back, researchers have constructed accurate pedigrees and specific maternal and paternal lineages. A 2004 Y-Chromosome study concluded that the majority of Samaritans belong to haplogroups J1 and J2, while the Samaritan Kohanim belong to haplogroup E1b1b1a."[19]

Michael held both hands in the air and looked at Vivi with his eyes wide, waiting for a similar shocked expression from her, which never came. Finally, he explained: "The Samaritans, who claimed to have never left the area from the very earliest days of Judaism, are proven right by genetics. Samaritan men primarily carry the J1 and J2-Y haplogroups, two haplogroups native to the Middle East; the men also carry deeper genetic markers found only in their Jewish neighbors. There is one surviving Kohen family, though, and that family carries the same haplogroup as me: E1b1b1a, or EV12. When I read that, I nearly fell out of my seat, because I remembered that the dollar bill in my Bible marked the 'Good Samaritan' parable, which is why I took a closer look at the dollar again and found the Egyptian Eye of Horus."

"You think someone was trying to tell you something about the Samaritans? It doesn't seem very meaningful, just having the same Y haplogroup as you. You said this haplogroup is roughly 17,000 years old?" Vivi interrupted, in an attempt to try to understand all the information Michael was throwing at her.

"Yeah, you're right; on the surface it just means we have the same paternal ancestor somewhere up in our family trees. Although this haplogroup is found in trace amounts in all Jewish populations, it's a distinctly Egyptian haplogroup. Not only did it originate somewhere near Thebes, but it's still found today mostly in southern Egyptians and drifting into the northern part of Sudan. Sometime around 17,000 years ago, someone in Egypt was born, and his Y-chromosome underwent what's called a 'single nucleotide polymorphism mutation.' This guy then had a Y-chromosome that was distinctly different from those males who came before him, creating a new haplogroup. If someone else has the same Y-haplogroup as me, it just means we have a common paternal ancestor; but it could be someone all the way back near the creation of this haplogroup around 17,000 years ago.

"More in-depth testing can be done, though, Vivi! The Y-chromosome can be broken down even further to get more markers. This is Professor's Sisti's expertise, especially when it comes to extremely old DNA. I have no idea exactly what the professor's lab is capable of, but I do know it's one of the best in the world at pulling markers from ancient samples. I had my Y-DNA tested to over a 100 markers from an online service marketed to the general public, but I think Sisti's lab at Sapienza, or one like it, can pull out thousands of markers. I sent my results to Professor Sisti when I pitched my thesis idea on the Malavoltis and was shocked he responded at all, much less so promptly. Maybe his interest was due to something he saw in my Y-chromosome test results. Sometimes there are really unique mutations among the deeper markers that can further help geneticists construct a family tree."

Vivianna interrupted him again with another plea for clarity. "So if Egypt has kept Tut's Y-chromosome DNA secret, what do you think Sisti found that put him at risk? And how might that relate to you?"

Michael pulled up the long article on Tut he had shown Vivianna earlier. "There are a few things that stand out for me here, other than the paragraph stating they aren't publishing Tut's full DNA because they don't want to bolster the idea that he was Jewish. There was a mummy found from the Amarna period in a tomb called KV-55, which was discovered back in 1907 in the Valley of Kings. While that area is not near Amarna, some of the artifacts in the tomb were carbon dated to the time of the Akhenaten's reformation. When Egypt published some of Tut's genetic results in 2010, they said that this mummy was most likely the father of Tut, Akhenaten, based on their genetic work.

"This assertion was immediately questioned by several academics for a number of reasons. The mummy from KV-55 was in rough shape, unlike Tut, who was given a proper king's burial. The theory, if it really is Akhenaten, was that his original tomb in Amarna was ransacked sometime after his death, and his mummy was moved to this tomb and sealed off again during the Twentieth Dynasty. The first scientists to question the assertion the mummy was Akhenaten were the various forensic anthropologists who had studied the bones. They all had the same conclusion: the bones belonged to a male who died between the ages of nineteen to twenty-three. That's incredibly specific and straightforward science, but the written history indicates Akhenaten lived well into his thirties or older. Then geneticists pointed out that some of the genetic puzzle parts of this royal family made public by Egypt didn't add up. Tut was buried with two stillborn daughters, which were thought to be two miscarriages from his sister-wife Ankhesenpaaten.

"The mother of those two stillborns was found: a mummy known as KV21a from the Valley of the Kings. That would mean Kv21a is none other than Ankhesenpaaten, the daughter of Akhenaten and Nefertiti. The problem is that based on the genetic information Egypt has made available, the mummy in KV-55 cannot be the father of Ankhesenpaaten, the mummy KV21a.

"Another issue is that only a handful of labs in the world could reliably run samples this old without contamination, and the Egyptian Ministry of Antiquities was attempting to run the results in a lab they had set up themselves. The results were immediately disregarded by many in the field who thought the tests were done in an unreliable manner. One popular theory now is that if the KV-55 mummy is a young man closely related to Tut, then it is probably Semenkare, who was likely Tut's brother or half-brother."

"So?" Vivi demanded.

"So my theory is that the Ministry of Antiquities might have reached out to Professor Sisti because of his lab's capabilities and asked him to discreetly run a blind test on a sample, which was from Tut. He's also the foremost authority on some of the haplogroups native to Egypt—the same two reasons I reached out to him to help me with my thesis."

"So you think the professor saw something in your sample that matched with Tut's? But it would require him to have had access to King Tut, and you're only speculating that might have happened."

"Yes, that's my theory, which I would have called crazy until someone started shooting at me with an Uzi yesterday. If given a roughly 3,400-year-old sample and a modern sample, a lab like the one at Sapienza could tell with near certainty if two people were of the same male patrilineage within just a few generations—three or four at most. In other words, if the Samaritan and Malavolti samples are a perfect match with King Tut, it would mean they have all these deeper markers matching on the Y-chromosome. Except for thirty-four mutations, one mutation for every hundred years since, the rest of the long serial number is a match. Tut had no living children, so someone within three of four generations of him—a brother, father, uncle, or great uncle or grandfather—had to be that ancestor. When the recorded history of Egypt is combined with that specific genetic information, a strong case could be made that Akhenaten ultimately left Egypt, settled in the Holy Land, and had more children."

Michael reached out and grabbed Vivi's shoulders. "You're not going to believe this, but I think I have an idea where the *real* tomb of Akhenaten is located!"

CHAPTER THIRTY-THREE

Jerusalem, Israel

Rabbi Bein gently rocked back and forth in focused prayer. He had just received word that one of his disciples, Ishmael, had been killed while attempting to carry out a shooting in the cathedral of Siena at the behest of the man he had instructed them to take orders from. Bein was lost, depressed, and as confused as he had ever been in the realm of *Nefesh*, the plane of action and the physical world. He focused his mind and attempted to allow his soul to ascend the ladder of consciousness. Even with his mind in these dire straits his mastery of Kabbalah allowed him to pass quickly through the realms of *Nefesh* and *Ruach*.

As time fell away, he began to intermingle with light in the realm of Neshama; all darkness faded as he entered the highest plane of Chaya. It had been years since he'd experienced the plane of Chaya like this: it was pure light. Gone was the dark energy he believed the light had been surrounding him with in recent years. His prayers and focus continued to plead for direction; he didn't want to leave this plane of existence. Rabbi Bein felt the light coaxing his soul upward as he ascended to another level. He knew there was only one level above Chaya, and it was reserved for martyrs. The soul of Rabbi Bein entered the plane of Yechida as his body slumped over. He would not be returning to the plane of action because his soul was now bound to the Holy One. He was free at last.

Rome, Italy

General Garret moved through the streets of Rome in civilian clothing, using his phone to find the church he sought in a city of over 600 churches. He turned north on Via dei Cestari and saw the Elephant and Obelisk, a sculpture Bernini created that used an obelisk unearthed in Rome in the 1600s. The obelisk had originally been brought to Rome in the first century AD, when Egypt was part of its vast empire. Garret had a meeting in the church behind the obelisk, Santa Maria sopra Minerva. The church was built over what was believed to have been a temple to the Greco-Roman goddess Minerva and thus named for her. It was later discovered the church was actually built over an ancient temple dedicated to the worship of the Egyptian goddess Isis.

Garret checked the time as he entered, punctual as usual. The sheer beauty and craftsmanship of the church was something even an avowed atheist like Garret could appreciate and admire. He decided to make Patrick wait a bit while he walked around the church, admiring its various sculptures and altars. He walked past the body of St. Catherine of Siena as he located his rendezvous point. Entering a specific confessional booth, he took a seat. A small door covered by a dark screen that divided the small booth in two slid open.

"I hope you have some good news for me," Garret began.

"Come on now, General, that's no way to start a confession. You're supposed to tell me how long it's been since the last time you confessed your sins."

"Cut the crap, Davies. I'm the only reason you're still breathing. You can imagine how unhappy some powerful people are that our mission failed—using men you had selected, need I remind you."

"From what I understand, our man was being shadowed. Ordo has a leak, General. The mission was compromised, and it had nothing to do with the men we used. It appears powers are moving in the shadows who want to take on Ordo."

"Who? I want to know who took out our man Siena!? You told me you had a lead, or was that just more BS, buying time to stay alive."

"I don't know who, but I know a person who does: Alfonso Carpacci. I've just come from meeting with him this morning."

"Alfonso Carpacci? You can't be serious."

"I am serious. I don't know who is behind the shooting, but whoever it is has a growing list of allies—enemies of Ordo—and it appears they're making a move. Carpacci is holed up in Castel Gandolfo with a small army for security. I've suspected something has been in the works since he stepped down. You have to see the writing on the wall too,

General. Ordo has become too strong. They're making bolder and bolder moves out in the open, thereby creating stronger enemies. They want to consolidate power even more and begin open control over a world government.

"The people are starting to wake up, General. Absolute power corrupts absolutely; this won't end well for them or the world. And don't get me started on their religion; 'Do what thou wilt' is dangerous nonsense. Search your conscience, and look at the big picture. Even a pragmatist like you knows their long-term plans won't work. The people will rise up and cut the head off the snake eventually. If a centralized world government were installed and then failed, it will be total anarchy, survival of the strongest. Another Dark Ages! Not to mention the bloodshed and total chaos Ordo would create for the world to want a centralized government in the first place. Now is the time to take a stand."

The confessional booth prevented the men from seeing each other's facial expressions, so when General Garret was silent for a long moment, Patrick feared his speech had sealed his fate and the general would kill him.

Finally Garret spoke up: "Do you think the opposition has an insider in the capstone? No one has betrayed their oath in over 100 years. Who would give up all that power and wealth and betray their future generations by risking it all?"

"I don't know. For obvious reasons Alfonso wasn't too forthcoming with me. He seemed surprisingly at ease with his fate, though. He was bold enough to take a private meeting with me and then asked if I was there to kill him. I think he's a man with nothing to lose, one who has decided to go down swinging."

"What makes you so sure he's working to take down Ordo?"

"He was coy, but he didn't hide the fact that he knew what happened in Siena. I'm not sure how involved he is with whoever was behind it, but at the very least he is their ally. He's surrounded himself with more security than you can imagine. I've known something was up for some time now from rumors in the Vatican. I thought maybe he was organizing a group to take on Ordo's influence within the Holy See, but I think it's more than that. I told him I'm willing to help any way I can. I think you should too. History will be on our side, not theirs."

That admission brought another long pause. Davies pressed his ear to the wood and listened for the sound of a bullet being chambered. Instead all he heard was deep breathing for several minutes before Garret stood up to leave.

"You should disappear for awhile, Patrick," Garret advised before exiting the confessional and strolling back out into Piazza della Minerva.

CHAPTER THIRTY-FOUR

Siena, Italy

"Last night on *this* porch, you think you found the location of a missing pharaoh's tomb?" Vivi sounded less than convinced.

"Not exactly, but hear me out," Michael said as he released her. "If genetics can prove this alternate origin for the biblical Exodus story, think about where that genetic trail might lead historians and archeologists. Remember when I said the Samaritans' religious beliefs were very similar to other Jewish sects of the time? Well one of the differences was in their commandments. They have the same ten traditional commandments condensed into just nine, but the Samaritans have a completely unique tenth commandment. Here, take a look...

> '*Commandment 10*. It shall be when your god will bring you to the Canaanite land, which you are going to inherit, you shall set yourself up great stones, and plaster them with plaster, and

you shall write on them all the words of this law. It shall be, when you are passed over the Jordan, that you shall set up these stones, which I command you this day, in Mount Gerizim. There shall you build an altar to Yahweh your God, an altar of stones: you shall lift up no iron tool on them. You shall build the altar of Yahweh your God of uncut stones, and you shall offer burnt offerings thereon to Yahweh your God: and you shall sacrifice peace-offerings, and shall eat there, and you shall rejoice before Yahweh your God. That mount beyond the Jordan, behind the way of the going down of the sun, in the land of the Canaanites who dwell in the Arabah, over against Gilgal, beside the oaks of Moreh, against Shechem (Nablus).'"[20]

Vivi just shook her head, more confused than ever.

Michael explained, "The Samaritans maintain that Mount Gerizim, near the West Bank city of Neblus in Holy Land, is the holiest place on earth—*not* the Temple Mount in Jerusalem that has been fought over by Jews, Muslims, and Christians for more than a millennium. If genetics can prove the Samaritans' oral history and also that some Samaritans are descended from Akhenaten...well, do you see what I'm getting at?"

"You think Akhenaten and Nefertiti are buried on Mount Gerizim?" she asked, sounding intrigued. A red-eyed and drained-looking Michael offered a shrug and nodded. "But why is the Eye of Horus so significant?"

"I don't know! Horus and Set were rivals. I'd guess whoever helped us out in the cathedral and left this Bible in my room is the same person meant to receive the hieroglyphic message in blood left in the professor's lab. Maybe there's an organization or individual that uses the Eye of Horus as a symbol and wants this information to go public? If I'm right, someone has known about these connections for awhile. Maybe the Set message was simply letting them know there are still people willing to fight the information's release. If you were going to war with someone whose logo was the Eye of Horus, it would only make sense that you would pick Set to represent yourself. I don't know; it's just a theory."

"So, which one is Horus and which one Set? Who would know and be willing to kill to keep it quiet?" Vivi asked.

"You got me! Egypt has had Tut's genetic information for years. As far as who would want to keep it all secret, that would be a long list. Anyone with an interest in preventing biblical history from being exposed as political fiction and/or anyone with an orthodox view of the Bible, not to mention the ramifications for the geopolitics of the Middle East. The region has been unstable and on the precipice of war for generations; this information in the wrong hands could cause World War III."

"Whoever is behind this, whoever is masquerading as Horus or Set, how would they know what the professor had learned and about your genetic sample?" she asked.

"Maybe someone has been monitoring the online genetic companies? Someone could have direct access to

Professor Sisti's software, as well. Or the professor saw a unique mutation on my Y-chromosome that caused him to reach out to colleagues, asking for help in locating matches for certain markers—and that tipped his hand to whoever Set is. The possibilities are endless. I don't know if Sisti made the connection to the Holy Land or not, but it appears someone has and is pointing us to the Samaritan *kohen* sample as a link."

"You'd think whoever is playing Horus and Set would need ties back in the Egypt's Ministry of Antiquities, right? From what you could find online regarding Egypt's genetic testing, they have kept the Tut sample under tight wraps. And your theory is that they used the Sapienza lab as a blind control for further testing on such an old sample?" Vivianna was mentally trying to work through the information and create a path forward for the investigation.

"Yes, from what I could find online, that's my theory. The problem is that all the information is digital. I suppose the perpetrator could have accessed the various DNA labs remotely with the right hacking expertise. If the motive is tied to the veracity of the Bible or Middle East politics, our suspect list would be long. Hell, it could cause a large-scale questioning of many authorities and power structures in general, especially if there's evidence of a cover-up."

Vivianna got up to leave. "Get your things together, Michael, and meet me in the lobby. We need to get back to Rome."

"Please don't make me tell that story to your boss!"

"My boss will be no help to us. We have to give statements there tomorrow, but first, we need to talk to someone with better resources—my uncle."

"The Vatican? Vivi, there's more to my theory, and it's even further out there. I think you should hear it, though, and if you still want to go to your uncle, then I'll trust your judgment. Please give me a few more minutes."

Vivianna relented and stopped walking for the door. "If you think the Vatican could somehow be involved in this, I feel all the more certain my uncle is the only one who could help us. I trust him. What is the rest of your theory?"

"If I'm right, and this is about Akhenaten and the origins of the Bible, then the most logical conclusion is that a religious group or some state agency recently discovered there are living descendants of Akhenaten. Those descendants are scattered around the Middle East, Europe...the world, yet are *not* found in Egypt, thanks to the faith of one of their ancestors. The other possibility, which seems far-fetched on the surface, is that there has always been a small group that has known the true history of the Bible, but has kept it secret for various reasons over the past 3,000 years. Some of the Bible's authors may have been a part of this 'illuminated' group."

"That does seem out there, Michael. The true history of the Bible? So you think we're dealing with a conspiracy that involves more than just the early days of the Old Testament?" asked Vivi as she sat back down.

Michael posed another question: "Assuming Akhenaten himself fled to the Holy Land and began a movement that would become the foundation for monotheism *and* assuming he had more children there whose identities would need to remain secret...how long do you think it would take before the true history was twisted beyond recognition and lost to time?"

"Probably in the first few hundred years, not long at all. As you said, in those early years, writing would have been limited to hieroglyphs or cuneiform and only very few people were literate. History must have been passed along orally, but with the need to hide a fleeing royal family, fighting in the area, politics, and power struggles within this movement...I'd assume it wouldn't take too many generations before this story was changed beyond recognition and lost. It's just human nature. It starts as a whisper before 1300 BCE, and by the time things are written down hundreds of years later, the current Old Testament is what came out of that very long broken-telephone game."

"That's what I'd think, too," he added. "Remember, the whole point of the genetic component of my thesis was to demonstrate how forgetful we are. Five hundred years after the fall of Siena, it seems few members of my family know much of anything about its history and their ancestors' role in it. That's 500 years of people who could almost all read and write, aided by the technology and ease of living during the last 500 years, compared to, say, 1300–500 BCE.

"What if there's proof, though, there *were* people who knew the truth all along and protected it? What if the clues are right under our noses, but we're blinded by thousands of years of dogma? Egypt is mentioned over and over in the Bible, and almost every important character in the Old Testament can be found visiting Egypt at some point. Egypt clearly had a big influence on the Israelites—so, what if there was a group in the Holy Land that kept this secret alive about their faith's origins, about Egyptian royalty from the Eighteenth Dynasty living among them?"

"I'd say that's crazy."

"I know it sounds insane, but look at these links dealing with this theory, Vivi." Michael pointed at the dozens of downsized tabs open on his computer. "Once I went down that rabbit hole last night and realized science could prove a genetic thread that could be overlaid and sown through the Bible story, I started to look for it." Michael turned his laptop toward her and started clicking on some of the tabs.

"Let's start in the Old Testament. Look at all these different amateur investigators, all labeled crackpots, who think the Book of Ezekiel is talking about the Amarna period of Egypt. The Book of Ezekiel is thought to have been written during the Babylonian Exile, sometime between 593–571 BCE. It contains prophetic visions, visions of the fall of the Temple, and eventual salvation for the Israelites. The temple vision is bizarre, though; it doesn't resemble any temple ever built in Jerusalem, and some of the practices described in it were not typical in Israel. Like this passage here." He scrolled down the page of one the websites he had up on his computer.

Ezekiel 43:7–8

[7]"The House of Israel and their kings must not again defile My holy name by their apostasy and by the corpses of their kings at their death. [8]When they placed their threshold next to My threshold and their doorposts next to My doorpost with only a wall between me and them, they were defiling My holy name."

"This doesn't describe Israelite burial customs at all. Instead, it reads like something written at the time of the Amarna reformation in Egypt. In Egypt, there was a practice of kings building mortuary temples where they would be embalmed in front of the temple of the god they were associated with. The mortuary temples were to be done away with in Amarna.

"The details Ezekiel shares about the temple in his vision could only be the great temple built to Aten in Armarna, according to this researcher. Ezekiel describes details that weren't there for either the first or second temple built in Jerusalem but *were* there for the great temple to Aten. Things from the sheer size, to details of rooms for singers fit more closely with the great temple in Amarna than they do any temple in Jerusalem. Here, look at this passage."

Ezekiel 47:1–7

[1]"He led me back to the entrance of the Temple, and I found that water was issuing from below the platform of the Temple—eastward, since the Temple faced east...

[3]As the man went on eastward with a measuring line in his hand, he measured off a thousand cubits and led me across the water; the water was ankle deep. [4]Then he measured off another thousand and led me across the water; the water was knee deep. [5]He measured off a further thousand and led me across the water; the water was up to the waist. When he measured yet another thousand, it was a river I could not cross; for the stream had swollen

into a stream that could not be crossed except by swimming. ⁶'Do you see, O mortal?' he said to me: and led me back to the bank of the stream. ⁷As I came back, I saw trees in great profusion on both banks of the stream."

"There is obviously no river in or near the temples in Jerusalem. It's a hot, dry place—but there *was* a river near the temple in Amarna: the Nile, exactly where it's described here. The Nile is 500 meters from the Great temple to Aten, the same distance Ezekiel states as a 1,000 cubits."

"Okay, okay, I get it. This book in the Old Testament describes a temple that may be in Armarna, not Jerusalem. That's not much evidence to imply a conspiracy that's survived over 3,000 years." Vivi was ready to end the history lessons and get on the road back to Rome.

"I agree it's circumstantial, and there are more strange things about the Book of Ezekiel, but let me get to the point and move right along to the New Testament. What do you know about the Essenes and the Dead Sea Scrolls, Vivi?"

"Because my uncle's archeological work, I do know a bit. They're a collection of scrolls from around the time of Christ written by a sect of Jews called the Essenes. They were discovered around the mid-1900s, I think. How are they associated with this theory of yours?"

"I would have given a similar answer until last night, when I began reading every academic and conspiracy theory under the sun involving them. I always thought the Essenes were just one of a number of minor Jewish sects at the time of Christ. After all, I don't recall ever really hearing about them before, unless it was in the context of the discovery of the Dead Sea Scrolls. Certainly not in the Bible, unlike the Pharisees or Sadducees. That's not how the few historical sources we have from that time record them, though; the Essenes were apparently significant.

"The most prolific historian of that time was probably Flavius Josephus who lived in the first century AD. He was a Jew born in Roman-controlled Palestine and grew up to become a general for the Jewish forces in Galilee before Romans captured him. Eventually, he was able to ingratiate himself with his Roman captors and went on to become a member of the imperial court in Rome, where he lived out the rest of his life writing as a historian. He was an eyewitness to the destruction of the Second Temple in Jerusalem in AD 70. Josephus says quite a bit about the Essenes.

"Just tell me what the Dead Sea Scrolls have to do with Akhenaten!"

"Okay! According to Josephus, there were three distinct branches of Judaism at that time: Sadducees, Pharisees, and Essenes. Josephus himself says he was born a Pharisee. Essenes were divided up into two categories. One branch lived like modern-day monks, taking vows to give up marriage and all wealth, and they lived in ascetic communities out in the desert. The other branch lived in cities in traditional family structures like the other Jews. Although Josephus is perhaps the most prodigious historian of this time, there were others, and they all make note of the Essenes." Michael quickly opened, looked at, and closed several tabs on his computer as if he was trying to jog his memory from the previous night before continuing.

"Philo of Alexandria, another historian who lived from 20 BCE to AD 60, also wrote at great length about the Essenes. He notes that in Egypt the Essenes were called Therapeutae (physicians for the soul), just as they were called doctors or healers in the Holy Land as well.

"Pliny the Elder was a historian and geographer who wrote in AD 70 after the destruction of Judea in the Jewish war with the Romans. He wrote specifically about the Essenes at Qumran who wrote the Dead Sea Scrolls. He describes how they lived very structured, disciplined lifestyles and spent a great deal of time writing."

"We actually know exactly when the Essenes became organized and started out; their history is laid out in the Dead Sea Scrolls. There's one scroll referred to as *The Damascus Document* that explains the sect's origins. It says that 390 years after the Babylonian Exile, they were groping blindly for the true way when God raised a 'teacher of righteousness' for them who was well schooled in the Torah and able to teach them the hidden ways in which Israel had gone astray. His identity is unclear, as he is always referred to simply as 'the teacher of righteousness.' The teachers of the sect are identified as *kohen*-priests from the patrilineage of Zadok. Zadok was the first high priest of the first temple in Jerusalem, thought to be built around 1000 BCE. This first high priest would have claimed direct descent from Aaron. The 'teacher of righteousness' claiming to descend from Zadok would have lived around 150 years before the time of Christ." Michael flipped Vivi another of his hand-scribbled timelines.

"The Sadducees grew out of a political movement that started due to the wars and forced exiles; they were high priests who blamed the earlier high priests for losing the Holy Land during the Assyrian and Babylonian Exiles. The Essenes claimed to be taught by the descendants of the original *kohen*-priests from the first temple of Jerusalem. So, like the Samaritans, one group claimed to be practicing a purer, more original form of Judaism, with teachings and even genetic lines reaching back to the original temple built 1,000 years earlier!

"The 'teacher of righteousness,' the founder of the Essenes, was put to death for his teachings by the politically elite Jews in Jerusalem, the Sadducees. He prophesied that he would return forty years after his death to judge the wicked and usher in the end times—fulfilling the prophecy of the Old Testament of a messiah 'from Aaron and from Israel,' according to the scrolls. His following grew larger and larger during the forty years after his death, but once the timeframe of his prophecy passed without it coming to fruition, a divide formed in the community."

Vivi looked at her watch again and rolled her eyes, giving Michael a look he had seen a few times now: What is your point?

"Okay, okay...now that we know about the Essenes, let's take a look at the Dead Sea Scrolls they wrote." Michael set the paper in his hand down and turned the computer toward himself to read an open link. "These scrolls were found in caves near the north end of the Dead Sea between 1946 and 1956. The unique geography and atmosphere of the area allowed many of the scrolls to remain intact and legible for 2,000 years. They were hidden in the caves during the war between the Romans and Jews, which stretched from AD 66–73. There are over 100 scrolls consisting of over 900 texts. The scrolls are written on various animal skins and papyrus, except one, which was chiseled into copper. Roughly 40% of the scrolls are Hebrew books of the Bible; 30% are books that were not considered canonical and kept out of the Bible. Apocrypha, basically, such as the Books of Enoch, Jubilees, Tobit, and the Wisdom of Sirach. The other 30% of the writings are totally unique and focus on the history of the Essene sect, their rituals, and various events."[21] Michael stopped reading and stared at Vivi as if he were second-guessing himself for what he was about to say.

"My point is this, Vivi: If there were a group of kohen priests who passed down a secret history of Judaism's origins spanning back to Akhenaten, could it be they resided with the Essenes at the time of Christ and knew of that lineage? They were firmly on the outside of the political elite in Jerusalem, and much like the Samaritans, the Essenes claimed to be originalists. At least as far as their kohen-priests were involved, they professed to teach secrets from the line of high priests from the first temple of Jerusalem.

There are at least two scrolls that support my theory: the so-called Temple Scroll and the Copper Scroll. The Temple Scroll, like the Book of Ezekiel, describes a temple that doesn't match the temples of Jerusalem, but *does* match with the great temple of Aten in Amarna. It describes a great temple 800 meters long, way too big to be in Jerusalem, but archeologists have measured the longest wall in the Great Temple to Aten at 800 meters exactly. The Copper Scroll is the most confounding, though. Think about what an arduous task creating a copper scroll would have been in the ancient world. You'd have to mine or buy the copper, melt it down, roll it out very thin, and then chisel in the writing. There is no other known Hebrew scroll written on copper. In fact, that practice was only found in Egypt in an earlier time. The Dead Sea Copper Scroll is a treasure map that describes a temple building and various places where treasure was buried in and around it. Look at all these links, and even books, that have been written on the Copper Scroll mystery."

Michael showed her several websites and books dedicated to solving the mystery of the Copper Scroll. "Many hypothesize that the Copper Scroll is describing the temple to Aten in Amarna. The dashes numbering system they used seems to fit better with Egyptian than Hebrew. The weights of buried treasure also make no sense when the values given on the scroll are converted to the Hebrew kikha, which was 35kg. But if the K weight listed on the scroll really means the Egyptian kite, which was 10.2g, then the weights make sense. The reasons are numerous why the Copper scroll seems to be describing treasure buried in an Amarna temple and not a temple in Jerusalem. But why would a group of Jews around the time of Christ have a treasure map to a temple from over 1,300 years earlier?

"Even the language on the Copper Scroll is unique when compared to the other papyrus scrolls. It's an older form of Hebrew and has various grammatical errors, leading some to speculate that the original creator didn't even speak the language. Along with that mystery, random Greek letters are sprinkled throughout the scroll. Look at this guy's book. This metallurgist lays out his case for the scroll coming from the Amarna period, pointing out that if you pull out the first three groupings of Greek letters they spell KEN XAT HN.[22] Could that be an early Greek interpretation of Akhenaten?"

"You can find a pattern in anything if you look hard enough," Vivi said skeptically.

"Of course," Michael smiled, "which is why this kind of speculation has been easy for mainstream biblical scholars to write it off as a wild conspiracy. But what if it becomes less wild when supported by genetic proof that Akhenaten had children in the Holy Land, and his offspring were instrumental in the religious movement that would become Judaism and Christianity? Think about the royal family having to flee Egypt in a hurry; they couldn't carry all their valuables, so they took what they could and had a scribe write down where some of their other deposits are stashed. Over centuries, the list might have been recopied and cherished for where it came from, even if the treasure was long gone."

"Michael, I'm following your connections of the genetic trail of Akhenaten to the Essene branch of Judaism, but how are you connecting that to the Vatican?" Vivi was obviously doing her best to understand Mike's train of thought.

He took a long swallow of bottled water before continuing. "Okay. Hypothetically speaking, let's assume we have a group of known facts in a routine detective case, except this case spans roughly 3,400 years. Let's further assume that Akhenaten and his most loyal followers settled in the Holy Land to practice their newly formed monotheistic faith and that he had children there. The boy or boys he fathered there had more children, extending his male patrilineage bloodline, some of which still survives today, as can be proven with Y-chromosome analysis. If we are to assume the secret origin of the world's three largest monotheistic religions was known and passed down through a small group of Judaic Levitical priests elected to protect that knowledge, where did the group reside at the time of Christ?"

"You're saying you think they were priests within the community of Essenes, based on the Dead Sea Scrolls. But you still haven't told me what you think it has to do with the Vatican," she huffed.

"Was Jesus raised a Jew?" Michael asked abruptly.

"Yes, of course."

"Well, then, what type of Jew was he? Remember, historians tell us there were three distinct philosophies amongst Jews in the Kingdom of Judah at that time: Pharisee, Sadducee, and Essene."

"So you think Jesus was an Essene, and the highest-ranking members of the Essenes were the keepers of this secret about the Egyptian royal family? Therefore, if there's a group that has continued to pass on this secret information, it would be traced to the religion Jesus inspired, the Catholic Church, correct? Am I following your logic? That seems more than a little out there, Michael. Can we start back for Rome now?"

"I agree it's more than a little out there, but something doesn't smell right here. Where are the Essenes in the Bible? If you wanted to make an argument that Jesus was not an Essene, you could—because there are some differences in his teachings and theirs—but it would be impossible not to admit they must have influenced him quite a bit. And yet they're conspicuously absent from the New Testament. Jesus is seen many times teaching the Pharisees and Sadducees and challenging their beliefs at temple, but he says nothing of the third distinct philosophy of Judaism present at that time. Why? The Pharisees embraced the entire Old Testament and believed in an afterlife for the soul. The Sadducees only embraced the teachings thought to come from Moses; they were more political and wealthy and didn't believe in an afterlife. After the Jewish-Roman war (AD 70), the Pharisee philosophy dominated Judaism and was the greatest influence on modern Judaism, but what happened to the Essenes? They just seem to disappear. All three of those sects were competing to create the doctrine of Judaism." Michael picked up a sheet of paper he had scribbled notes on from the night before and began to read it to Vivi.

"The Essenes believed in an afterlife and that your faith and deeds done in your life on Earth would affect whether or not your soul lived on in paradise or was tortured in hell to atone for your sins. It was the only group we know of that performed a ritual of baptism by water to purify the soul. Jesus's cousin John the Baptist was almost certainly an Essene, based on what we know of him, not only from the Bible but from historical sources as well—and Jesus was a follower of John. The Essenes refer to their beliefs as 'the Way' and 'the Light'; they call themselves that over and over in the Dead Sea Scrolls. They were the only group that shunned wealth and worldly ways altogether, focusing on the reward of the afterlife by denying themselves many worldly pleasures as vices. Any of this sounding familiar?

"They state in the scrolls that their teachings are to be done in parables, so as to not reveal their innermost secrets. The Essenes were also known to be healers of the sick. Of the three major sects, they were the only group that had many of their followers living celibate, ascetic lives—and the only group against any form of slavery, and they did not practice animal sacrifice.

"The Essenes refer to themselves as 'Teachers of the Light.' They thought there was a cosmic battle between good (Light) and evil (Darkness), and that they were living in the end days of that battle. They were waiting for the return of the prophet who would judge the wicked and usher in the end times. The sect practiced leaving your worldly life behind, even your family, if you wanted to join their order. They were fishers of men." Michael stopped reading and looked up at Vivi for a reaction. She stared back at him, seemingly lost in thought. Michael tossed his notes on the table and clicked another open tab on his laptop to continue making his case.

"There's now a debate among some archeologists as to whether or not Nazareth was even a town at the time of Jesus. Some claim that Jesus of Nazareth, as in the town of Nazareth, is a twisting of facts—that Jesus was, in fact, part of a subsect of Essenes from the north of Judah known as Nazarenes. Pliny the Elder, whom I mentioned wrote about the Essenes, was a geographer who made detailed maps of northern Judah, and he makes no mention of a town called Nazareth. Archeologists have been digging there for years now, and their findings support the theory that Nazareth did not exist at the time of Christ. The earliest pottery shards come from a few hundred years later. Take a look at this passage from the book of Acts, which seems to support this theory that the Nazarenes were a religious sect."

Acts 24:5

"For we have found this man a real pest and a fellow who stirs up dissension among all the Jews throughout the world, and a ringleader of the sect of the Nazarenes."

"Do you know who wrote Acts?" Michael asked.

"Luke," Vivi answered.

"That's right. Do you know who Luke was?"

"Skywalker?"

"Oh, you've actually seen that one, eh? No, but very funny. The author Luke was known as Luke the Physician. It's thought that he wrote the Gospel of Luke and Acts both. He was a follower of St. Paul, also known as Saul of Tarsus. Paul refers to Luke as 'Luke the Doctor' once, and that's why it is thought he was a physician by profession; but remember who else were called doctors—the Essenes! The earliest writings on Christ come to us from St. Paul, thought to have been written around AD 50. There are no firsthand accounts from people who witnessed or interacted with Jesus.

Paul was born a Pharisee, and the Bible says he persecuted early Christians until he was visited by a vision of Christ while on his way to kill Christians. He was blinded by a bright light for three days before being healed and becoming the greatest driving force in the new religion, Christianity. Check out this passage in Acts describing that day."

Acts 9:1–3

Meanwhile, Saul was still breathing out murderous threats against the Lord's disciples. He went to the high priest [2] and asked him for letters to the synagogues in Damascus, so that if he found any there who belonged to *the Way*, whether men or women, he might take them as prisoners to Jerusalem. [3] As he neared Damascus on his journey, suddenly a light from heaven flashed around him. [4] He fell to the ground and heard a voice say to him, 'Saul, Saul, why do you persecute me?'

"Are you seeing this, Vivi? They describe these early Christians as followers of 'the Way!' Remember who else used that exact phrase to describe their teachings in the Dead Sea Scrolls? It's very possible that the Nazarenes were a growing sect within the Essene movement. What if this sect had a secret, one about the origins of their faith and the messiah?

"By the way, did you know that the Joseph of the Holy Family is only mentioned in *two* of the gospels, Matthew and Luke? Curiously, they both offer a genealogy for the human father of Jesus, and those genealogies greatly differ.

Isn't it strange that a genealogy is offered at all for the human father of a messiah born of a virgin through miraculous conception? The Gospel of Luke offers a much longer genealogy then Matthew, listing seventy-five generations back to Adam. Now, humor me and imagine the name *Adam* is a Hebrew version of the Egyptian *Aten*. That just happens to give you about eighteen years per generation between the birth of Jesus and the time of Akhenaten, roughly 1,350 years earlier.

Luke 3:23–38

23 Jesus, when he began his ministry, was about thirty years of age, being the son (as was supposed) of Joseph, the son of Heli, 24 the son of Matthat, the son of Levi, the son of Melchi, the son of Jannai, the son of Joseph, 25 the son of Mattathias, the son of Amos, the son of Nahum, the son of Esli, the son of Naggai, 26 the son of Maath, the son of Mattathias, the son of Semein, the son of Josech, the son of Joda, 27 the son of Joanan, the son of Rhesa, the son of Zerubbabel, the son of Shealtiel,[a] the son of Neri, 28 the son of Melchi, the son of Addi, the son of Cosam, the son of Elmadam, the son of Er, 29 the son of Joshua, the son of Eliezer, the son of Jorim, the son of Matthat, the son of Levi, 30 the son of Simeon, the son of Judah, the son of Joseph, the son of Jonam, the son of Eliakim, 31 the son of Melea, the son of Menna, the son of Mattatha, the son of Nathan, the son of David, 32 the son of Jesse, the son of

Obed, the son of Boaz, the son of Sala, the son of Nahshon, [33] the son of Amminadab, the son of Admin, the son of Arni, the son of Hezron, the son of Perez, the son of Judah, [34] the son of Jacob, the son of Isaac, the son of Abraham, the son of Terah, the son of Nahor, [35] the son of Serug, the son of Reu, the son of Peleg, the son of Eber, the son of Shelah, [36] the son of Cainan, the son of Arphaxad, the son of Shem, the son of Noah, the son of Lamech, [37] the son of Methuselah, the son of Enoch, the son of Jared, the son of Mahalaleel, the son of Cainan, [38] the son of Enos, the son of Seth, the son of Adam, the son of God.

"So you think the author of the gospel of Luke was trying to tell us that Jesus was in the male line of Akhenaten?" Vivi deadpanned, sounding as if she believed Michael's theories had gone off the rails.

"Well...yes, if there were never an Abraham, Isaac, the twelve tribes of Jacob, Moses, and the priestly class from Aaron, but they were just names and stories used to cover up the 'real' story. There was only a king/pharoah who was thrice great: the greatest philosopher, priest, and ruler. Then *his* offspring would have been the most important people in the early movement, and the rest was invented political fiction to mask their true identities. If a group within Judaism believed they were the keepers of this great secret, even *they* would be at the mercy of several hundred years of the telephone game. I think it's possible that the writers of the New Testament thought Jesus was from this male lineage, or needed to be anyway. Both genealogies for Joseph make sure to trace him back to King David, which was the important connection for Jesus. The King of the Jews had to be from this royal line.

"King David is considered a great Jewish king who unified the tribes of Israel around 1000 BCE. He was so important that Charlemagne felt the need to link his family to David's line more than 1,700 years later. The only problem is that outside of biblical stories, no record of a King David exists. Archeologists and historians have come up empty when looking for traces of him or his kingdom. Maybe he's just a metaphor for a king who lived a few hundred years earlier. Or maybe he *was* a king around 1000 BCE who unified some Semitic tribes, but his right to rule came not from slaying a giant, but from the fact he'd descended from the king of Egypt who fled his country and founded a kingdom commanded to him by God in the Holy Land.

"You have to at least admit *something* doesn't add up with the Essenes and the origins of Christianity. Maybe the Church has always known more about this than anyone could ever suspect. And I just learned something else last night about the Dead Sea Scrolls, which was, apparently, just in the news. Relatively recently, another cave was discovered at Qumran, one that had been purposely caved in to disguise its entrance. Inside the cave, picks and other digging tools were found and carbon dated to the 1950s.

"Sometime around the discovery of the known scrolls, someone else had obviously found something in a different cave there, as well, and hid that fact. Why? It's thought there are likely more scrolls and artifacts from the Essene community at Qumran out there on the shadowy black market. Those scrolls might clarify some of these things. Or perhaps the Vatican has squirreled them away. Maybe the Church has been looking into what genetics might someday prove in order to get out in front of a scandal that could rock its foundation. I don't know what to believe anymore. I just thought we should talk about where the clues lead before we ask a senior Vatican official for help."

Vivi sighed. "I still think my uncle is our best hope, Michael. Get your things and meet me in the lobby in twenty minutes. We'll have a police escort back; you can sleep in the car."

CHAPTER THIRTY-FIVE

Castel Gandolfo, Italy

Sister Mary Margarita shot upright in bed. Someone was knocking at her door before dawn. "Alfonso, what are you doing up?" she asked, after peering through crack between door and jamb.

"I'm leaving, Mary. I've made arrangements for your return to your convent in Rome whenever you desire. I want to thank you for your company here the last few weeks; it has meant a great deal to me."

"Where will you go? Back to your home in the Vatican?"

"No, I have some business to attend to first. I'll be traveling to Basel, Switzerland today, and then taking a trip to Malta. May I sit down?" Alfonso motioned to the small table and chairs that sat near the window of her bedroom.

"Of course." Mary pulled back the drapes, revealing that it was still dark outside as a drizzle fell, tapping on the window.

"Mary, I've never stopped loving you," Alfonso said, "and before I leave, I wanted to see you one more time and tell you how much I appreciate our friendship." Taking a seat across from Alfonso, she reached out and embraced both of his hands.

"And I have never stopped loving you from afar," she admitted.

"You followed Mother Teresa into a life of service because you felt called to give everything you had to God. Your soul is as pure and full of light as anything I have ever known." Alfonso paused, as if he were confessing something that anguished him. "Mother Teresa once said, 'I am a pencil in the hand of a writing God, who is sending a love letter to the world.' I have not allowed God to write through me; I have forced his hand and scribbled where I thought I knew best."

"Alfonso, you have been an inspiration to the faith of millions of people around the world. Your impact on souls is greater than you could ever know!"

"I had a reoccurring nightmare shortly after I was elected to the papacy. I was a wolf on the outside of a large herd of sheep. There were other wolves too, and they were circling the sheep, occasionally attacking them and violently feasting while the terrified sheep made this horrible bleating sound. The sheep were all huddled together and fearful. I could see from my vantage point a small lamb in the middle that suddenly looked to the sky, and I heard a voice say, 'You are not a lamb; you are a lion.' The lamb then transformed into a mighty lion and charged to the edge of the herd, where he began ripping apart the many wolves. At this point I felt an overwhelming sense of fear and dread, and a shepherdess appeared out of nowhere. The shepherdess approached me and pulled back her hood, which was masking her face. Looking down at me was you, Mary; with a look full of grace and mercy, you reached down and stroked my face. In that instant, I transformed from a wolf into a sheep." Alfonso stopped himself, sensing how ridiculous he sounded.

"And then what happened?"

"I don't know. I always woke up then." Alfonso chuckled at himself. "I just wanted to let you know before I leave that I never stopped thinking about you, wondering what our lives could have been like had we chose different paths. I also wanted to tell you that I hope you never change, never lose your faith, no matter what might happen and what you may learn. Your radiance and grace could only come from God. I am trying to allow God to write through me now...but I am afraid it is not a love letter I will be used to pen."

"And what is it that God is calling you to write now, after you have given so much to the Church?"

"A reckoning," Alfonso answered, as he squeezed Mary's hands and stood up to leave. Mary stood and moved to stop him.

"You've seen the lion, haven't you?"

Alfonso froze in his tracks, unsure how his dear friend could read him so well.

"Perhaps," Alfonso answered, while taking one last long look into Mary's eyes. Mary returned his gaze with warmth and compassion before reaching up and caressing his face lovingly.

"Goodbye, Alfie," she whispered.

CHAPTER THIRTY-SIX

Rome, Italy

Michael was startled awake by a loud noise. His phone read 4:00 a.m.; they weren't due at the police station for another five hours. The night before, he had timidly laid out to Cardinal Franco his Y-chromosome theory involving King Tut and the religious and geopolitical ramifications that would certainly follow such a discovery. To his surprise, the cardinal merely listened with what appeared to be a genuine concern, even as Michael quickly went through his more controversial theory involving the Essenes and the foundation of Christianity. When he finished, the cardinal had simply thanked him for his work and said he would do everything in his power to help locate Professor Sisti.

Michael now peered down from the loft to see Vivi coming out of her room in a bathrobe, gun in hand. The booming voice coming from the other side of the door was unmistakable. "Vivi, Vivi! It's Franco, open up!"

Franco burst into the room as she opened the door. "I have wonderful news! Professor Sisti is safe and sound. He was rescued in a raid just a couple hours ago. Thanks to some excellent police work by the Mossad!"

"Mossad? Where is he?" Vivi interrupted.

"That's why I'm here! Please get ready; we need to go to him. He is safe, but he is in Israel. They are asking for you to come there and identify the man who was following you." Franco directed his next comment to Michael: "I understand they also want you to sign some release forms due to the sensitive nature of the professor's work."

"Release forms? Who needs me to sign release forms?" Michael didn't like the sound of that.

"The Egyptian government, I'm told. I'll explain everything on the way. I've secured a Vatican plane; it's waiting for us at Leonardo da Vinci airport right now. We'll be there and back today with the professor."

Michael trusted Vivi. He was too tired and sleepy to demand more clarification, and since she went into her room to get dressed, he groaned and did the same.

It was still dark, overcast, and drizzling as a large sedan with Vatican plates pulled onto the tarmac next to a waiting jet adorned with the papal seal. Franco, Michael, and Vivianna scrambled up the steps and into the plane, strapping themselves in for the short flight across the Mediterranean to Israel.

"You want to tell us what's really going on now?" Vivi directed the question at her uncle, who was sitting across a small table from her and Michael.

"I will tell you all I know. The Holy See and the state of Israel have had official diplomatic relations since 1993, and I have become good friends with Israel's ambassador to the

Vatican since that time. He was one of the first persons I contacted last night after I met with the two of you.

"I explained to him that this incident might involve our shared Judeo-Christian roots, and asked if he could discreetly reach out to his contacts in their intelligence community. It didn't take long for him to get back to me; perhaps they were already looking into it? Every country has their own homegrown zealots and terror groups they try to keep an eye on. Israel is no different, except they are very good at it because they face threats on several fronts. Apparently, there is a small but well-funded group that calls itself 'Gideon's Sword,' a militant group of ex-soldiers and mercenaries who use the guise of defending Israel to justify their bloodlust. Israel deems them a terrorist group. The ambassador tells me that a wealthy businessman, who has long been suspected of financing this group, owns a yacht that makes port in Haifa. His yacht was in port in Ostia near Rome the day the professor was abducted. Mossad raided that boat last night in Haifa. On board, they found two members of Gideon's Sword and the professor. He was restrained, but relatively unharmed."

"Why did they take him? If this has something to do with the Y-chromosome of King Tut, with the Bible...how did they know?" Vivi asked.

"I don't know. I was only told what I shared, and that we would be fully briefed on the investigation once we landed."

CHAPTER THIRTY-SEVEN

Jerusalem, Israel

As Michael, Vivianna, and Franco were escorted into a government building in Jerusalem, they were greeted by a host of men in suits. One man stepped forward to welcome them, introducing himself as being from the Israeli Department of International Affairs. They were escorted to a conference room, where they sat around a large conference table and with a few men in suits, who seemed content to observe without introducing themselves. A man in his late fifties entered, wearing a navy-blue pinstriped suit. He did not address the group, but instead found the open chair next to Michael. "Hello, Michael, I'm Jeremy Goeshen, American ambassador stationed here in Israel. If you should need anything, I'm here for you."

"Great, Mr. Goeshen. Thank you. Is Professor Sisti here? Is he doing okay? When can I see him?" Michael asked.

"Yes, of course. I understand he's fine and will be here shortly. I'll take you to see him as soon as I can. I'm just waiting on a call to let me know he's arrived."

Another man entered the room and walked to the head of the conference table, "Cardinal Colombi, Detective Giuseppe, Mr. Malavolti, welcome to Israel—and thank you for your help in this investigation. I'm Associate Director Geoff Linden with Israeli Intelligence, and I'll explain where we are in our investigation."

Linden sighed deeply and began: "There is a small domestic group of radical zealots our intelligence agencies have long feared might turn militant. It's led by an ex-rabbi named Isaac Bein; he refers to his group of devout followers as 'Gideon's Sword.'" Mr. Linden clicked something in his hand and the lights dimmed. A photo of an elderly bald man appeared on a wall. "Isaac Bein was once a respected rabbi, but he grew increasingly radical and militant with age. Bein was a Kabbalist from the most extreme fringe aspects of Kabbalah, who thought he could tell the future from esoteric interpretations of Holy Scripture and meditative prayer. He was convinced we are living in the end days of civilization with bloodshed soon to be widespread. He had attracted a militant following of ex-soldiers and mercenaries willing to adhere to his fanatical beliefs."

Another click and a second man's face appeared on the wall. "This is David Horowitz, thought to be second-in-command and chief recruiter for Gideon's Sword. Here are two of his other known associates." Two more men's pictures appeared on the wall, both of them instantly recognizable to Michael. "These men are Ely Green and Ishmael Khan."

Ambassador Goeshen's phone buzzed; after reading the text, he leaned over to whisper to Michael. "Professor Sisti is here. I'm going to take you just down the hall to meet with him now."

As the ambassador and Michael got up to leave, Vivi shot Michael a concerned look. "Where are you taking him?" Vivi directed her question to Goeshen.

"It's okay, Vivi, Professor Sisti is here. I'm going to meet with him," Michael answered.

"I'm coming with," she said, standing to leave with Michael.

"I'm sorry, Detective Giussepe. I'm told the professor has done some contracted work for Egypt that is deemed classified. He's bound by a nondisclosure agreement. They've prepared nondisclosure documents for Michael as well, so he and Professor Sisti can discuss his work. I can only bring Michael to discuss this matter."

Vivi remained standing, staring incredulously at the ambassador as if she wouldn't take no for an answer.

"I'll be fine. We'll just be down the hall, and we'll come right back here, correct?" Michael asked the ambassador, who nodded. Vivi sat back down to listen to the intelligence briefing, but her displeasure was clearly noted by her facial expression.

While walking to meet the professor, Michael said, "Look, I'll sign whatever they want me to. This isn't my fight, but just so you know where I stand: this is *not* okay. History should never be considered a classified state secret."

The ambassador simply nodded in a placating manner before opening the door to another conference room. Michael was oblivious to the other men sitting around the table and immediately locked eyes with Professor Sisti. "Federico!" Michael rushed in and hugged the professor.

"Michael! I'm so sorry we are meeting like this." The professor stood and reciprocated the firm embrace.

Before he could reply, Ambassador Goeshen interrupted, pointing to a man seated across from the professor. "Michael, this is Dr. Ali Zafar from Egypt's Ministry of Antiquities."

Michael took a seat next to Professor Sisti as Dr. Zafar addressed him: "Mr. Malavolti, as you know, Egypt has a long, rich history that we are tasked with preserving and guarding as its caretakers. Professor Sisti has been contracted by us to run genetic tests on various antique samples, using proprietary techniques developed in his laboratory in Rome. I'm told that Professor Sisti and you planned to work on a joint academic project together, and you are worried this unfortunate event that has befallen Professor Sisti has something to do with research his lab has done on our behalf. I assure you that this cannot be possible. I will leave the investigation to Israel, but I can tell you that any work he did for our agency is strictly protected by a nondisclosure agreement, and the professor assures me has never violated his contracts. Egypt has no ties to these terrorists and abhors terrorism in all its ugly forms. This nondisclosure agreement will also legally bind you to secrecy regarding any research discussed with Professor Sisti that has been contracted by us. Is that understood?"

"Yes." Michael began to read the five-page document full of tiny print and verbose legal verbiage. "So if I sign this, I can discuss with Professor Sisti the classified work he's done for the government of Egypt, but not with anyone else without violating international law? Even if that work involves, say…my great uncle?"

Ambassador Goeshen spoke up and answered, "That's right, Michael. This is a standard NDA written to incorporate any work done under the umbrella of the contract between Egypt and the Sapienza lab."

Michael again turned to look at the ambassador. "Do *you* think history should be classified?"

Ambassador Goeshen began to stammer, "Well, I...I... this is just a standard legal..."

Dr. Zafar, who now spoke in a louder, agitated tone, interrupted: "Egypt has been plundered by foreign invaders for centuries! We can no longer allow foreign interests to come in and rape our antiquities, to create their own narratives about our rich history. Egypt alone owns this heritage, and it is up to Egypt to study, catalog, document, and preserve our antiquities, our culture. Any research contracted out to foreign universities or scientists is due to our limited resources in certain areas. The genetics lab at Sapienza is the gold standard for sequencing ancient DNA samples, and we have therefore used the professor's expertise to bolster our own lab's research in Cairo. How that data fits into the greater puzzle of Egyptian history and how it will then be conveyed and disseminated is up to Egypt and Egypt alone. Your clearance to discuss this research is a gift, not a restraint. Frankly, if it were up to me, you would not be signing these documents today. We don't typically grant classified status to foreign students, even if this genetic research *is* purely academic."

Michael let the last statement sink in, wondering who above Zafar had set this up and what the goal was. In the interest of getting the professor home, he found the lines that required his signature and scribbled his autograph. "Can we go back with the rest of the group now?"

"Yes, of course. I'll take you back down the hall now. There's one more thing they want today: for you to ID one of the men they have in custody believed to be the person stalking you in Italy." Ambassador Goeshen rose.

"Yeah, sure. He was on my flight from Chicago to Rome as well, so he's recently been in the United States." The ambassador just motioned toward the door with his arm to direct them toward the exit.

Michael's frustration turned to excitement as he exited with Sisti—a man he'd been so nervous to meet, then thought was dead. "I'm here with one of the detectives assigned to your case, Vivianna Giuseppe, Dr. Sisti. You'll get to meet her now. Her uncle is here, too. I think you've met him before—Cardinal Franco Colombi, the head of the Sacred Archaeology Department at the Vatican. We flew here on a Vatican jet!"

As Michael talked to Sisti, Ambassador Goeshen, who was just a few feet in front of them, started a conversation with their armed escort. Seeing this, Sisti leaned in close to Michael and whispered, "We need to talk in private. Don't trust *anyone*."

As they reentered the investigation briefing room, it was immediately clear that Vivi was furious. "So that's *it*? A radical group already known to you was allowed to carry this out? Move freely between various countries? But whoever was directing them, financing them, giving them all their information is still a mystery, and the only man who would know the answers to these questions is now dead! Isn't that convenient? No loose ends!" Vivi continued grilling Mr. Linden from Israeli intelligence as Michael and Federico took their seats.

"I've shared everything we have up to this moment, Detective Giuseppe. It is an ongoing investigation, and we're doing everything in our power to find everyone behind this crime and bring them to justice. Now if you'll excuse me, I'll be back shortly to bring you all to the holding center." With that, Mr. Linden closed his dossier and exited the room, a trail of men in suits following him out.

"What's going on?" Michael asked.

Cardinal Colombi moved toward the exit, punching keys on his phone as he said, "If you'll excuse me, I need to make a call. Professor Sisti, so good to see you again."

Vivi summarized: "Rabbi Bein is dead. Apparently, they found him slumped over at his desk when they went to take him into custody. The initial report indicates he died of a heart attack, but they are performing a full autopsy now. A man named David, who's in custody now, claims someone called 'Seth, the Egyptian' was directing this operation. Says he only met him once, at Rabbi Bein's office; all communication after that was electronic. David says their organization took orders from Bein, who told them to trust this man Seth and do exactly as he said—that this man was privy to information very few people in the world have. David thinks Seth was some kind of government spook. The three Gideon's Sword members were each paid $50,000 with the promise of more work in the near future. Of course they claim it wasn't about the money; it was about protecting 'God's chosen people' in the impending apocalypse, end times, or whatever these nut jobs call it." Her words erased any sense of relief Michael had been feeling.

"So whoever is behind this, whoever this Seth or Set is, he's still out there. Do they have any leads? Do they think we're still in danger?" he asked, motioning to himself and Federico.

"Linden just gave us the standard 'we're doing all we can' pep talk. Hello, Professor Sisti, I'm detective Vivianna Giuseppe with the Roman Police Department."

"Nice to meet you. From what I understand, I owe you a great debt as your detective work helped lead the authorities here to my rescue."

"No, that was all Michael, and I think the two of you have much to discuss. Is there anything you can add to what I told you?"

"I'm afraid not; it sounds like I was given the same briefing. It's a bit of a blur right now, though…"

Professor Sisti was interrupted by Cardinal Colombi and Mr. Linden returning to the conference room. "We're ready for you, Michael. If you'll all come with me," said Director Linden.

As they walked through a labyrinth of hallways, Linden addressed Michael: "I want you to know that this man will be tried for several serious crimes, including terrorism, kidnapping, and human trafficking. He won't be getting out anytime soon, so you don't have to worry about seeing him again."

Vivi spoke up, "I'd like to be in the room with Michael when he identifies him."

"Did you get a look at him as well, that day on the highway, detective Giuseppe?"

"No but I'd like see the man who nearly killed us, and to support Michael. In fact, I'd like to ask him a question about that day."

Director Linden nodded in approval. "Ok, you two follow me, we'll be entering his holding cell now."

Franco and Federico took a seat in a waiting area, while Vivi and Michael followed Linden and another man into a room where Ely sat behind a small table, shackled to the floor.

"Yes, that's him," Michael said before he was asked.

Ely sat staring at Michael, who held his eye contact to show that he was not intimidated. Director Linden looked at the other man in a suit, who was holding some files and a recorder, and nodded as if to say, *We got what we need.* "Detective Giuseppe, you wanted to ask him something?"

Vivi took a step forward. "Ely Green," she said with disgust while leaning in closer. Putting both her hands on the table, their faces only a couple feet apart now, Ely let out a taunting laugh. Then, in the blink of an eye, her right hand came off the table and cracked him across the face with an open hand so hard that his head violently recoiled to the right.

"That's enough, Detective!" Director Linden grabbed Vivi by the arm and directed everyone toward the door with his other hand.

"*That* was for my car!" she said while being pulled out of the holding room. Michael was unable to wipe the grin off his face.

As they stood on the tarmac later, waiting to board the jet for their return to Rome, Professor Sisti found himself standing next to Michael, no one within earshot. His eyes darted around, making sure no one was listening. "I have no idea what you found that led the authorities here to me," he murmured. "They only said that someone came to your aid when you were attacked in Siena and left a clue pointing you toward religious zealots. I want to tell you what I found in your DNA, what started all this, but we need to talk in private. I don't understand how, but it seems you were able to piece together some of the truth."

The professor paused, looking around again. Vivianna and Franco were a distance away having a conversation of their own. "Okay, here's the short version: When I ran a full scan on your sample my software alerted me to a unique marker embedded in your Y chromosome. Well, not totally unique: it matched only one other ev12 sample in my database, which is probably the largest database of this haplogroup anywhere. The other sample that carried this marker was a 3,400-year-old sample I ran for Egypt's Ministry of Antiquities, which I am fairly certain belongs to King Tut.

CHAPTER THIRTY-EIGHT

Jerusalem, Israel

"I'm sorry I've been on my phone so much today, Vivi," Cardinal Franco said. "I wear several hats in the Vatican, and it seems we can't go a day without political infighting. There has been tension building between the Holy See and the Knights of Malta, and I'm being called to attend meetings regarding it."

"The Knights of Malta? I thought they were autonomous?"

"It's a complicated relationship between the Church and the order. They are sovereign, but they are also tied to their history and to the Church. Soon you'll be reading about the pope asking their grandmaster to step down. It's nothing to worry about; I just wanted to let you know why I've been so distracted today. Please, invite the gentlemen to the villa, Vivianna; it's wide open for the next month."

Across the tarmac, Professor Sisti was finishing his short synopsis on the events leading up to his abduction: "For now I think it's important we keep all these events as quiet as possible."

Michael responded, "Professor, the shooting in Siena is being billed as religious terrorism. According to the authorities, I was just 'a tourist in the wrong place at the wrong time,' but whoever's behind this is still out there. I can't imagine what you've been through. You need to rest, but just let me know as soon as you have time to meet, and I'll be there. We need to talk about the safest way to move forward."

"I have to see what kind of damage was done to my lab and my flat, and that will take some time. We need an insurance policy, Michael, some way to protect..." Professor Sisti stopped midsentence as Vivi walked over to them.

"We'll be ready to board in five minutes. I've talked to my uncle, and we would like to extend an invitation to you both. There's a beautiful old villa on the sea that has been in our family for several generations. It's secluded in Montemarcello Park, overlooking the Bay of Poets, not far from your relatives up north, Michael. It's open for the next few weeks, and you are both welcome to use it, get some rest, and catch up on things."

"Thank you, Vivianna, that's very kind, but I'm afraid I need to get back to Rome and put my life back together first, though," answered the professor.

"Will you come too?" Michael asked her.

Pausing, as if she hadn't thought about it, she answered, "I could use a few days of relaxation. I'll see. Well, the offer stands. If you would like to take advantage of it, just let me know." She walked back to her uncle, who was talking to the pilot and organizing their bags to board.

"Oh come on, Professor. You deserve a vacation, and we can talk about my thesis," Michael pleaded.

"Do you trust them?"

"I do. I trust Vivi, anyway, with my life. Plus, she's beautiful and carries a gun."

Sisti chuckled. "Okay...maybe. Give me a few days to get organized in Rome." Turning more serious, the professor continued, "Michael, we have to consider that we are up against state-level actors here. I'm not sure you totally understand where this could go, but the ramifications could destabilize the world. We have to proceed with extreme caution." He paused again, eyes darting around their vicinity, seemingly unable to shake his sense of paranoia. "Okay, yes. I'll meet you up north for a few days to discuss how we are going to move forward. Now if you'll excuse me, I'm going to sleep." With that, he headed toward the idling jet, which had just lowered its stairs for boarding.

As Michael climbed aboard the jet, he could see Vivi and Franco seated at a table talking. Rather than joining them, he found an open recliner and planned to follow the professor's lead.

Vivi took the seat next to him. "Michael, you're still in danger," she said in a hushed tone.

"I know," he answered, hoping she would let him drift off to sleep.

"I don't think an NDA is going to satisfy whoever is behind this crime," she whispered. He opened his eyes a slit once again and nodded in agreement, thinking their talk could wait until later. "The professor already had an NDA in place, and look where that got him."

He relented and returned his chair to its upright position. "I know, Vivi. Professor Sisti took a risk. When he ran a full scan on my DNA sample, there *were* a number of markers that matched another sample in his hard drive that he believes belongs to King Tut, and he was bound to secrecy regarding those test results. He was *not* bound by any agreement regarding my sample, however, so he used it as an opportunity to try to trace that paternal line, which history says should be extinct. He told me that he sent out emails and made some posts on research boards asking for help from other anthropological geneticists who may have E1b1b1a samples on hand. He was looking for samples that contained the various markers I carry, including a mutation he had never seen before other than on what he assumed was the Tut sample.

"He received an email from a professor in Israel working on the 'Y-chromosome Aaron' project, who said he had seen a match for all the markers on a sample from Samaria in the *kohen* study. Professor Sisti explained he was working on a project tracing the lineage of a prominent medieval family in Tuscany and asked for a raw sample from the Samarian subject to run it through his tests. That was the week before he was abducted."

Michael sighed. "The truth will come out eventually, Vivi; it always does. For now, we'll just have to focus on the Malavoltis from the Italian peninsula though."

She stared at him intensely, as if she had more to say. "Look," he said firmly, "I know I'm not out of the woods yet, but I have to get on with my life. We can talk about it more when we get back to Rome. Besides, the Mossad are pretty good at their jobs. Hopefully, they can find out who this Seth guy is and get to the bottom of the attack."

Vivi leaned closer and whispered, "I don't think there is a Seth."

"What do you mean?" He was wide awake now.

"Michael, those men were low-level muscle. Whoever was controlling them didn't care if they were caught and wouldn't have given them anything of value that could be traced. Whoever is behind this has great resources at their disposal, including the shooter who helped us in the dome of the Siena Cathedral. He was conveniently in a position to take a perfect shot and get out undetected. You're caught up in something with powerful people fighting to control some very valuable information. At least I hope."

"What do you mean 'you hope'? You hope I'm caught between two warring groups using trained assassins?" Michael was shocked by her attitude.

"No. I just mean, hopefully, we have an ally with good intentions. But what if there never *was* a 'Horus' helping us or a 'Set' out to get us? What if just one entity is behind the entire operation? They controlled these Gideon's Sword patsies and had them leave the Set clue in the lab. They placed the Bible in your room and the sniper in the church, leaving behind the Horus clues. What if we're not looking at a Seth or a Horus."

"Then who should be looking for?"

"Thoth," she whispered.

"Thoth?" Michael snickered.

"Yes—Thoth. You told me he's the god that oversees the struggle between good and evil, controlling *both* Horus and Set when he needs to. I've been thinking about everything that's happened to us, and it all fits together too neatly."

"Ummm, okay. But what does Thoth want, then? Why kidnap the professor and lead us around by our noses until we figure out why? Gideon's Sword is eliminated, then what's next? We know about the Tut match and Akhenaten lineage in the Holy Land. So what? Professor Sisti already knew about it, or at least he was well on his way to figuring it out."

"But he was bound by an NDA and couldn't mention anything regarding the Tut sample, not even to you," she pointed out.

"Yeah, and now I'm bound by the same NDA, so we still can't publish anything about the Tut sample. No Tut sample, no proof his father founded the three largest monotheistic religions in history. I don't understand; what would Thoth want at *this* point?"

After a moment of reflection, she replied, "I don't know yet. Get some rest." With that, she pushed the button to recline Michael's chair and pulled his blanket back up to his chest as she got up and returned to the front of the cabin.

CHAPTER THIRTY-NINE

Astana, Kazakhstan

Kazakh Eli monument and Palace of Peace and Reconciliation in Astana [23]

The members of the capstone were seated in a room on the top floor of the Pyramid of Peace and Reconciliation. The lights were dimmed, yet an electric buzz murmured throughout the room as they awaited one of the most senior members of the capstone, Barron Henrik Von Brunstein, to address the group and clarify his most unprecedented call to assemble on short notice.

Before them stood a podium by windows that looked out on the Presidential Palace; beyond the palace were two golden glass towers that framed the sun or golden egg floating atop the Tower of Baiterek high in the sky. A screen lowered as a spotlight gently shown on the podium. Henrik entered, taking his position behind the podium. He was tall and long limbed yet moved with grace, despite his age. He wore a dark suit, his pale gray eyes matching his gray hair, which he wore combed straight back and uniformly cut at the collar. The Relic Hunter began:

"Ladies and gentlemen of the capstone, acolytes of Thelema, I know we did not intend to convene here so soon, so I am thankful for your prompt reply and attendance tonight to address a most dire situation. We stand at the precipice of a new day. Our destiny has always been clear: One day we will oversee the greatest era of peace and prosperity our planet has ever known. As you know, we began building this city center over twenty years ago for that very destiny.

"We in the capstone have studied and debated how and when to reveal that destiny for over fifty years. *Operation Chaos* has been analyzed and contemplated ad nauseam. On some issues, we've reach a uniform consensus. We all know the global population must be taken back under 5 billion, and the collateral damage to the Earth's ecological system must be minimized. Industries wholly controlled and run by members of the capstone must also be preserved, so we are positioned to make the transition into the new Golden Age as seamlessly as possible.

"Throughout the end of the twentieth century and into the new millennium, one trend has indicated we were not yet ready. All of the statistical models for success had been showing yearly improvement. We were successfully consolidating power and moving toward our goal without a single bomb or biological contagion from *Operation Chaos* needed. In recent years, however, the statistical models have plateaued and become stagnant. This fact has created a fissure between those capstone members who find it prudent to wait—thinking the stagnation is temporary—and those who think it is time to fulfill our destiny and unleash the full scope of *Operation Chaos*.

"I called this meeting to present truly great and historic news from our very own Ordo prophet to the capstone today. The prophet has spoken, and the universe has once again confirmed him as the one true prophet for mankind—given unto us true believers to guide and usher us into the Golden Age of Man."

As the Relic Hunter spoke, an image of a rotating globe in the dark appeared on the screen behind him. The globe began to flash light in the Nile Valley and in Mesopotamia. The light quickly spread to other areas of the globe, brighter in ancient civilization centers, such as Athens and Rome. Eventually all the modern capital cities of the world were flashing lights, and the current countries' borders were delineated by lines of light.

Then streaks of light, representing air traffic connecting every region of Earth to show the interconnectedness of modern man, began flashing across the entire globe. The air-traffic streaks disappeared, and the bright border and capital lights slowly began to fade. As those lights faded, one began to grow in a singular spot, Astana, Kazakhstan. Eventually, all light was consolidated on Astana, the capital city in which they were gathered. The light became brighter and brighter...until it shot up from Astana into the heavens. The image then gave way to a picture of the prophet, Aleister Crowley.

Henrik continued: "Today I bring remarkable news from our prophet that may lay any fear about timing to rest; the time to initiate our plan for a world rebirth and seize our destiny is now. What I am about to read is one of the last prophecies we were blessed to have received from the prophet. The vision was written in his diary while he was in the throes of death."

The image of Aleister Crowley gave way to a passage the Relic Hunter read aloud: "There will come a time when the progeny of the patriarch will reveal himself. This man will make manifest the lineage of the patriarch and founder of the Aeon of Osiris. Follow the rituals laid down before you, and spill his blood in the King's Chamber. So begins the Aeon of Horus."

The Relic Hunter paused after reading the prophecy, letting the inevitable murmurs spread throughout the room and quiet again before continuing. "Recent advances in the science of genetics have made many things clear, and the universe has once again confirmed Crowley to be the one true prophet. I believe we need to prepare for this most sacred ritual now which will bless our plans and guarantee us success as we execute operation chaos, ushering in a new age." He clicked a button on the podium and a picture of a man appeared on the screen. "This is Michael Malavolti. I believe his sacrifice will usher in the Aeon of Horus!"

CHAPTER FORTY

Tellaro, Italy

There was standing room only in the small church of Stella Maris to see Mass said by the visiting Cardinal Colombi. Michael gazed out over the Bay of Poets from his perch in front of the church, as the crowd of locals and tourists began to dissipate. Tellaro sits at the end of a string of small villages that cling to the jagged shore on the eastern side of a bay anchored by the port city of La Spezia. Directly across the bay, Michael could see Porto Venere and the island of Palmaria.

The Colombi family villa is south of Tellaro in a national park only accessible by a footpath from the village. The park of Montemarcello lay on a peninsula cut off from the mainland by the River Magra. From the park looking east, you can see the river flowing into the sea at the peninsula's southern tip, framed beyond by the Carrara Mountains, where white marble has been mined for centuries, giving them the appearance of being snowcapped even in the warm summer months. Looking west is the breathtaking view of the Bay of Poets; the famed pastel villages of the

Cinque Terre cling to the coast beyond the western side of the bay. If there were a more beautiful place on Earth, Michael was having a hard time imagining it as he waited for Vivi. He watched as the tiny old woman she was talking to pulled Vivi's face down and kissed her good-bye on the cheek.

"Should we wait for your uncle?" he asked as Vivi joined him.

"No, he'll be awhile yet. He's been coming here a few weeks a year his whole life, so he knows half the village and will be chatting them up. The woman I was just talking to was a friend of my grandmother. Let's head back and make breakfast. Professor Sisti is probably up and wondering where we are."

To get to the villa, Michael and Vivi headed down the walking path that traversed the craggy terrain. Up and down they hiked, surrounded by olive trees, citrus trees, and flowering bougainvillea. The foliage would occasionally open to give them a postcard view of the bay. "Growing up, I'd get to spend a month or so here every summer," Vivi recalled fondly. "I have so many great memories of racing down this path with my cousins, trying to keep up and lick my gelato at the same time. Were you still up when Professor Sisti got in last night?"

"Yes, it was shortly after you turned in. We stayed up two more hours, had a bottle of wine, and talked."

"And?"

"And what?"

"What's going on with your thesis? Any more you can tell me about what started all this trouble?"

"Not really. I was surprisingly right on with some of my assumptions back in Siena. There *is* a mutation in my Y-chromosome, and it matched with only one sample in his database. It's a sample that wasn't part of any larger subset and hadn't been cataloged. Professor Sisti says he knew right away whose it was, because it was the only sample run on that date, and he'd done it himself. It wasn't cataloged as part of any larger study because he'd run it on behalf of the Antiquities Department of Egypt. I was a complete match, except for 3,400 years of mutations—thirty-four unmatched markers. So someone within just a few generations of King Tut was my paternal grandfather. The match in Samaria I told you about is also a complete match. On top of that, the professor thinks he could prove that a number of other Kohens who carry Y-DNA from my haplogroup could be traced to a small number of men from right around the same time, 3,400 years ago—probably the early priests of Aten. My haplogroup is ubiquitous in small frequencies in all sects of Judaism."

"So you really are a descendant of Pharaoh Akhenaten!" Vivi said with amazement.

"Looks like it. And Federico thinks he could trace a number of those in this haplogroup to a small Diaspora, a spreading out, right around the time of Akhenaten's religious reformation. We aren't looking into this at all, though, and have given up on even addressing the Malavoltis' origins before their presence in Italy. He feels the safest way to proceed is to try to keep the pressure on Egypt to publish more of their results regarding Tut...and eventually they will. I'd also like to mention that you shouldn't bring this up with him at all or mention we've talked about it. He's still paranoid, understandably so after what he's been through."

"How are you holding up?" she asked.

"I'm fine, really. Thanks for inviting us to your family's villa. It's incredible here; I'm really enjoying myself."

"No crisis of faith?" asked Vivi.

"Nope." Michael kept walking on the path, gathering his thoughts, and occasionally looking out at the bay. "The historicity of the Bible has never been important to me. I know that's grounds for excommunication in some circles, but so be it. Hey, did you know 'Amen' means 'so be it'? It was always thought to have a Hebrew origin, but there's a similar word in nearly every early language from the area. Even some Islamic prayers end with 'Amin.'"

"I suppose that came from Egypt too? Tut's grandfather was Amenhotep III, and Akhenaten himself was even named Amenhotep IV at birth, right?" noted Vivi.

"Yeah, Amen was a form of Amun, the official state god at the time of Akhenaten's religious reformation. Once you know these things, the connections become obvious. Understanding the natural evolution of mankind better doesn't hurt my faith, though. Religion has been good for me; it's provided structure for my faith and for my attempt at communing with a higher power. It feeds my good wolf! I've never been good at meditating, but I can say a few memorized prayers and feel my mind more in tune with God. Every week, I set an hour aside to be in awe of this power. I never leave Mass feeling more anxious than I entered. The message of the gospels is pretty amazing. Do you know what Einstein said about religion?"

"E=mc²?" she stated dryly.

"Ha, you're funny...sometimes. I think that answer is probably right on a number of levels, but he also said," as he pulled his phone out to read the quote: "'The most beautiful emotion we can experience is the mystical. It is the power of all true art and science. He to whom this emotion is a stranger, who can no longer wonder and stand rapt in awe, is as good as dead. To know that what is impenetrable to us really exists, manifesting itself as the highest wisdom and the most radiant beauty, which our dull faculties can comprehend only in their most primitive forms—this knowledge, this feeling, is at the center of true religiousness. In this sense, and in this sense only, I belong to the rank of devoutly religious men.'"[24]

"In a strange way, I've never felt closer to God," Michael mused. "You know what a miracle it was that Howard Carter found King Tut's tomb in the Valley of Kings? His perseverance and faith that something was still there, when everyone else was sure there wasn't, is the stuff of movies. Think about how many things had to fall into place for us to be here at this moment knowing what we think we know. The Samaritan story itself seems miraculous, surviving two exiles and all the turmoil of the region over the last 3,000 years, to have their story verified by science now when there are less than 1,000 Samaritans remaining.

"The Essenes at Qumran who stashed their scrolls in caves to protect them from war just happened to live near the lowest point on earth. The Dead Sea is over 400 meters below sea level. The extremely low altitude combined with the desert climate created a unique environment for parchments to survive for thousands of years, only to be found in the last century.

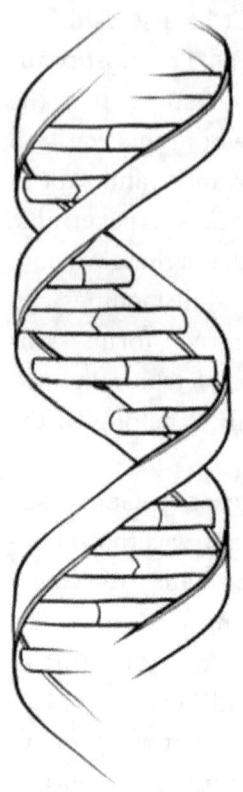

"Even the Malavolti ladder... Why is it in black and white with a little black line in the middle of every rung, as if breaking up the light segments? It seems like an unlikely way to stylize a ladder to me, yet it was drawn that way roughly 1,000 years ago, at least. Knowing what I do now, I can't help but think that if you give the ladder a little twist, it looks just like DNA: the double helix with nitrogenous bases bound together in the middle.

"Do you think whoever wrote the Gospel of Luke could have known the Good Samaritan parable would serve to make the Samaritan name synonymous with doing a good deed? People the world over know what the term 'Good Samaritan' means even if they've never read any of the Bible. It seems highly unlikely that whoever picked the surname 'Malavolti' would have known his most famous ancestor was called 'the evil-doer' for several centuries after his rule, yet somehow that's the name they picked. Now the truth is found through these descendants of Akhenaten. The name contrasts like black and white—those who do good deeds and those who do evil deeds—the duality of man. Mankind has always had tremendous capability for both, and religion has played a critical role in feeding the good and bad wolf alike."

"Science can't tell us what a thought is, or what the source of the innate intelligence that flows throughout all living things is. We know so little; at any point in history as we look back, it's easy to see how ignorant we were of things we know now. It's hard to realize how ignorant we *still* are. Science can't tell us why it hurts so much to lose a loved one, only the mechanism by which we process that emotion. I should be scared to death of whoever is out there pulling the strings behind what happened to the professor and us, but for some reason, I'm not. I've never felt more at ease that I'm in the place I'm supposed to be at the moment I'm supposed to be."

Michael looked up from the path at Vivi walking by his side; her eyes held a hint of pain, and then she unexpectedly reached out and held his hand. The two walked the remaining path back to the villa in silence, hands held firmly.

After breakfast, Federico, Michael, and Vivianna sat sipping their coffee, taking in the view of the bay. The cardinal walked around the garden, talking on his cell phone; his free hand held a cigar, the ember dancing around as he talked and made dramatic motions.

"What is it about Italians needing to move their hands to talk?" Michael asked as the three sat watching Franco.

"I think it's genetic," quipped Vivi, looking at Federico.

"Don't look at me," said Federico with a shrug as they all chuckled. "Hey, Vivianna, is there any way you could discreetly get me a sample of the blood that was used to paint the hieroglyphs in my lab? I asked around, and all anyone could tell me is that it was all cleaned up as evidence and that the crime lab had run tests on it."

"I could look into it."

"I'd like to run some different tests, ancestry tests. If it's from a male, I'll run the entire single copy euchromatic portion of the Y-marker, roughly 10 Mbase," explained Federico.

Vivi, looking bewildered, but responded, "I'll see what I can do."

"Professor Sisti is fluent in nerd in multiple languages," said Michael, hoping his ribbing of the professor would be okay.

To his relief, the professor smirked before adding, "I just doubt the crime lab did an in-depth analysis of the Y-chromosome."

Cardinal Colombi entered with his phone in one hand, and a large bouquet of flowers in the other. "Michael, these were left at the gate with your name on them!" Franco laid the flowers in front of him: white irises wrapped in black cellophane with a small piece of paper stapled to the cellophane.

"From your family?" asked Vivi.

"I...doubt it," answered a confused Michael as he picked up the strange bouquet and inspected it. Peeling back the black cellophane, he pulled out a small black card with white text on one side and a figure on the other. The color began to drain from his face.

"What does it say? Who are they from?" demanded Vivi, growing more anxious.

Michael read aloud what was printed on the card: "Luke 8:17: For nothing is hidden that will not be made manifest, nor is anything secret that will not be known and come to light."

As Michael flipped the card over, he immediately recognized the figure printed on the card, and his heart sank. He tossed the card onto the table, picture side up. She looked down at it, then back at Michael, who held an expression of disbelief and vulnerability. Finally, he nodded as if to confirm what was left unsaid.

"Who are they from?!" demanded Professor Sisti.

"Thoth," Vivi answered.

To be continued...

"The great enemy of truth is very often not the lie—deliberate, contrived and dishonest—but the myth—persistent, persuasive and unrealistic. Too often we hold fast to the clichés of our forebears. We subject all facts to a prefabricated set of interpretations. We enjoy the comfort of opinion without the discomfort of thought."

—John F. Kennedy, June 11, 1962

AUTHOR'S NOTE

Like Michael Malavolti, I became interested in my paternal ancestors because I was amazed that such a fascinating family history could ever cease to be passed down to new generations. Over the course of a few years of passive research, I accumulated a decent amount of disjointed trivia about the Malavoltis and the Republic of Siena. After having my ancestry test done, I became particularly interested in my Y-DNA haplogroup due to my family's history and mysterious origins in Siena.

Upon discovering that my Y-DNA belonged to the rare E-V12 haplogroup, I let my imagination run wild, trying to figure out how my ancestors became wealthy counts of Siena as far back as the 800s. There's a scene in the book where Michael points out that the haplogroup occurs in higher numbers in southern Italy (carried by 1%–2% of men), yet becomes rarer as you move north (in Tuscany, for example, it has a frequency of around 0.5%). This is true, but there's one exception I know of. Although there's a smattering of E-V12 throughout Europe, in southwestern

France among the Basques, it reaches a concentration of 5%–6% of men.

Might the higher concentration in this region be genetic remnants of the Jewish kingdom of Septimania or the larger Jewish population who lived in this region even earlier? Possible, but science could probably answer that question. The following link is to a study published in *Molecular Biology and Evolution* on the distribution of haplogroup E-M78, of which E-V12 is a derivation. As you can see on the study's chart, outside of a logically decreasing frequency away from its epicenter in southern Egypt, that small area in southwest France is the only place saturation reaches over 3%.

https://academic.oup.com/mbe/article/24/6/1300/984002

For the most part, the historical persons, events, legends, and places described in this book are accurate to the best of my knowledge. I did, however, take some liberties in describing places that I could not find images of online, such as the museum for the *Contrada del Drago*. Also, while the Republic of Siena was generally a Ghibelline stronghold, as mentioned in the book, over the course of hundreds of years, cities and even families switched allegiances back and forth. The knight from Dante's *Inferno* I mentioned— Catalano de Malavolti, the *podesta* of Bologna who was appointed to corule the Knights of St. Mary—was actually a representative of the Guelf faction at the time.

A secretive cabal called Ordo and the capstone that operates as the upper level of Ordo Templi Orientis is a creation of fiction for this novel, as is the prophecy attributed to Aleister Crowley. Astana, Kazakhstan is a planned city and the capital of Kazakhstan; most of its city center was built in the late 1990s. The connection to O.T.O. is fictitious, yet the architecture with occult Masonic imagery does exist as described.

ENDNOTES

1. John Adams, *A Defence of the Constitutions of Government of the United States of America: Volume II* (Quincy, MA: Liberty's Lamp Books, 1778).

2. Wikipedia.org, "Ordo Templi Orientis," accessed September 2018, https://en.wikipedia.org/wiki/Ordo_Templi_Orientis.

3. Wikipedia.org, "Aeon (Thelema)," accessed September 2018, https://en.wikipedia.org/wikipedia.org/wiki/Aeon_(Thelema).

4. Image credit: AgeFotoStock.com De Agostini/G. Nima, https://www.agefotostock.com/age/en/StockImages/Rights-Managed/DAE-10327712/1.

5. Image credit: Shutterstock.com, ermess, https://www.shutterstock.com/image-photo/montalcino-siena-tuscany-italy-medieval-fortress-659291965?src=xKg_jOyW-MtCjDDxYDN38Q-3-93.

6. Image Credit: Agefotostock.com, Alinari/Permission of Ministero Beni Culturali, https://www.agefotostock.com/age/en/Stock-Images/Rights-Managed/AHV-AGC-F-002013-0000/1.

7. Image credit: iStock by Getty Images, georgeclark, https://www.istockphoto.com/photo/ancient-capitoline-wolf-statue-in-siena-gm933682474-255751240.

8. Wikipedia.org, "St. George," accessed January 2017, https://en.wikipedia.org/wiki/Saint_George.

9. Image credit: izanbar, iStock by Getty Images, https://www.istockphoto.com/photo/siena-dome-cathedral-external-view-detail-of-statue-wolf-with-romolus-and-remus-gm829246518-134875463.

10. Image credit: Alamy Stock Photo, Science History Images, https://www.alamy.com/stock-photo-mosaic-floor-inlay-in-the-cathedral-of-siena-of-hermes-mercurius-trismegistus-151887395.html.

11. Image credit: iStock by Getty Images, boggy22, https://www.istockphoto.com/photo/siena-cathedral-in-italy-gm641942672-116392763.

12. Chakazul, "World Map of Y-Chromosome Haplogroups —Dominant Haplogroups in Pre-Colonial Populations with Possible Migrations Routes," Wikimedia.com (September 18, 2013) https://commons.wikimedia.org/wiki/File:World_Map_of_Y-DNA_Haplogroups.png.

13. James Henry Breasted, *The Dawn of Conscience* (New York: Charles Scribner's Sons, 1933).

14. Raymond Faulkner, Ogden Goelet, translators, *The Egyptian Book of the Dead: The Book of Going Forth by Day* (San Francisco: Chronicle Books LLC, 1994).

15. Sigmund Freud, *Moses and Monotheism* (New York: Knopf, 1939).

16. Douglas A. Knight and Amy-Jill Levine, *The Meaning of the Bible: What the Jewish Scriptures and Christian Old Testament Can Teach Us* (New York: HarperCollins Publishers, 2012).

17. Joseph Davidovits, *De cette fresco naquit la Bible* (Paris: Editions Jean-Cyrille Godefroy, 2009), https://www.davidovits.info/the-lost-fresco-and-the-bible-my-new-book-in-french.

18. Jo Marchant, "Tutankhamun's Blood," Medium.com, March 6, 2014, https://medium.com/matter/tutankhamuns-blood-9fb62a68597b.

19. Wikipedia.org, "Y-chromosomal Aaron," accessed September 2018, https://en.wikipedia.org/wiki/Y-chromosomal_Aaron.

20. Wikipedia.org, "Ten Commandments," accessed January 2017, https://en.wikipedia.org/wiki/Ten_Commandments#Samaritan.

21. Wikipedia.org, "Dead Sea Scroll," accessed September 2018.

22. Robert Feather, *The Mystery of the Copper Scroll of Qumran: The Essene Record of the Treasure of Akenaten* (Rochester, Vermont: Bear & Company, 2003).

23. Image credit: Shutterstock.com, Yury Shkrebiy, https://www.shutterstock.com/image-photo/kazakh-eli-monument-palace-peace-reconciliation-525234595?src=QFXsFX7GrH7qBvl491yuBw-1-0.

24. Albert Einstein, *Living Philosophies* (New York: Simon and Schuster, 1931).

ABOUT THE AUTHOR

Aaron Malavolti is a chiropractor who has been in private practice in Chicago for over a decade.